INSIDE STORIES

3

Peter and Susan Benton

Hodder & Stoughton

LONDON SYDNEY AUCKLAND TORONTO

Illustration acknowledgements:

pp. 14, 15, 16, 19 woodcuts from *1800 Woodcuts by Thomas Bewick and His School*, ed. Blanche Cirker, Dover Publications; pp. 33 and 56 Peanuts cartoons, © 1952, 1956 by United Syndicate Features Inc; p. 37 drawing by Herbert Goldberg, copyright 1967 *Saturday Review*, Inc.

British Library Cataloguing in Publication Data
Inside stories.
3.
1. Short stories in English – Anthologies
I. Benton, Peter *1942–*   II. Benton, Sue
823.0108

ISBN 0 340 50358 0

First published 1991

Typeset by Wearside Tradespools, Fulwell, Sunderland
Printed in Great Britain for the educational publishing division of Hodder and Stoughton Ltd, Mill Road, Dunton Green, Sevenoaks, Kent by The Bath Press, Avon

INSIDE STORIES

♣

Contents

CONTENTS

♣

ACKNOWLEDGMENTS

The publishers would like to thank the following for their kind permission to reproduce material in this volume:

Angus and Robertson (UK) Publishers for 'Kid in a Bin' from *The Pleasure Within* by Robert Carter; Annick Press for 'The Paper Bag Princess' from *The Paper Bag Princess* by Robert N. Munsch (1982); The Bodley Head for 'Like Immortality Almost' from *Enough Is Too Much Already* by Jan Mark (1983) © Jan Mark, The Bodley Head; Lorna Callender for 'An Honest Thief' by Timothy Callender from Anne Walmsley (ed.) *The Sun's Eye*, published by Longman; Cambridge University Press for 'The Difference' by Denys Thompson from *Readings* (1976); Collins Publishers for 'The White Trousers' from *Anatolian Tales* by Yashar Kemal; Rupert Hart Davies for 'The Flying Machine' from *Golden Apples of the Sun* by Ray Bradbury; J. M. Dent and Sons Ltd for 'The House of Coloured Windows' from *The Door in the Air and Other Stories* by Margaret Mahy; Faber and Faber Ltd for 'The Star Beast' from *Mainly in Moonlight* by Nicholas Stuart Gray and 'The Healing' from *First Fictions: Introduction 9* by Dorothy Nimmo (1986); Farrar, Straus and Giroux Inc for 'Boating' and 'Perfection' from *The Devil's Other Storybook* by Natalie Babbitt; Leon Garfield/John Johnson Ltd for 'Surprised' by Catherine Storr from Leon Garfield (ed.) *Baker's Dozen* (1973); Hamish Hamilton for 'The Best Day of My Easter Holidays' from *Black Faces, White Faces* by Jane Gardam; William Heinemann Ltd/Diogenes Verlag for 'The Snail-Watcher' from *Eleven* by Patricia Highsmith, copyright © 1945, 1962, 1964, 1965, 1967, 1968, 1970, originally printed in *Gamma*; Langston Hughes/David Higham Associates Ltd for 'Thank you M'am' from *Sudden Fiction* by Langston Hughes, published by Penguin Books Ltd (1958); Longman Group UK Ltd for 'Do Angels Wear Brassieres?' from *Summer Lightning* by Olive Senior; Macmillan Ltd for 'The Wolf and His Gifts' by Catherine Storr from Anne Thwaite (ed.) *Allsorts 3* (1974); Mayer, Brown and Platt/Macmillan Ltd for 'A Day's Wait' from *Winner Take Nothing* by Ernest Hemingway (1933); Oxford and Cambridge University Presses for the extract from the *New English Bible*, Second edition © 1970; Peters, Fraser and Dunlop Group Ltd for 'The Genius' by Frank O'Connor from *The Stories of Frank O'Connor*, published by Hamish Hamilton Ltd; Murray Pollinger for 'The Landlady' from *Kiss, Kiss* by Roald Dahl, published by Michael Joseph Ltd and Penguin Books Ltd; Random Century Group/Scholastic Inc for 'Petronella' from *The Practical Princess and Other Liberating Fairy Tales* by Jay Williams, published by Chatto and Windus Ltd (1979); Random House Inc for 'The Ring' from *Tales of the Hasidim: Early Masters* by Martin Buber (1947); Martin Secker and Warburg Ltd/A. M. Heath and Co. Ltd for 'Marcovaldo at the Supermarket' from *Marcovaldo* by Italo Calvino, copyright © 1963 Giulio Einaudi Editore SpA, Torino, English translation copyright © 1983 by Martin Secker and Warburg Ltd; Richard Scott Simon Ltd for 'The Bellows of the Fire' from *The Garden of Villa Molini* by Rose Tremain, published by Hamish Hamilton Ltd, copyright © 1987 by Rose Tremain; Iain Crichton Smith for 'The Blot'; Rosemary Thurber/Hamish Hamilton Ltd for 'The Princess and the Tin Box' from *The Beast in Me and Other Animals*, 'The Little Girl and the Wolf' from *The Thurber Carnival* and 'The Fox and the Crow' from *Further Fables of Our Time*, all by James Thurber.

Every effort has been made to trace and acknowledge ownership of copyright. The publishers will be glad to make suitable arrangements with any copyright holders whom it has not been possible to contact. Every endeavour has been made to trace the copyright holder of 'Woof' by Jan Dean.

♣

To the Teacher

There are stories in every culture and, as far as we know, stories have existed in all past ages. A French or a Chinese child of the twelfth or the nineteenth century would hear stories just as surely as the child in medieval England or the Victorian nursery. Indeed, a child in ninth century China may have heard what is essentially the story of Cinderella a thousand years before his or her counterpart in Europe was delighted by the Perrault version. Aesop's fables of two thousand five hundred years ago were not even then altogether new and had their counterparts in tales from Egypt, Babylon, India and elsewhere. The parables and allegorical stories of the Bible often have their parallels in other faiths.

Today's children may hear stories read at bedtime, at school, in their place of worship, on tape, on radio, and on television. They will tell each other stories both real and imagined: as small children they may make up stories, imaginary friends, fantasies that may delight or frighten. Later, they may become voracious readers devouring stories from the printed pages of books and magazines. Some may enjoy writing their own stories from a very early age. In a sense, the play of making up stories is the work of the child, for through story we make sense of the world. We have an insatiable appetite for stories whether as children or as adults: even those who are not great readers of books may well be passionately committed to following the twists and turns of the soap opera on television, the daily unfolding of a seemingly endless story – which may possibly extend over twenty years or more. All the time we are absorbing the structures and patterns of stories and many people who would never be great *writers* of stories have a skill as story *tellers* that makes them popular wherever they go. For the world loves a good story.

It seems that human beings *need* stories and, whatever our age or whatever our role, we are the main characters in the story we weave about ourselves. Stories are a way in which we represent the world to ourselves and, in the stories we tell ourselves or others, stories also become a way in which we represent ourselves to the world. They also help us to understand experiences we may never have had personally – of another time, another place, another culture. Stories allow us to speculate about 'what if . . . ?' Stories are the foundations of religions and of history. The culture and the beliefs of a society are deeply embedded in its stories. For both individuals and societies live by the stories they tell themselves.

Stories delight, entertain, relax, and instruct but they are not value-free. It is important to be able not only to enjoy the stories we read but to see where they are coming from and where they would lead us. To do this we need to have some understanding of how stories work, how their effects are achieved.

Inside Stories 3, the third book in this four-volume series, is concerned to assist students explore the nature and roots of story, the act of reading and their own critical response rather than to offer merely 'comprehension-type' activities. It is geared to the needs of pupils working towards Key Stage 4 and it reflects, we believe, the needs of the teachers of such groups. The range of authors represents some of the best of modern story writers from several nationalities, reflecting the view that the range of stories presented in classrooms should be diverse, multicultural, and include American and Commonwealth writers as well as translations. In addition, we have throughout the series attempted to promote an awareness of the roots of story such as those in fairy story, classical myth and legend, and the Bible. This volume also includes fables and parables which have their roots in the oral tradition.

In common with the other books of this series, *Inside Stories 3* is divided into two main sections. In each volume, *Section A – Exploring Stories* is a 'teaching section' which focuses on specific aspects of storytelling or on types of story. Thus, for example, *Section A* of this volume offers teaching sections on fables, on parables and allegorical stories, and on fairy stories. The material on fairy stories asks pupils to articulate their implicit knowledge about the conventions of this genre and to consider some modern alternative views. Here, though not only here, we have been alert to the Cox Report and National Curriculum recommendations that pupils should be encouraged to think critically about stories, question authorial stance and intention, recognise that attitudes and beliefs expressed are not necessarily those of the author, and be aware of the choices made by writers with regard to vocabulary, imagery, genre, form and style. *Section B* is a teaching anthology of stories loosely linked by theme into sections. While acknowledging that any such sectionalisation is far from perfect, it does, we believe, help the teacher to present disparate material in a manageable fashion. Teachers should not feel bound by the sections, however, and should cut across these artificial boundaries – or introduce other material from outside – whenever it seems appropriate.

Each story is accompanied by a teaching section – *Inside the Story*. The aim of this section is to prompt students to think more deeply about what they have read, about how it operates and about how they respond. In almost every case we have suggested pair or group discussion as a way into the text in the firm belief that one has to start with the student's own perceptions about the story before one can proceed further and that the sharing of such perceptions is, in itself, a valuable activity. Nonetheless, we recognise that there may be occasions when the teacher judges that a preliminary written response may be more appropriate for a particular group. There are, of course, suggestions for students' own writing as well as for oral work at the end of each story.

The activities related to the text are wide ranging and are designed to further understanding of the structures and techniques used by tellers and writers of stories. They offer opportunities for creative and critical responses, for discussion, writing, interviewing, tape recording and performance. These tasks cover the range of activities which are seen as being appropriate at all levels for the National Curriculum in English. We share the belief that pupils should be encouraged towards an active engagement with stories which stresses reading and response rather than comprehension and criticism. Small group work and shared experiences of stories are valuable, and wide ranging writing tasks – such as pastiche and genre transformation – as well as the more common writing of stories and reviews are encouraged. We believe that pupils should increasingly be made aware of the elements of story structure and encouraged to use more consciously crafted techniques in their own writing of stories and we have designed the talking and writing assignments

with this end in view. The teaching sections give the student the opportunity to develop skills which will provide a sound grounding in the variety of tasks appropriate to their GCSE work. Given the different levels of sophistication at which the same stories may be approached, the book should also be valuable with students up to GCSE. The stories and tasks proposed vary greatly in difficulty and complexity; thus the book aims to cater for a very wide range of readers and it will be possible for individuals to follow their own interests at their own level – perhaps branching out beyond the immediate context of this collection where they find an area that they wish to explore further.

We have suggested ways in to the material but the teacher is the best judge of what is appropriate for which students and will modify the approaches in the light of his or her close knowledge of the class. This is not a course to be followed slavishly and, for all its serious purpose, we hope it is a book to be enjoyed.

Peter and Susan Benton, Oxford 1991

SECTION A:
EXPLORING STORIES

1
ANIMAL FABLES

A fox praises a crow for his fine singing voice. The crow is flattered and opens his beak to sing, thus dropping the food he is carrying which is promptly snapped up by the fox.

A lion catches a mouse and is persuaded to let it go. Later, when he himself is caught in a trapper's net, the mouse frees him by gnawing through the cords that bind him.

The fox outwits the foolish crow and maybe the crow learns a lesson. The lion learns that even the strongest may have need of the weak and should not despise them.

These two stories are probably known to many of you for they are examples of *fables* – and fables, like nursery rhymes, folk-tales and fairy stories are common in young children's books around the world, handed down from generation to generation.

These stories may appear to be about animal characters but they are really aimed at telling us something about ourselves, illustrating the way humans, not animals, behave. They laugh at our vanity or our foolishness, for example, or they warn us about where our thoughtless actions may lead. And they achieve all this in a neat, witty and clever way which invites us to recognise ourselves and to smile as we recognise our own faults.

In this way, animal fables are universal. They are easily understood by everyone and have a simple folk wisdom of the kind that is found in proverbs. It is not surprising to find that they are among the very earliest forms of storytelling and that they endure for centuries. In fact, the fable of the Lion and the Mouse quoted above dates back some thousands of years and a version has been found inscribed on an ancient Egyptian papyrus.

The ancient Greek, Aesop, is probably the best known teller of fables. Fables told by this man, who lived some 2,500 years ago and who never wrote or published anything, have been translated into over 250 languages, with many new editions appearing each year. The tales were originally passed on by word of mouth and it was several centuries before anyone recorded them in writing. Even Aesop may have been retelling some much older stories which came from other countries. We know for certain that collections of fables written down in the third century BC are based on Buddhist stories from even earlier and on stories from India, Persia and Arabia.

THE CROW AND THE PITCHER

A thirsty crow suddenly spied a pitcher some way off and flew to it with delight.

When he looked inside he saw that there was, as he had hoped, some water in it. But it was a large and deep pitcher, and the water remained quite beyond the reach of his beak no matter how much he twisted and strained to get at it.

'Perhaps,' he thought to himself, 'if I can overturn the pitcher, the water would lie on the side and be within reach.' But the pitcher was too heavy and he had not the strength to move it.

He was just about to give up when, seeing some pebbles nearby, he had an idea. Several times he fluttered down picking up the pebbles one by one and dropping them into the vessel. With the addition of each pebble, the water level rose a little and before long it was within reach of his beak.

Perched happily on the rim of the pitcher, the crow drank his fill, well pleased with his ingenuity.

Moral: Never give up. There is always a way.
or:
What we cannot do by strength, we can often achieve by intelligence.

THE JACKDAW'S FINE FEATHERS

A Jackdaw, a plain black bird of no great distinction, was rather discontented with his life; he was also more than a little vain. Seeing a number of brilliant peacocks' feathers lying on the ground, he resolved to change his dull appearance and stuck the bright plumes in among his own.

'Now,' said the Jackdaw proudly, 'I am exceedingly well dressed and all the birds will admire my handsome appearance.' And he strutted haughtily across the grass to join the peacocks' company.

The other birds were not deceived and in any case the borrowed plumes soon began to fall out. The peacocks mocked him, pecked him and tore the remaining feathers from him.

The wretched jackdaw went back to his old companions, hoping to rejoin the flock, but the other jackdaws remembered how proudly he had behaved and wanted no more to do with him.

'You could have stayed with us and been content,' they said, 'but you choose to give yourself airs and to spurn us.' As we were not good enough for you yesterday, so today you are not good enough for us.'

Moral: Be yourself. Fine feathers do not always make fine birds.

THE FOX AND THE CROW

A crow, who had stolen a large piece of cheese from an open cottage window, carried it in his beak high into a tall tree. Seeing this, the fox said to himself, 'If I am clever, I can have that cheese for myself.' After a little thought he decided on a plan.

'Good afternoon,' he called up to the crow. 'How very beautiful you look today. And what delicate feathers you have; finer and more glistening than any I have ever set eyes on! Your neck is more graceful than a swan's, your wings mightier than those of an eagle. Surely, if you were blessed with a voice, you would sing more sweetly than any nightingale!'

Very pleased to hear such fine words, the crow hopped along the branch and then, in order to prove what a sweet voice he had, opened his beak to sing. A raucous 'Caw!' came from his throat and the cheese dropped to the ground where the fox swiftly snapped it up.

As he trotted off, he turned and called back to the crow, 'I may have said much of your beauty, but I said nothing at all about your brains.'

Moral: Don't be deceived by flattery.

FABLES RETOLD

The twentieth century American writer, James Thurber, enjoyed rewriting the classic fables and produced two collections called *Fables For Our Time* and *Further Fables For Our Time*. In this example he takes Aesop's old story of the Fox and the Crow and develops it in directions that Aesop could never have imagined . . .

THE FOX AND THE CROW

James Thurber

A crow, perched in a tree with a piece of cheese in his beak, attracted the eye and nose of a fox. 'If you can sing as prettily as you sit,' said the fox, 'then you are the prettiest singer within my scent and sight.' The fox had read somewhere, and somewhere else, that praising the voice of a crow with a cheese in his beak would make him drop the cheese and sing. But this is not what happened to this particular crow in this particular case.

'They say you are sly and they say you are crazy,' said the crow, having carefully removed the cheese from his beak with the claws of one foot, 'but you must be nearsighted as well. Warblers wear gay hats and colored jackets and bright vests, and they are a dollar a hundred. I wear black and I am unique.' He began nibbling the cheese, dropping not a single crumb.

'I am sure you are,' said the fox, who was neither crazy nor nearsighted, but sly. 'I recognize you, now that I look more closely, as the most famed and talented of all birds, and I fain would hear you tell about yourself, but I am hungry and must go.'

'Tarry awhile,' said the crow quickly, 'and share my lunch with me.' Whereupon he tossed the cunning fox the lion's share of the cheese, and began to tell about himself. 'A ship that sails without a crow's nest sails to doom,' he said. 'Bars may come and bars may go, but crow bars last forever. I am the pioneer of flight, I am the map maker. Last, but never least, my flight is known to scientists and engineers, geometrists and scholars, as the shortest distance between two points. Any two points,' he concluded arrogantly.

'Oh, every two points, I am sure,' said the fox. 'And thank you for the lion's share of what I know you could not spare.' And with this he trotted away into the woods, his appetite appeased, leaving the hungry crow perched forlornly in the tree.

THE MORAL: *'Twas true in Aesop's time, and La Fontaine's, and now, no one else can praise thee quite so well as thou.*

VARIATIONS ON THE THEME

I

A fox, attracted by the scent of something, followed his nose to a tree in which sat a crow with a piece of cheese in his beak. 'Oh, cheese,' said the fox scornfully. 'That's for mice.'

The crow removed the cheese with his talons and said. 'You always hate the thing you cannot have, as, for instance, grapes.'

'Grapes are for the birds,' said the fox haughtily. 'I am an epicure, a gourmet, and a gastronome.'

The embarrassed crow, ashamed to be seen eating mouse food by a great specialist in the art of dining, hastily dropped the cheese. The fox caught it deftly, swallowed it with relish, said *'Merci,'* politely, and trotted away.

II

A fox had used all his blandishments in vain, for he could not flatter the crow in the tree and make him drop the cheese he held in his beak. Suddenly, the crow tossed the cheese to the astonished fox. Just then the farmer, from whose kitchen the loot had been stolen, appeared, carrying a rifle, looking for the robber. The fox turned and ran for the woods. 'There goes the guilty son of a vixen now!' cried the crow, who, in case you do not happen to know it, can see the glint of sunlight on a gun barrel at a greater distance than anybody.

III

This time the fox, who was determined not to be outfoxed by a crow, stood his ground and did not run when the farmer appeared, carrying a rifle and looking for the robber.

'The teeth marks in this cheese are mine,' said the fox, 'but the beak marks were made by the true culprit up there in the tree. I submit this cheese in evidence, as Exhibit A, and bid you and the criminal a very good day.' Whereupon he lit a cigarette and strolled away.

IV

In the great and ancient tradition, the crow in the tree with the cheese in his beak began singing, and the cheese fell into the fox's lap. 'You sing like a shovel,' said the fox, with a grin, but the crow pretended not to hear and cried out, 'Quick, give me back the cheese! Here comes the farmer with his rifle!'

'Why should I give you back the cheese?' the wily fox demanded.

'Because the farmer has a gun, and I can fly faster than you can run.'

So the frightened fox tossed the cheese back to the crow, who ate it, and said, 'Dearie me, my eyes are playing tricks on me – or am I playing tricks on you? Which do you think?' But there was no reply, for the fox had slunk away into the woods.

Inside the story

In pairs or small groups

1 Thurber gives us a Moral for his first new version. Decide on a suitable Moral to go at the end of each of the others. (They don't have to be in rhyme like Thurber's!)

2 Try to think of other variations on the theme of the Fox and the Crow that Thurber might have written.

In pairs or on your own

1 Invent your own animal fable complete with Moral ending. You may find it helps to take a well-known proverb or saying as your Moral: for example, 'he who hesitates is lost', or 'too many cooks spoil the broth' or 'the grass is always greener on the other side of the hill', or 'who dares, wins' . . . and so on.

The accompanying illustrations are all from old books of fables and you might like to use one or more of these pictures as a starting point for your own fables. In some cases you may know the traditional story they were intended to illustrate but there is no reason why you should not invent your own version.

2 Invent your own fable that reverses or changes the traditional idea in some way so that you may have 'the grass is always browner on the other side of the hill' or 'he who hesitates, wins' or even 'who dares, dies' . . . and so on.

If the class produces enough new fables, collect them together as a booklet – complete with illustrations if you like.

2
PARABLES, ALLEGORIES AND MORAL TALES

Parables are closely related to fables. A parable is a story told with the purpose of illustrating some spiritual or moral point. Its aim is to teach us something. It does so by relating a story which, at first reading, may seem to have nothing to do with us but which, on reflection, forces us to think about whether or not it relates to our own behaviour. 'Am I like that?' we ask. 'What would I have done in a similar situation?' Parables require us to ask ourselves about how we live. They are common in all sorts of religious teaching for they are a simple way of holding the attention of an audience and of making complicated ideas easy to grasp. Parables are often remembered by people of many different faiths because they communicate essential ideas simply and dramatically.

Parables often make use of *allegory* – that is, where something concrete and everyday really stands for something more abstract and spiritual. Thus, when Jesus counsels his followers to be like the wise man who builds his house firmly upon a rock which can outface any storm, rather than like the foolish man who builds his house upon shifting sand, we know that it isn't really houses that are being talked about, but lives. The 'rock' is an allegory (or metaphor) for the foundation of his teaching.

A parable tends to answer a single moral question or to suggest a single principle by which to live. Usually there is a definite moral message attached. All of the stories in this section have a moral message: some, like 'The Good Samaritan', are unquestionably parables and similar stories may be found in other religious teachings; the basic message of the Korean parable, 'The Difference', could equally well have come from any one of the major religions as could the Jewish story of 'The Ring'.

The remaining stories in this section, although not parables, are certainly moral tales. The two stories by Natalie Babbitt, 'Perfection' and 'Boating', although they are modern, have much in common with parables and could come from almost any age. Saki's story about a storyteller typically manages to be both moral and faintly immoral at the same time.

The first three stories are offered without comment or instruction other than that you read them and discuss what each suggests about how we might live better.

THE GOOD SAMARITAN

On one occasion a lawyer came forward to put this test question to him: 'Master, what must I do to inherit eternal life?' Jesus said, 'What is written in the Law? What is your reading of it?' He replied, 'Love the Lord your God with all your heart, with all your soul, with all your strength, and with all your mind: and your neighbour as yourself.' 'That is the right answer,' said Jesus: 'do that and you will live.'

But he wanted to vindicate himself, so he said to Jesus, 'And who is my neighbour?' Jesus replied, 'A man was on his way from Jerusalem down to Jericho when he fell in with robbers, who stripped him, beat him, and went off leaving him half dead. It so happened that a priest was going down by the same road: but when he saw him, he went past on the other side. So too a Levite came to the place, and when he saw him went past on the other side. But a Samaritan who was making the journey came upon him, and when he saw him was moved to pity. He went up and bandaged his wounds, bathing them with oil and wine. Then he lifted him onto his own beast, brought him to an inn and looked after him there. Next day he produced two silver pieces and gave them to the innkeeper, and said, "Look after him: and if you do spend any more, I will repay you on my way back." Which of these three do you think was neighbour to the man who fell into the hands of the robbers?' He answered, 'The one who showed him kindness.' Jesus said, 'Go and do as he did.'

New English Bible, Luke, Chapter 10 vv 25–37

THE RING

A poor man came to Rabbi Schmelke's door. There was no money in the house, so the rabbi gave him a ring. A moment later, his wife heard of it and heaped him with reproaches for throwing to an unknown beggar so valuable a piece of jewelry, with so large and precious a stone. Rabbi Schmelke had the poor man called back and said to him: 'I have just learned that the ring I gave you is of great value. Be careful not to sell it for too little money.'

Martin Buber (trans.), Tales of the Hasidim

THE DIFFERENCE

In Korea there is a legend about a native warrior who died and went to heaven. 'Before I enter,' he said to the gate-keeper, I would like you to take me on a tour of hell.' The gate-keeper found a guide to take the warrior to hell. When he got there he was astonished to see a great table piled high with the choicest foods. But the people in hell were starving. The warrior turned to his guide and raised his eyebrows.

'It's this way,' the guide explained. 'Everybody who comes here is given a pair of chopsticks five feet long, and is required to hold them at the end to eat. But you just can't eat with chopsticks five feet long if you hold them at the end. Look at them. They miss their mouths every time, see?'

The visitor agreed that this was hell indeed and asked to be taken back to heaven post-haste. In heaven, to his surprise, he saw a similar room, with a similar table laden with very choice foods. But the people were happy; they looked radiantly happy.

The visitor turned to the guide. 'No chopsticks, I suppose?' he said.

'Oh yes,' said the guide, 'They have the same chopsticks, the same length, and they must be held at the end just as in hell. But you see, these people have learned that if a man feeds his neighbour, his neighbour will feed him also.'

Anonymous, retold by Denys Thompson

BOATING

Natalie Babbitt

Some people think Hell is dry as crackers, but this is not the case. There are four nice rivers inside the walls, and a fifth, called the Styx, that flows clear round the place outside.

Hell has the Styx the way castles have moats, but there isn't any drawbridge. Intead, you have to come across the water on a ferryboat run by a very old man named Charon. Most of the time Charon does his job all by himself, but it happened one day that he came to the throne room with a problem.

'What's wrong?' said the Devil, putting aside the novel he was reading.

'Why,' said Charon, 'they're having some kind of fuss in the World, in case you didn't know it.'

'They're always having fusses in the World,' said the Devil with a yawn. 'What of it?'

'Well, whatever sort of fuss it is,' said Charon, 'they're coming down in droves and I can't keep up. You'll have to lay on another ferryboat.'

'You don't say!' said the Devil. 'That's splendid! I'll come and take a look.'

And sure enough, there were hordes of people on the far side of the Styx, waiting to get across. Some of them were quite put out to be kept there cooling their heels, and wouldn't stay nicely in line for a minute. And what with their birdcages, boxes, and bags all piled and getting mixed, the confusion was indescribable.

'I'm doing the best I can,' said Charon to the Devil, 'but you see the way things are.'

'Hmmm,' said the Devil. 'Well now. I'll give you a hand myself. It looks like fun.'

He called for a second ferry – which was, like Charon's, more of a raft than a boat – and, climbing aboard, seized the pole and pushed out cross-current into the river Styx. He wasn't as good at it as Charon, not having had the practice, but still arrived not too long after at the opposite bank, where all the people were waiting.

'Ahoy,' said the Devil. 'Women and children first.' And since there weren't any children – indeed, there never are – three old women stepped onto the raft, which was all there was room for, and off they started back across the river.

'And who, my dears, may you be?' asked the Devil, eyeing their silks and feathers.

'We're sisters,' said the first old woman. 'The last of an important old family. The sort of people who matter.'

'We can't imagine what we're doing here with all these common types,' said the second.

'It's all a terrible mistake,' said the third.

'Indeed!' said the Devil, with a smile. 'I'll have someone look into it.'

'I should hope so,' said the first old woman. 'Why, we can't put up with this! Look at these dreadful people you've got coming in – riffraff of the lowest sort! It would appear that anyone at all can get in.'

'We can't be expected,' said the second, 'to mingle with peasants and boors.'

'Never in the World,' said the third.

'It's true,' said the Devil, 'that we do have every class down here. But so, I've heard, does Heaven.'

'I don't believe it,' said the first old woman. 'Not Heaven.'

'You must be misinformed,' said the second. 'Only the best people go to Heaven.'

'Otherwise,' said the third, 'whyever call it Heaven?'

'An interesting point,' said the Devil. 'Why, indeed!'

And all the way across the river Styx the three went on protesting and explaining.

When the raft at last scraped up before the gates, the sisters refused to get off. 'We simply can't go in,' said the first old woman. 'I'm sure you understand.'

'Oh, I do,' said the Devil. 'I do.'

'Not our grade of people in the least,' said the second.

'Look into it for us, won't you?' said the third. 'We'll just wait here and catch the next boat back.'

Now, the river Styx flows round the walls of Hell in a wandering clockwise direction, and a long way round it is, too, which will come as no surprise. And though the current isn't swift, it's steady. So the Devil, disembarking, put his pole against the ferry and simply shoved it out again so that the current bore it off, turning it gently in circles, with the sisters still on board. And then he went back to his throne room and sent a minor demon out to give a hand to Charon. For the Devil had had enough and wanted to finish his novel.

Years went by, and dozens of years, with the sisters still floating round the walls of Hell. Every once in a while, in the beginning, the Devil would remember them and go out when it was time for them to pass. And as they came along, he could hear their protestations, steady as the current of the Styx.

'Ragtag and bobtail,' they'd be saying. 'Waifs and strays. Quite beneath contempt! Commoners, upstarts, people of the street. Not our sort at all.' And they would say, 'There's been some mix-up, certainly. Why don't they get it straightened out?'

Sometimes they saw the Devil standing on the banks, and the first old woman would call to him, 'Yoo-hoo! I say, my good man – have you made inquiries concerning our situation?' And the Devil would wave and nod, and watch as they slowly circled by and disappeared. And then he would smile and go back through the gates for a nice cold glass of cider. But after a time he forgot the three completely. This was not because he was too busy to remember. No, indeed. He forgot them because they weren't the sort of people who matter.

Inside the story

In pairs or small groups

'Some people think hell is as dry as crackers,' begins the story; however, Natalie Babbitt describes a hell which isn't the traditional fiery furnace but which is particularly appropriate for its new arrivals. Discuss why their situation is hell for the three ladies.

On your own

What other hells might there be appropriate for other people? Invent your own versions of hell for people with other failings: a vain person too proud of their beauty or their strength, a bully, a successful, rich and selfish businessman, a perfectionist for whom everything must be *just so*, a sarcastic teacher. . . . There are lots of other possibilities. When you have decided on your character, write your own story of what happens when they meet the Devil. You could start your version from the point in Natalie Babbitt's story where the Devil asks 'And who, my dears, may you be?'

Make sure that in the reply and in everything your character says and does it is clear what sort of person is being ferried and why the punishment you have decided upon will be appropriate.

In groups

Dramatise Natalie Babbitt's story of the three ladies and act it out. Think carefully about the ladies' actions and their tone of voice. You may want to add some additional dialogue for each time the Devil appears on the bank. If you have the use of a drama room, you could find that illuminating the raft in a pool of light and fading it out with the fading voices helps the illusion. The playlet is also simple enough to lend itself to tape recording or, more ambitiously, to videotaping.

If you have developed your own scripts for other characters in hell, you could also dramatise these.

The nineteenth century saw the publication of many strict moral tales intended to act as good examples to naughty children. The writer H.H. Munro, who wrote under the pen-name of 'Saki', was brought up on such moral tales and in adult life gleefully took his revenge and revolted against them. In 'The Story-Teller' he pokes delicious fun at the highly moral stories he himself had endured as a child.

THE STORY-TELLER

'Saki'

It was a hot afternoon and the railway carriage was correspondingly sultry, and the next stop was at Templecombe, nearly an hour ahead. The occupants of the carriage were a small girl, and a smaller girl, and a small boy. An aunt belonging to the children occupied one corner seat, and the further corner seat on the opposite side was occupied by a bachelor who was a stranger to their party, but the small girls and the small boy emphatically occupied the compartment. Both the aunt and the children were conversational in a limited, persistent way, reminding one of the attentions of a house-fly that refused to be discouraged. Most of the aunt's remarks seemed to begin with 'Don't', and nearly all of the children's remarks began with 'Why?' The bachelor said nothing out loud.

'Don't, Cyril, don't,' exclaimed the aunt as the small boy began smacking the cushions of the seat producing a cloud of dust at each blow.

'Come and look out of the window,' she added.

The child moved reluctantly to the window. 'Why are those sheep being driven out of that field?' he asked.

'I expect they are being driven to another field where there is more grass,' said the aunt weakly.

'But there is lots of grass in that field,' protested the boy; 'there's nothing but grass there. Aunt, there's lots of grass in that field.'

'Perhaps the grass in the other field is better,' suggested the aunt fatuously.

'Why is it better?' came the swift, inevitable question.

'Oh, look at those cows!' exclaimed the aunt. Nearly every field along the line had contained cows or bullocks, but she spoke as though she were drawing attention to a rarity.

'Why is the grass in the other field better?' persisted Cyril.

The frown on the bachelor's face was deepening to a scowl. He was a hard, unsympathetic man, the aunt decided in her mind. She was utterly unable to come to any satisfactory decision about the grass in the other field.

The smaller girl created a diversion by beginning to recite 'On the Road to Mandalay'. She only knew the first line, but she put her limited knowledge to the fullest possible use. She repeated the line over and over again in a dreamy but resolute and very audible voice; it seemed to the bachelor as though someone had a bet with her that she could not repeat the line aloud two thousand times without stopping. Whoever it was who had made the wager was likely to lose his bet.

'Come over here and listen to a story,' said the aunt, when the bachelor had looked twice at her and once at the communication cord.

The children moved listlessly towards the aunt's end of the carriage. Evidently her reputation as a story-teller did not rank high in their estimation.

In a low, confidential voice, interrupted at frequent intervals by loud, petulant questions from her listeners, she began an unenterprising and deplorably uninteresting story about a little girl who was good and made friends with every one on account of her goodness, and was finally saved from a mad bull by a number of rescuers who admired her moral character.

'Wouldn't they have saved her if she hadn't been good?' demanded the bigger of the small girls. It was exactly the question the bachelor had wanted to ask.

'Well, yes,' admitted the aunt lamely, 'but I don't think they would have run quite so fast to help her if they had not liked her so much.'

'It's the stupidest story I've ever heard,' said the bigger of the small girls, with immense conviction.

'I didn't listen after the first bit, it was so stupid,' said Cyril.

The smaller girl made no actual comment on the story, but she had long ago recommenced a murmured repetition of her favourite line.

'You don't seem to be a success as a story-teller,' said the bachelor suddenly from his corner.

The aunt bristled in instant defence at this

unexpected attack.

'It's a very difficult thing to tell stories that children can both understand and appreciate,' she said stiffly.

'I don't agree with you,' said the bachelor.

'Perhaps *you* would like to tell them a story,' was the aunt's retort.

'Tell us a story,' demanded the bigger of the small girls.

'Once upon a time,' began the bachelor, 'there was a little girl called Bertha, who was extraordinarily good.'

The children's momentarily-aroused interest began at once to flicker; all stories seemed dreadfully alike, no matter who told them.

'She did all that she was told, she was always truthful, she kept her clothes clean, ate milk puddings as though they were jam tarts, learned her lessons perfectly, and was polite in her manners.'

'Was she pretty?' asked the bigger of the small girls.

'Not as pretty as any of you,' said the bachelor, 'but she was horribly good.'

There was a wave of reaction in favour of the story; the word horrible in connection with goodness was a novelty that commended itself. It seemed to introduce a ring of truth that was absent from the aunt's tales of infant life.

'She was so good,' continued the bachelor, 'that she won several medals for goodness, which she always wore, pinned on her dress. There was a medal for obedience, another medal for punctuality, and a third for good behaviour. They were large metal medals and they clicked against each other as she walked. No other child in the town where she lived had as many as three medals, so everybody knew that she must be an extra good child.'

'Horribly good,' quoted Cyril.

'Everybody talked about her goodness, and the

Prince of the country got to hear about it, and he said that as she was so very good she might be allowed once a week to walk in his park, which was just outside the town. It was a beautiful park, and no children were ever allowed in it, so it was a great honour for Bertha to be allowed to go there.'

'Were there any sheep in the park?' demanded Cyril.

'No,' said the bachelor, 'there were no sheep.'

'Why weren't there any sheep?' came the inevitable question arising out of that answer.

The aunt permitted herself a smile, which might almost have been described as a grin.

'There were no sheep in the park,' said the bachelor, 'because the Prince's mother had once had a dream that her son would either be killed by a sheep or else by a clock falling on him. For that reason the Prince never kept a sheep in his park or a clock in his palace.'

The aunt suppressed a gasp of admiration.

'Was the Prince killed by a sheep or by a clock?' asked Cyril.

'He is still alive, so we can't tell whether the dream will come true,' said the bachelor unconcernedly; 'anyway, there were no sheep in the park, but there were lots of little pigs running all over the place.'

'What colour were they?'

'Black with white faces, white with black spots, black all over, grey with white patches, and some were white all over.'

The story-teller paused to let a full idea of the park's treasures sink into the children's imaginations; then he resumed:

'Bertha was rather sorry to find there were no flowers in the park. She had promised her aunts, with tears in her eyes, that she would not pick any of the kind Prince's flowers, and she had meant to keep her promise, so of course it made her feel silly to find there were no flowers to pick.'

'Why weren't there any flowers?'

'Because the pigs had eaten them all,' said the bachelor promptly. 'The gardeners had told the Prince that you couldn't have pigs and flowers, so he decided to have pigs and no flowers.'

There was a murmur of approval at the excellence of the Prince's decision; so many people would have decided the other way.

'There were lots of other delightful things in the park. There were ponds with gold and blue and green fish in them, and trees with beautiful parrots that said clever things at a moment's notice, and humming birds that hummed all the popular tunes of the day. Bertha walked up and down and enjoyed herself immensely, and thought to herself: "if I were not so extraordinarily good I should not have been allowed to come into this beautiful park and enjoy all there is to be seen in it," and her three gold medals clinked one against another as she walked and helped remind her how very good she really was. Just then an enormous wolf came prowling into the park to see if it could catch a fat little pig for its supper.'

'What colour was it?' asked the children, amid an immediate quickening of interest.

'Mud-colour all over, with a black tongue and pale grey eyes that gleamed with unspeakable ferocity. The first thing that it saw in the park was Bertha; her pinafore was so spotlessly white and clean that it could be seen from a great distance. Bertha saw the wolf and saw that it was stealing towards her, and she began to wish that she had never been allowed to come into the park. She ran as hard as she could, and the wolf came after her with huge leaps and bounds. She managed to reach a shrubbery of myrtle bushes and she hid herself in one of the thickest of the bushes. The wolf came sniffing among the branches, its black tongue lolling out of its mouth and its pale grey eyes glaring with rage. Bertha was terribly frightened, and thought to herself: "If I had not been so extraordinarily good I should have been safe in the town at this moment." However, the scent of the myrtle was so strong that the wolf could not sniff out where Bertha was hiding, and the bushes were so thick that he might have hunted about in them for a long time without catching sight of her, so he thought he might as well go off and catch a little pig instead. Bertha was trembling very much at having the wolf prowling and sniffing so near her, and as she trembled the medal for obedience clinked against the medals for good conduct and punctuality. The wolf was just moving away when he heard the sound of medals clinking and stopped to listen; they clinked again in a bush quite near him. He dashed into the bush, his pale grey eyes gleaming with ferocity and triumph and dragged Bertha out and devoured her to the last morsel. All that was left of her were her shoes, bits of clothing, and the three medals for goodness.'

'Were any of the little pigs killed?'

'No, they all escaped.'

'The story began badly,' said the smaller of the small girls, 'but it had a beautiful ending.'

'It is the most beautiful story that I ever heard,' said the bigger of the small girls, with immense decision.

'It is the only beautiful story that I ever heard,' said Cyril.

A dissentient opinion came from the aunt.

'A most improper story to tell to young children! You have undermined the effect of years of careful teaching.'

'At any rate,' said the bachelor, collecting his belongings preparatory to leaving the carriage, 'I kept them quiet for ten minutes, which was more than you were able to do.'

'Unhappy woman!' he observed to himself as he walked down the platform of Templecombe station; 'for the next six months or so those children will assail her in public with demands for an improper story!'

Inside the story

In pairs or small groups

1 Discuss what appeals to the children about the story of Bertha and the wolf.

2 What does the bachelor understand about children that the aunt does not?

3 Discuss what makes the bachelor a good storyteller and the methods he uses to keep the children's attention.

4 Although the aunt says it is 'a most improper story to tell young children', the story of Bertha and the wolf does, in fact, have a traditional moral which even the aunt might approve of – if she could see it. What would you say it was?

On your own

Write your own moral tale about a sickeningly good person – young or old – who comes to a sticky end as a result of being too good to be true. Of course, the outcome of your story doesn't have to be as final as having the main character eaten up by a wolf. There are other fates that some might think equally trying, particularly as they can go on for years – as the following story about another perfect little girl might suggest.

Perfection

Natalie Babbitt

There was a little girl once called Angela who always did everything right. In fact, she was perfect. She had better manners than anyone, and not only that, but she hung up her clothes and never forgot to feed the chickens. And not only *that*, but her hair was always combed and she never bit her fingernails. A lot of people, all of them fair-to-middling, disliked her very much because of this, but Angela didn't care. She just went right on being perfect and let things go as they would.

Now when the Devil heard about Angela, he was revolted. 'Not,' he explained to himself, 'that I give a hang about children as a rule, but *this* one! Imagine what she'll be like when she grows up – a woman whose only fault is that she has no faults!' And the very thought of it made him cross as crabs. So he wrote up a list of things to do that he hoped would make Angela edgy and, if all went well, even make her lose her temper. 'Once she loses her temper a few times,' said the Devil, 'she'll never be perfect again.'

However, this proved harder to do than the Devil had expected. He sent her chicken pox, then poison ivy, and then a lot of mosquito bites, but she never scratched and didn't even seem to itch. He arranged for a cow to step on her favorite doll, but she never shed a tear. Instead she forgave the cow at once, in public, and said it didn't matter. Next the Devil fixed it so that for weeks on end her cocoa was always too hot and her oatmeal too cold, but this, too, failed to make her angry. In fact it seemed that the worse things were, the better Angela liked it, since it gave her a chance to show just how perfect she was.

Years went by. The Devil used up every idea on his lists but one, and Angela still had her temper, and her manners were still better than anyone's. 'Well, anyway,' said the Devil to himself, 'my last idea can't miss. That much is certain.' And he waited patiently for the proper moment.

What do *you* think the Devil's final idea will be?

When that moment came, the Devil's last idea worked like anything. In fact, it was perfect. As soon as he made it happen, Angela lost her temper once a day at least, and sometimes oftener, and after a while she had lost it so often that she was never quite so perfect again.

And how did he do it? Simple. He merely saw that she got a perfect husband and a perfect house, and then – he sent her a fair-to-middling child.

Inside the story

In pairs or small groups

1 Discuss why being the parent of an ordinary child should prove so infuriating to Angela. (Why do you think the author chose to call her Angela, by the way?)

2 'Perfection' is a neat little moral fable where we are left to work out a moral for ourselves. Decide what you think a suitable moral for the story might be.

3
SOME DAY MY PRINCE WILL COME?

In the previous section on fables it was suggested that, like fables, folk and fairy stories are well known to people in many different countries and cultures and that they were passed down from generation to generation. Whether we know these stories from childhood story-telling sessions at home or school or from picture books or cartoon films, we have a knowledge of many folk and fairy stories by the time we are seven or eight years old. The story that follows in some ways provides a bridge between the world of the fable and that of the fairy story.

THE PRINCESS AND THE TIN BOX

James Thurber

Once upon a time, in a far country, there lived a king whose daughter was the prettiest princess in the world. Her eyes were like the cornflower, her hair was sweeter than the hyacinth, and her throat made the swan look dusty.

From the time she was a year old, the princess had been showered with presents. Her nursery looked like Cartier's window. Her toys were all made of gold or platinum or diamond or emeralds. She was not permitted to have wooden blocks or china dolls or rubber dogs or linen books, because such materials were considered cheap for the daughter of a king.

When she was seven, she was allowed to attend the wedding of her brother and throw real pearls at the bride instead of rice. Only the nightingale, with his lyre of gold, was permitted to sing for the princess. The common blackbird, with his boxwood flute, was kept out of the palace grounds. She walked in silver-and-samite slippers to a sapphire-and-topaz bathroom and slept in an ivory bed inlaid with rubies.

On the day the princess was eighteen, the king sent a royal ambassador to the courts of five neighbouring kingdoms to announce that he would give his daughter's hand in marriage to the prince who brought her the gift she liked the most.

The first prince to arrive at the palace rode a swift white stallion and laid at the feet of the princess an enormous apple made of solid gold which he had taken from a dragon who had guarded it for a thousand years. It was placed on a long ebony table set up to hold the gifts of the princess's suitors. The second prince, who came on a grey charger, brought her a nightingale made of a thousand diamonds, and it was placed beside the golden apple. The third prince, riding on a black horse, carried a great jewel box made of platinum and sapphires, and it was placed next to the diamond nightingale. The fourth prince, astride a fiery yellow horse, gave the princess a gigantic heart made of rubies and pierced by an emerald arrow. It was placed next to the platinum-and-sapphire jewel box.

Now the fifth prince was the strongest and handsomest of all the five suitors, but he was the son of a poor king whose realm had been overrun by mice and locusts and wizards and mining engineers so that there was nothing much of value left on it. He came plodding up to the palace of the princess on a plough horse and he brought her a small tin box filled with mica and feldspar and hornblende which he had picked up on the way.

The other princes roared with disdainful laughter when they saw the tawdry gift the fifth prince had brought to the princess. But she examined it with great interest and squealed with delight, for all her life she had been glutted with precious stones and priceless metals,

but she had never seen tin before or mica or feldspar or hornblende. The tin box was placed next to the ruby heart pierced with an emerald arrow.

'Now,' the king said to his daughter, 'you must select the gift you like best and marry the prince that brought it.'

The princess smiled and walked up to the table and picked up the present she liked the most.

Stop! What do you think her decision will be? Why do you think so?

It was the platinum-and-sapphire jewel box, the gift of the third prince.

'The way I figure it', she said, 'is this. It is a very large and expensive box, and when I am married, I will meet many admirers who will give me precious gems with which to fill it to the top. Therefore, it is the most valuable of all the gifts my suitors have brought me and I like it the best.'

The princess married the third prince that very day in the midst of great merriment and high revelry. More than a hundred thousand pearls were thrown at her and she loved it.

Moral: All those who thought the princess was going to select the tin box filled with worthless stones instead of one of the other gifts will kindly stay after class and write one hundred times on the blackboard 'I would rather have a hunk of aluminium silicate than a diamond necklace.'

Inside the story

As a group

1 Did you expect the story to end like this? Why did/didn't you?

2 Go back to the beginning of the story and list the things that made you realise that this was a fairy tale princess.

3 Discuss the way in which the king and the princes regard the princess.

When we read or listen to a folk-tale or fairy story, we remember other stories of a similar type and so we know what to expect when we come across a prince, a fairy godmother, a dragon, an enchanter or a stepmother. We are not unduly surprised by animals who behave and talk like humans – after all, they may turn out to be humans under a spell. Even if the talking frog really is just a talking frog that's all right because we know that one of the rules of such tales is that frogs, or any other

"I was happier when I was a frog."

creatures, are allowed to talk. Whatever the setbacks, we know that the hero will win in the end, through bravery or cunning or a mixture of both. Questions, riddles, impossible tasks, magic and evil characters are all common features of the fairy tale world. We know that princes have to prove themselves worthy to inherit their kingdoms and/or marry their princesses – though by the time they actually become kings they seem to change into capricious or incompetent characters, forever at the mercy of dragons, enchanters and misfortunes.

The story which follows contains many of the stock characters and basic structures found in fairy stories. Before you read the story itself, look at the lists of characters and events given below, bearing in mind what you already know about this type of story.

Characters	Events
a King	a Marriage
a Queen	Three Questions to be asked
an Enchanter	a Rescue
a Princess	Three Tasks to be performed
Three Princes	a Quest
a Spellbound Old Man	Three Magical Objects to be won

On your own

1 Write a sentence about each of the characters in the first list – what would you expect each to be like? How might each behave in the story?

2 Arrange the Events in the order in which you think they might happen in the story.

Working with a partner

Compare what you have written for 1 and 2 above. Discuss any differences between your answers. Agree on a version of the story together. Either together or individually, write your own version of a story containing these characters and events.

Now read the story.

PETRONELLA

Jay Williams

In the kingdom of Skyclear Mountain, three princes were always born to the king and queen. The oldest prince was always called Michael, the middle prince was always called George, and the youngest was always called Peter. When they were grown, they always went out to seek their fortunes. What happened to the oldest prince and the middle prince no one ever knew. But the youngest prince always rescued a princess, brought her home, and in time ruled over the kingdom. This was the way it had always been. And so far as anyone knew, that was the way it always would be.

Until now.

Now was the time of King Peter the twenty-sixth and Queen Blossom. An oldest prince was born, and a middle prince. But the youngest prince turned out to be a girl.

'Well,' said the king gloomily, 'we can't call her Peter. We'll have to call her Petronella. And what's to be done about it, I'm sure I don't know.'

There was nothing to be done. The years passed, and the time came for the princes to go out and seek their fortunes. Michael and George said good-bye to the king and queen and mounted their horses. Then out came Petronella. She was dressed in travelling clothes, with her bag packed and a sword by her side.

'If you think,' she said, 'that I'm going to sit at home, you are mistaken. I'm going to seek my fortune, too.'

'Impossible!' said the king.

'What will people say?' cried the queen.

'Look,' said Prince Michael, 'be reasonable, Pet. Stay home. Sooner or later a prince will turn up here.'

Petronella smiled. She was a tall, handsome girl with flaming red hair and when she smiled in that particular way it meant she was trying to keep her temper.

'I'm going with you,' she said. 'I'll find a prince if I have to rescue one from something myself. And that's that.'

The grooms brought out her horse, she said good-bye to her parents, and away she went behind her two brothers.

They travelled into the flatlands below Skyclear Mountain. After many days, they entered a great dark forest. They came to a place where the road divided into three, and there at the fork sat a little, wrinkled old man covered with dust and spiderwebs.

Prince Michael said haughtily, 'Where do these roads go, old man?'

'The road on the right goes to the city of Gratz,' the man replied. 'The road in the centre goes to the castle of Blitz. The road on the left goes to the house of Albion the enchanter. And that's one.'

'What do you mean by "and that's one"?' asked Prince George.

'I mean,' said the old man, 'that I am forced to sit on this spot without stirring, and that I must answer one question from each person who passes by. And that's two.'

Petronella's kind heart was touched. 'Is there anything I can do to help you?' she asked.

The old man sprang to his feet. The dust fell from him in clouds.

'You have already done so,' he said. 'For that question is the one which releases me. I have sat here for sixty-two years waiting for someone to ask me that.' He snapped his fingers with joy. 'In return, I will tell you anything you wish to know.'

'Where can I find a prince?' Petronella said promptly.

'There is one in the house of Albion the enchanter,' the old man answered.

'Ah,' said Petronella, 'then that is where I am going.'

'In that case I will leave you,' said her oldest brother. 'For I am going to the castle of Blitz to see if I can find my fortune there.'

'Good luck,' said Prince George. 'For I am going to the city of Gratz. I have a feeling my fortune is there.'

They embraced her and rode away.

Petrolla looked thoughtfully at the old man, who was combing spiderwebs and dust out of his beard. 'May I ask you something else?' she said.

'Of course. Anything.'

'Suppose I wanted to rescue that prince from the enchanter. How would I go about it? I haven't any experience in such things, you see.'

The old man chewed a piece of his beard. 'I do not know everything,' he said after a moment, 'but I do know that there are three magical secrets which, if you can get them from him, will help you.'

'How can I get them?' asked Petronella.

'Offer to work for him. He will set you three tasks, and if you can do them you may demand a reward for each. You must ask him for a comb for your hair, a mirror to look into, and a ring for your finger.'

'And then?'

'I do not know. I only know that when you rescue the prince, you can use these things to escape from the enchanter.'

'It doesn't sound easy,' sighed Petronella.

'Nothing we really want is easy,' said the old man. 'Look at me – I have wanted my freedom, and I've had to wait sixty-two years for it.'

Petronella said good-bye to him. She mounted her horse and galloped along the third road.

It ended at a low, rambling house with a red roof. It was a comfortable-looking house, surrounded by gardens and stables and trees heavy with fruit.

On the lawn, in an armchair, sat a handsome young man with his eyes closed and his face turned to the sky.

Petronella tied her horse to the gate and walked across the lawn.

'Is this the house of Albion the enchanter?' she said.

The young man blinked up at her in surprise.

'I think so,' he said. 'Yes, I'm sure it is.'

'And who are you?'

The young man yawned and stretched. 'I am Prince Ferdinand of Firebright,' he replied. 'Would you mind stepping aside? I'm trying to get a suntan and you're standing in the way.'

Petronella snorted. 'You don't sound like much of a prince,' she said.

'That's funny,' said the young man, closing his eyes. 'That's what my father always says.'

At that moment the door of the house opened. Out came a man dressed all in black and silver. He was tall and thin, and his eyes were as black as a cloud full of thunder. Petronella knew at once he must be the enchanter.

He bowed to her politely. 'What can I do for you?'

'I wish to work for you,' said Petronella boldly.

Albion nodded. 'I cannot refuse you,' he said. 'But I warn you, it will be dangerous. Tonight I will give you a task. If you do it, I will reward you. If you fail, you must die.'

Petronella glanced at the prince and sighed. 'If I must, I must,' she said. 'Very well.'

That evening they all had dinner together in the enchanter's cozy kitchen. Then Albion took Petronella out to a stone building and unbolted its door. Inside were seven huge black dogs.

'You must watch my hounds all night,' said he.

Petronella went in, and Albion closed and locked the door. At once the hounds began to snarl and bark. They bared their teeth at her. But Petronella was a real princess. She plucked up her courage. Instead of backing away, she went toward the dogs. She began to speak to them in a quiet voice. They stopped snarling and sniffed at her. She patted their heads.

'I see what it is,' she said. 'You are lonely here. I will keep you company.'

And so all night long, she sat on the floor and talked to the hounds and stroked them. They lay close to her, panting.

In the morning Albion came and let her out. 'Ah,' said he, 'I see that you are brave. If you had run from the dogs, they would have torn you to pieces. Now you may ask for what you want.'

'I want a comb for my hair,' said Petronella.

The enchanter gave her a comb carved from a piece of black wood.

Prince Ferdinand was sunning himself and working at a crossword puzzle. Petronella said to him in a low voice, 'I am doing this for you.'

'That's nice,' said the prince. 'What's "selfish" in nine letters?'

'You are,' snapped Petronella. She went to the enchanter. 'I will work for you once more,' she said.

That night Albion led her to a stable. Inside were seven huge horses.

'Tonight,' he said, 'you must watch my steeds.'

He went out and locked the door. At once the horses began to rear and neigh. They pawed at her with their iron hoofs.

But Petronella was a real princess. She looked closely at them and saw that their coats were rough and their manes and tails full of burrs.

'I see what it is,' she said. 'You are hungry and dirty.'

She brought them as much hay as they could eat, and began to brush them. All night long she fed them and groomed them, and they stood quietly in their stalls.

In the morning Albion let her out. 'You are as kind as you are brave,' said he. 'If you had run from them they would have trampled you under their hoofs. What will you have as a reward?'

'I want a mirror to look into,' said Petronella.

The enchanter gave her a mirror made of silver.

She looked across the lawn at Prince Ferdinand. He was doing exercises leisurely. He was certainly handsome. She said to the enchanter, 'I will work for you once more.'

That night Albion led her to a loft above the stables. There, on perches, were seven great hawks.

'Tonight,' said he, 'you must watch my falcons.'

As soon as Petronella was locked in, the hawks began to beat their wings and scream at her.

Petronella laughed. 'That is not how birds sing,' she said. 'Listen.'

She began to sing in a sweet voice. The hawks fell silent. All night long she sang to them, and they sat like feathered statues on their perches, listening.

In the morning Albion said, 'You are as talented as

you are kind and brave. If you had run from them, they would have pecked and clawed you without mercy. What do you want now?'

'I want a ring for my finger,' said Petronella.

The enchanter gave her a ring made from a single diamond.

All that day and all that night Petronella slept for she was very tired. But early the next morning, she crept into Prince Ferdinand's room. He was sound asleep, wearing purple pajamas.

'Wake up,' whispered Petronella. 'I am going to rescue you.'

Ferdinand awoke and stared sleepily at her. 'What time is it?'

'Never mind that,' said Petronella. 'Come on!'

'But I'm sleepy,' Ferdinand objected. 'And it's so pleasant here.'

Petronella shook her head. 'You're not much of a prince,' she said grimly. 'But you're the best I can do.'

She grabbed him by the wrist and dragged him out of bed. She hauled him down the stairs. His horse and hers were in a separate stable, and she saddled them quickly. She gave the prince a shove and he mounted. She jumped on her own horse, seized the prince's reins, and away they went like the wind.

They had not gone far when they heard a tremendous thumping. Petronella looked back. A dark cloud rose behind them, and beneath it she saw the enchanter. He was running with great strides, faster than the horses could go.

'What shall we do?' she cried.

'Don't ask me,' said Prince Ferdinand grumpily. 'I'm all shaken to bits by this fast riding.'

Petronella desperately pulled out the comb. 'The old man said this would help me!' she said. And because she didn't know what else to do with it, she threw the comb on the ground. At once a forest rose up. The trees were so thick that no one could get between them.

Away went Petronella and the prince. But the enchanter turned himself into an axe and began to chop. Right and left he chopped, slashing, and the trees fell before him.

Soon he was through the wood, and once again Petronella heard his footsteps thumping behind.

She reined in the horses. She took out the mirror and threw it to the ground. At once a wide lake spread out behind them, gray and glittering.

Off they went again. But the enchanter sprang into the water, turning himself into a salmon as he did so. He swam across the lake and leaped out of the water on to the other bank. Petronella heard him coming – *thump! thump!* – behind them again.

This time she threw down the ring. It didn't turn into anything, but lay shining on the ground.

The enchanter came running up. And as he jumped over the ring, it opened wide and then snapped up around him. It held his arms tight to his body in a magical grip from which he could not escape.

'Well,' said Prince Ferdinand, 'that's the end of him.'

Petronella looked at him in annoyance. Then she looked at the enchanter, held fast in the ring.

'Bother!' she said. 'I can't just leave him here. He'll starve to death.'

She got off her horse and went up to him. 'If I release you,' she said, 'will you promise to let the prince go free?'

Albion stared at her in astonishment. 'Let him go free?' he said. 'What are yout talking about? I'm glad to get rid of him.'

It was Petronella's turn to look surprised. 'I don't understand,' she said. 'Weren't you holding him prisoner?'

'Certainly not,' said Albion. 'He came to visit me for a weekend. At the end of it, he said, "It's so pleasant here, do you mind if I stay on for another day or two?" I'm very polite and I said, "Of course." He stayed on, and on, and on, and on. I didn't like to be rude to a guest and I couldn't just kick him out. I don't know what I'd have done if you hadn't dragged him away.'

'But then –' said Petronella, 'but then – why did you come running after him in this way?'

'I wasn't chasing him,' said the enchanter. 'I was chasing *you*. You are just the girl I've been looking for. You are brave and kind and talented and beautiful as well.'

'Oh,' said Petronella. 'I see.'

'Hmm,' said she. 'How do I get this ring off you?'

'Give me a kiss.'

She did so. The ring vanished from around Albion and reappeared on Petronella's finger.

'I don't know what my parents will say when I come home with you instead of a prince,' she said.

'Let's go and find out, shall we?' said the enchanter cheerfully.

He mounted one horse and Petronella the other. And off they trotted, side by side, leaving Prince Ferdinand of Firebright to walk home as best he could.

Inside the story

Talking – in pairs

1 Discuss with your partner (a) whether the story was different from what you expected; (b) how it differed from your own version.

Why do you think the author chose to make Petronella different from the stereotype of a fairy tale princess?

In her introduction to *Clever Gretchen and Other Forgotten Folktales*, Alison Lurie writes:

In the fairy tales we know best today, the heroes seem to have all the interesting adventures. They get to kill dragons and outwit giants and rescue princesses and find the magic treasure. As for the heroines, things just happen to them: they are persecuted by wicked stepmothers, eaten by wolves, or fall asleep for a hundred years. All most of them ever seem to do is wait patiently for the right prince to come, or for someone else to rescue them from dangers or enchantments. This has made some people say that modern children ought not to read fairy tales, because they will get the idea that girls are supposed to be beautiful and good and helpless and dull.

Do you think that readers of fairy stories get ideas about expected behaviour from characters in the tales?

2 You will have noticed from the lists at the beginning of this section that things tend to go in threes in the story – three tasks, three questions, three magic objects, three princes. Think of other tales that you may know and see how many of them contain things or people that come in threes. Make a list, like the one on p. 46, showing the story titles and the groups of three in each story. We have suggested a few titles to set you off.

TITLE

Goldilocks   Three Little Pigs   Billy Goats Gruff   Cinderella   Others?

3 Bears

3 Chairs

3 Bowls of
   Porridge

3 Beds

Whoever heard of a fairy giving more or less than three wishes? Why do you think that the number three crops up so often in magical tales? Can you think of other instances where the number three is associated with powerful forces? Are there any other numbers associated with magical power?

3 The first paragraph of any folk-tale usually sets up in two or three sentences the key points in the story. From these we know immediately who the main characters are, what the situation is, and we can, from our past experience of such stories, predict the kinds of things that are likely to happen. In a way, they are quite comforting, because the reader can say to him or herself right from the outset, 'Oh, yes, it's *that* sort of story and, whatever dreadful things happen, all will come right in the end . . .' Folk-tales and fairy stories may appear dangerous because they can give their readers a fright and a warning, but they are at the same time safe because they work to rules and patterns from long ago and have predictable endings. Look at the following first paragraphs:

(a) *A certain poor miller had only his mill, his ass and his cat to bequeath to his three sons when he died. The children shared out their patrimony and did not bother to call in the lawyers; if they had done so they would have been stripped quite bare, of course. The eldest took the mill, the second the ass and the youngest had to make do with the cat.*

(b) *Once upon a time, there lived a king and a queen who were bitterly unhappy because they did not have any children. They visited all the clinics, all the specialists, made holy vows, went on pilgrimages and said their prayers regularly but with so little success that when, at long last, the queen finally did conceive and, in due course, gave birth to a daughter, they were both wild with joy. Obviously, this baby's christening had to be the grandest of all possible christenings; for her godmothers, she had to have as many fairies as they could find in the entire kingdom. According to the magic custom of those times, each fairy had to make the child a magic present, so that the princess could acquire every possible perfection. After a long search, the king and queen managed to trace seven suitable fairies.*

You may recognise the openings; it doesn't matter if you do. In any case, try to decide what happens in each story and share your predictions with the class.

In small groups

Because most people – young or old – remember some fairy stories, it is interesting to do a survey of what people recall and to find out what they liked or disliked.

Try to recall any fairy stories you remember from your own childhood which made an impression on you. Talk about the stories you remember.

- Which of the stories frightened you?
- Did any of them make you sad? Why?
- Did any of them make you happy? Why?
- Did you want to be like any of the characters?
- Did you have a favourite story? Why did you like it?

On your own

1 If you are able to talk to a younger child, perhaps a smaller brother or sister, ask them the same questions about fairy stories and record their answers. If you are talking to a much younger child don't challenge them with 'Do you believe in fairies . . .'; instead, try asking them where Cinderella lives, how they would get there and so on. Try to collect the children's answers and see if you can write about How Young Children See Fairy Stories. If you are fortunate enough to be able to work with young children from a local infant/primary school or playgroup you may be able to develop quite an interesting project from this activity.

2 It's not just young children who can be surveyed in the ways outlined above: you can undertake similar surveys of first year pupils in your own school or you can ask older people, parents, grandparents, teachers – adults you know well – and build up a picture of the way fairy stories continue through the generations.

Writing

Another project which perhaps works best if you can talk to a class in a local infant/primary school or playgroup is to write your own fairy story and to make it into a small book suitable for young children. You will need to think about a simple story which they can follow and find satisfying. It has to be short enough to keep their attention, have an exciting cover and illustrations, and be printed simply and boldly enough for them to be able to follow the words if they can read. As well as the story itself, a piece of writing on how you wrote it, what problems you had and how you solved them, and how the children received it when you read it to them, could also be part of the assignment.

As you might guess from its title, the story which follows also takes a different view of a stock fairy tale situation, whilst relying for its effect on the reader's knowledge of what *usually* happens in this sort of story.

THE PAPER BAG PRINCESS

Robert H. Munsch

Elizabeth was a beautiful princess. She lived in a castle and had expensive princess clothes. She was going to marry a prince named Ronald.

Unfortunately, a dragon smashed her castle, burned all her clothes with his fiery breath, and carried off Prince Ronald.

Elizabeth decided to chase the dragon and get Ronald back.

She looked everywhere for something to wear but the only thing she could find that was not burnt was a paper bag. So she put on the paper bag and followed the dragon.

He was easy to follow because he left a trail of burnt forests and horses' bones.

Finally, Elizabeth came to a cave with a large door that had a huge knocker on it.

She took hold of the knocker and banged on the door.

The dragon stuck his nose out of the door and said, 'Well, a princess! I love to eat princesses, but I have already eaten a whole castle today. I am a very busy dragon. Come back tomorrow.'

He slammed the door so fast that Elizabeth almost got her nose caught.

Elizabeth grabbed the knocker and banged on the door again.

The dragon stuck his nose out of the door and said, 'Go away. I love to eat princesses, but I have already eaten a whole castle today. I am a very busy dragon. Come back tomorrow.'

'Wait,' shouted Elizabeth, 'Is it true that you are the smartest and fiercest dragon in the whole world?'

'Yes,' said the dragon.

'Is it true,' said Elizabeth, 'that you can burn up ten forests with your fiery breath?'

'Oh, yes,' said the dragon, and he took a huge, deep breath and breathed out so much fire that he burned up fifty forests.

'Fantastic,' said Elizabeth, and the dragon took another huge breath and breathed out so much fire that he burned up one hundred forests.

'Magnificent,' said Elizabeth, and the dragon took another huge breath, but this time nothing came out.

The dragon didn't even have enough fire left to cook a meat ball.

Elizabeth said, 'Dragon, is it true that you can fly around the world in just ten seconds?'

'Why, yes,' said the dragon and jumped up and flew

all the way round the world in just ten seconds.

He was very tired when he got back, but Elizabeth shouted, 'Fantastic, do it again!'

So the dragon jumped up and flew around the whole world in just twenty seconds.

When he got back he was too tired to talk and he lay down and went straight to sleep.

Elizabeth whispered very softly, 'Hey, dragon.' The dragon didn't move at all.

She lifted up the dragon's ear and put her head right inside. She shouted as loud as she could, 'Hey, dragon!'

The dragon was so tired he didn't even move.

Elizabeth walked right over the dragon and opened the door to the cave.

There was Prince Ronald.

He looked at her and said, 'Elizabeth, you are a mess! You smell like ashes, your hair is all tangled and you are wearing a dirty old paper bag. Come back when you are dressed like a real princess.'

'Ronald,' said Elizabeth, 'your clothes are really pretty and your hair is very neat. You look like a real prince, but you are a toad.'

They didn't get married after all.

Inside the story

In pairs or small groups

1 Robert N. Munsch wrote this story for children much younger than yourselves. Discuss what features of the language and style would lead you to guess that this is a story from a young children's picture book.

2 List the ways in which Elizabeth is like/not like a traditional princess.

3 How does Elizabeth get the better of the dragon?

4 What is *your* opinion of Ronald?

5 Decide whether there is a moral at the end of the story and, if so, what it is.

6 Why do you think the author wrote this story for very young children? (Look back at the quotation from Alison Lurie on p.45.)

Catherine Storr's story which follows, 'The Wolf and his Gifts', refers directly or indirectly, to a whole range of traditional stories with which she assumes the reader is already familiar. As you read through the story, make a mental note of any features from stories you recognise.

THE WOLF AND HIS GIFTS

Catherine Storr

The wolf, who had failed to catch Polly so many times, was feeling discouraged.

'There must be something wrong with her,' he thought. 'No ordinary girl could have escaped me so often. But she looks all right. Delicious, in fact. It's just that she doesn't seem to know the rules. She never does what the books say she should.'

He remembered gloomily the time he'd met Polly on her way to her grandmother. She hadn't played the part of Red Riding Hood at all properly. Then there'd been the time he'd tried to blow her house down; if she'd only been one of those succulent little pigs in the story, he'd certainly have had her. And it hadn't been any better when he'd tried the trick his ancestor had so ingeniously played on seven stupid little kids. Somehow those old stories didn't work out right nowadays.

'Things aren't what they were in the Good Old Days,' the wolf sighed. He leafed through his book of folk and fairy tales for the hundredth time.

Suddenly his eye brightened, and his ears pricked. His long red tongue curled round his black lips.

'Hah! I believe I see where I went wrong. I've been trying to *catch* Polly. I've been behaving like a – well, like a wolf. Quite unsuitable for an educated, well-born animal like myself. From now on I am a different creature. I am a suitor. I shall play the part of a Prince. I shall put in my claim, and I shall *win* the girl.'

A few days later, while Polly's family were at breakfast, the doorbell rang.

'Post! I'll go,' Jane said. She always hoped there might be some exciting letter for her, but there practically never was.

'Nothing for me. Two letters for Mum. And this for you,' she said, putting a badly-wrapped parcel by her father's plate. He opened it doubtfully.

'What is it?'

'Extraordinary! It can't be meant for me.'

'It said Mr. None of the rest of us are Misters,' Jane said.

'But who would send me a purse?'

'Anything in it?' Polly asked.

'Couldn't be. Someone's cut the bottom off.'

'But it looks quite new!' Polly's mother said.

'That's what's so extraordinary.'

'Isn't there a letter to explain?'

'Not a word.'

'Look! There's something written on the brown paper, only it's so torn it's difficult to read.'

'Let's see.' Polly's father said. 'It doesn't make sense,' he said.

'What does it say?'

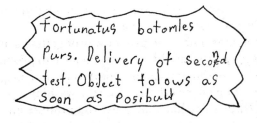

Fortunatus botomles Purs. Delivery of secod test. Object folows as Soon as Posibull

'Whoever wrote it can't spell.'

'Horrible writing too,' said Polly's mother.

'Must be a practical joke. I shan't take any notice.'

After her father had gone to work, Polly took the bottomless purse out of the wastepaper basket and put it away in a safe place. She had an idea. Something outrageously stupid about the whole business reminded her of the friend she hadn't seen for such a long time.

It was the following week, just as it was getting dark one evening, when there was a knock on the door.

'I'll go!' Jane said, as she always did.

'Can't be the post at this time of night,' her father said.

'It's for you, Father,' Jane called from the front door.

'Most extraordinary thing,' he said, coming back into the sitting room.

'What on earth have you got there?' his wife asked.

'Dog!' Lucy said.

'It's a very tiny dog,' Jane said.

'Says here it's the smallest dog in the world,' Polly said, reading a card tied on the dog's collar.

'What's that?'

The smorlest dog in the world Sorry There wasnt a warnut shell big enuff to Put it In.

Polly read from the card.

'Horrible writing,' Polly's mother said.

'Can't spell, either. Same practical joker as last time. But why me?' Polly's father said.

The smallest dog in the world was not happy. He wouldn't sit down and he wouldn't keep quiet. He either whined or he yapped. When Polly and her sisters tried to stroke him, he snapped at their fingers. When their mother offered him a piece of meat, he bit at it once or twice in a haughty manner, and then dropped it nastily into a shoe which Lucy had taken off a moment before.

'Want my shoe,' Lucy immediately said. But the smallest dog in the world now looked on it as his shoe. He would not let anyone near it. When Jane tried to take it from him, he growled, showing horrid, pointed little teeth. Lucy burst into tears and the smallest dog barked himself into a sort of fury, so that none of them could hear themselves speak.

'He'll have to go,' Polly's father said.

'Into a walnut shell?' Polly asked.

'Out. Tonight. Either that dog goes, or I do.'

The RSPCA came in a van and took the horrid little dog away. 'Wurry small dog. I don't know when I've seen a smaller,' the van driver said.

'You've never seen a nastier,' Polly's father said. (The van driver would have agreed with this before his evening was over, but that would be another story.)

'Let's hope that that's the end of that,' Polly's father said thankfully, when the last yap had died away. But of course it wasn't.

It must have been the following weekend that Polly's father came out of his front gate to find a long dark person digging industriously in the road just outside.

'Good morning,' he said.

'May you live for ever,' said the person.

'What's this? Gas? Electricity? Drains? Telephone?'

'Nothing so boring.'

'Perhaps you're digging for treasure?' Polly's father asked politely.

'Not exactly.'

'Don't keep me guessing, there's a good chap. What exactly are you doing? You're making a horrible mess of the road. I'll be lucky if I get my car out over that.'

'Don't step on it,' said the person in a panic.

'On what?'

'On that. It's the beginning of a palace. It was supposed to be finished by sunrise, but it's taken longer than I expected.'

'A palace? Here? Just outside my front gate?'

'Certainly. Marble, porphyry, gold and lapis lazuli, I think the specification was. To be completed overnight. As I was saying, it's proved rather more of a business than I'd anticipated. However, I expect I shall have it all ship-shape in a day or two.'

'And when it's up and ship-shape, how do I get my car in and out of the garage?' Polly's father asked, now really annoyed.

'Don't be petty,' the person said indignantly. 'How can you drivel on about your miserable car, when I'm building you the castle of your dreams in front of your house?'

'But I do want to get my car in and out of the garage, and I don't want the castle of my dreams.'

'You're impossible!' the wolf said angrily. 'You'll be telling me next you didn't want Fortunatus' purse, or the smallest dog in the world.'

'So it was you! What on earth persuaded you to play a silly practical joke like that?'

'You must know the proper way of getting someone to give you his daughter. First you have to produce a magic something; it can be a tinderbox, or a magic sword, or a tablecloth that does the washing-up, or some little thing like that. Next you produce an out-of-the-way animal. I did think of a goat that sneezes gold, but then I didn't want to catch its cold. Beastly infectious creatures, goats; and there seemed to be a shortage of talking horses and birds with fiery tails and that sort of thing, so I settled for a small dog. Then we all know about the last task. It's always the palace to be built overnight outside the king's house. Why he should want another palace just there is something I've never understood. Still there it is. This,' said the wolf, indicating a mound of yellow mud dotted with untidy lumps of brick and stone, 'is the palace.'

'And when you've got my daughter? What happens then?' Polly's father asked.

'Well. In the old stories I marry her. But we mustn't be old-fashioned, must we? Other times, other customs. Each man to his taste. Your Polly is very much "to my taste", I must say.'

'Polly,' said her father, seeing her at the window, 'I think you'd better come and explain the situation to this friend of yours.'

'Nearly ready for you, as you see,' the wolf said, as Polly joined him at the garden gate.

'I don't see the palace of ivory and gold that my father has a right to expect,' Polly said.

'Rome wasn't built in a day,' the wolf said hopefully.

'Don't tell me that this pile of mud is going to be Rome.'

'You are ungrateful. I've already given your father a bottomless purse . . .'

'A purse with the bottom cut off isn't exactly a purse which is always full of money.'

'. . . and a very small dog.'

'A horrid little dog. He bit Lucy.'

'That could have shown his perception. On the one occasion when I met your sister I felt like biting her myself.'

'I know what you mean,' Polly said. 'However, don't let's argue about that. A moment ago you said something about "nearly ready". What exactly did that mean?'

'Now who's being stupid? I've done the three tasks. Purse, dog, palace. This is the last. Then you are mine.'

'When?'

'When I've finished building Rome. I mean, of course, when I've built this palace.'

'How long do you suppose that's going to take?' Polly asked.

'I've only been working for about an hour or two, and I've made what you could call a promising start,' the wolf said smugly.

'It's more of a promise than a start,' Polly said.

'Deep foundations are necessary to support the noble edifice which I have designed,' the wolf said dreamily.

'After digging these foundations, you'll no doubt be raising the walls.'

'Colossal walls,' the wolf agreed.

'Then there'll be a roof?'

'With gilded turrets and battlements of steel,' the wolf promised.

'Windows?'

'Of the finest crystal.'

'A moat?'

'Certainly, A moat both wide and deep to keep out invaders.'

'A drawbridge?'

'We don't want to be over-elaborate, do we?' the wolf asked, with a hint of uneasiness in his voice.

'If you have a moat you must have a drawbridge. What about the inside of the palace?'

'Everything a moderately priced, well-stocked palace ought to have, this palace will contain,' the wolf said glibly.

'Have you anyone working for you, Wolf? Any friends? Relations? Labourers? Hired assassins?'

'With the sweat of my brow, with the honest toil of my own four paws I am going to win you for my own,' the wolf said earnestly.

'And you calculate that you are nearly ready for me. When precisely do you imagine that will be?'

The wolf looked up at the sky and down at the ground; he consulted a small diary and looked at a large old-fashioned silver watch. Then he said, 'Sunrise tomorrow morning. Sharp. Please be ready punctually.'

'My calculations,' said Polly, who had meanwhile been doing sums with a sharp stick on the mound of mud, 'come to something quite different.'

'Oh? What do your calculations tell you?'

'On the basis of the work already done, I calculate that to finish this palace and to equip it adequately is going to take you approximately six hundred and thirteen thousand hours, starting now.'

'Say that again,' the wolf said, after a moment of disbelieving silence.

'Six hundred and thirteen thousand hours.'

'It's a great many hours,' the wolf said.

'You're right, Wolf. It is.'

'How many days is that, Polly?'

Polly did another sum.

'It's over twenty-five thousand days, Wolf.'

'What's that in years?' the wolf asked rather faintly.

'Getting on for seventy years, Wolf.'

'Seventy years of work! I shall be exhausted!' The wolf sat down on the edge of the foundations as if the thought alone tired him. He looked across at Polly. 'Would you wait for me?' he asked wistfully.

'You've forgotten something, Wolf. Even if I waited, do you think after all that time you'd still want me?'

'You will never look old to me, Polly.'

'I wouldn't be too sure of that. What I meant, though, was, don't you think by then I might be a trifle tough?'

'You'll be how old?'

'Getting on for seventy-seven.'

'It would be an advanced age for a wolf, but perhaps it's different for humans.'

'Do you know old Miss Spinnaker who lives at the corner house? That'll give you some idea of what I'll be like.'

'Looks like a shrivelled spider in a purple hat?'

'That's the one.'

'Couldn't we deep-freeze you to keep the juices in?' the wolf suggested hopefully.

'That's not part of the bargain in any story I've ever heard of,' Polly said firmly. 'No, Wolf.'

'You're quite sure you've calculated right?'

'I generally get ten out of ten for my number work,' Polly said. 'But if you don't believe me, work it out for yourself.'

'You'd better let your father know that the bargain's off,' the wolf said, sullenly. 'I've been misled, that's what I've been. I should never have gone in for this competition in the first place if it had been made clear to me that all I was going to get at the end of it would be a bony, indigestible old windbag like that one on the corner. Sharp practice some people might call it, and they'd be right. It isn't the first time I've suffered through having such a trusting nature. Small minds some people have, I must say.'

'Others have large stomachs,' Polly murmured, but the wolf pretended not to hear.

'I shan't ask for the return of the purse or the dog. I hope I know how to be generous,' the wolf said. 'I shan't fill in the foundations either.'

'Are you just going to leave that hole there, Wolf? It's not very safe. Anyone might fall into it,' Polly said.

'Of course I don't want to cause any unpleasantness,' the wolf said, with a disagreeable smile. 'I thoughtfully brought a notice with me for just this purpose, which I'm sure will meet with your approval.'

From the bag containing his tools, he drew out a board and propped it up against the stones above the hole. It said,

'The story of my life,' thought Polly.

Inside the story

In pairs or small groups

1 Discuss which features of the story you recognise from other traditional fairy stories and fables and together make a list of them.

2 The wolf says of Polly near the beginning of the story: 'she doesn't seem to know the rules. She never does what the books say she should'. Discuss how Polly's behaviour is different from what the wolf expects and decide whether it is true that she doesn't know the rules.

3 The wolf decides to 'play the part of a Prince'. How does he change his behaviour to fit in with his idea of the role he has chosen for himself?

4 List the three tasks the wolf sets himself to gain the Princess/Polly and explain how he gets it wrong each time.

5 Pick out those things Polly's father says that best show *his* view of the wolf and his gifts.

6 In the end, Polly gets the better of the wolf – but not in quite the traditional way. How would you describe her tactics?

7 When she sees the wolf's notice DANGER. WOLF AT WORK, Polly sighs and thinks 'The story of my life'. What does this suggest to you about Polly and the wolf – and, perhaps, about girls and wolves generally?

On your own

1 This story relies for its effect on putting the accepted conventions and unreal situations of a traditional fairy story into a modern setting with common-sense characters. Try writing a story of your own based on a fairy story with which you are familiar, but putting it into a modern setting.

2 As you read the story, clear pictures begin to form in your mind of the different scenes. You might like to try drawing the story as a strip cartoon with thought and speech bubbles.

In a group

Much of the story is written as a direct conversation between the wolf and Polly's family, or as the wolf's inner thoughts. This makes it suitable to perform as a radio play. You will need people to play Polly, Jane, Lucy, their mother and father, the wolf, and the RSPCA man; you might also decide you need a narrator for the linking bits. You will probably need somebody to be in charge of the sound effects and the tape recording.

Making a radio play: some points to bear in mind

- Work out your script together, deciding who says what. For instance, in paragraph 2 of the story do you want the wolf to murmur his inner thoughts to himself? Do you want him to take over the narrator's bit in paragraph 3 and remember aloud to himself just how Polly hasn't behaved as she should, or will you leave paragraph 3 to a narrator? Or will you skip paragraph 3 altogether?

- Can any bits be cut to make the script tighter? For example, perhaps you can dispense with the RSPCA man after all?

- Are there any parts that need some additional dialogue to help the listener understand what is happening? For example, in paragraph 4 does the wolf need to mention that he's looking at his book of folk and fairy tales?

- Decide what sound effects are called for. For example, do you want the listener to hear the pages of the wolf's book being turned? Sometimes, a sound effect can help you get round the problem of having a narrator. For example, if we can hear the wolf digging, we may not need to be *told* what he is doing. Assemble all your sound effect materials in advance. Write them into your script.

- Think about the impression you have of the various characters to help you get the right expression in your voices. You won't have any actions to show how you feel, just the way you say things. Rehearse your lines (and get over your giggles at this stage!).

- Are you going to have any music and/or announcements to open and close your broadcast play? For example, 'Radio Four Schools Broadcasting. Storytime. This morning's story is 'The Wolf and his Gifts' by Catherine Storr.' You need to think of something suitable and may find that a few notes on a recorder or flute will be quite sufficient. Such little musical interludes, gradually faded out, are quite useful in the course of the play if you want to indicate that some time has passed.

- Rehearse your version and, when you are happy with it, tape record it. Remember to find a quiet spot for your recording, preferably one without too many hard echoing walls and surfaces. Use as good a quality tape and recording machine as you can. Place the machine and the microphone where they will not get knocked and where they will not pick up vibrations from furniture being moved. Sit or stand around the microphone as close as you reasonably can. You may find it helps to have the sound recordist move the microphone towards each speaker in turn. Keep movement to a minimum and avoid rustling scripts by the microphone. Be as professional as you can.

- Play your tape to the class on as large a recorder as you can. A little machine may be fine for making the tape but you will need good amplification if a whole class is to hear it.

- You might like to offer your 'broadcast' to a younger class in your school or to a nearby primary school if you think it is good enough.

In the story which follows, James Thurber presents a twentieth century version of an old fairy story and in doing so produces a tale which is a cross between a fairy story and a fable. (The Metro-Goldwyn lion he refers to is the roaring lion symbol which was the trademark of Metro-Goldwyn films in Hollywood. Calvin Coolidge was a former President of the USA.)

THE LITTLE GIRL AND THE WOLF

James Thurber

One afternoon a big wolf waited in a dark forest for a little girl to come along carrying a basket of food to her grandmother. Finally a little girl did come along and she was carrying a basket of food. 'Are you carrying that basket to your grandmother?' asked the wolf. The little girl said yes, she was. So the wolf asked her where her grandmother lived and the little girl told him and he disappeared into the wood.

When the little girl opened the door of her grandmother's house she saw that there was somebody in bed with a nightcap and nightgown on. She had approached no nearer than twenty-five feet from the bed when she saw that it was not her grandmother but the wolf, for even in a night cap a wolf does not look any more like your grandmother than the Metro-Goldwyn lion looks like Calvin Coolidge. So the little girl took an automatic out of her basket and shot the wolf dead.

Moral: It is not so easy to fool little girls nowadays as it used to be.

SECTION B:
INSIDE STORIES

1
PRESENT IMPERFECT: PARABLES FOR THE PRESENT DAY

The four stories in this section all invite us to look at the way human beings behave and warn us of faults in our society. Two of them tell us stories which are apparently set in the future but they are really comments on the way human beings are today. One is set in the distant past of imperial China but it too relates to twentieth century life. The fourth is set in a strangely magical present and is perhaps more of an allegory than a parable.

Nicholas Stuart Gray's story, 'The Star Beast', uses the simple, direct language which reminds us of the fable. From its opening 'Soon upon a time, and not so far ahead . . .' we can hear the voice of the traditional storyteller drawing us into a tale. A desperately sad tale it is too, and one which reminds us that although we claim to be human we are capable of great cruelty and that our so-called superiority and intelligence may mask arrogance and stupidity.

A similar theme is taken up in John Christopher's story, 'Blemish', where humans' pride in their technology is judged by a set of values it has tended to ignore. We are invited to see ourselves in another light – and it is not a very flattering one.

Technological achievement is the downfall of the inventor in Ray Bradbury's story of 'The Flying Machine'. The emperor, seeing the possible loss of his power and position, the end of his cherished 'civilisation' as a result of the inventor's genius, feels that there is only one harsh course of action he can take to ensure that his world does not change. To his mind, a lesser evil is justified if it prevents a greater one. Who is to say he is wrong?

Finally, Margaret Mahy's story, 'The House of Coloured Windows', is a magical story which you might feel provides a kind of balance to the rather pessimistic views of the three previous stories. A simple allegorical tale, it suggests that the present is perhaps not as imperfect as all that.

THE STAR BEAST

Nicholas Stuart Gray

Soon upon a time, and not so far ahead, there was a long streak of light down the night sky, a flicker of fire, and a terrible bang that startled all who heard it, even those who were normally inured to noise. When day came, the matter was discussed, argued, and finally dismissed. For no one could discover any cause at all for the disturbance.

Shortly afterwards, at a farm, there was heard a scrabbling at the door, and a crying. When the people went to see what was there, they found a creature. It was not easy to tell what sort of creature, but far too easy to tell that it was hurt and hungry and afraid. Only its pain and hunger had brought it to the door for help.

Being used to beasts, the farmer and his wife tended the thing. They put it in a loose-box and tended it. They brought water in a big basin and it drank thirstily, but with some difficulty – for it seemed to want to lift it to its mouth instead of lapping, and the basin was too big, and it was too weak. So it lapped. The farmer dressed the great burn that seared its thigh and shoulder and arm. He was kind enough, in a rough way, but the creature moaned, and set its teeth, and muttered strange sounds, and clenched its front paws. . . .

Those front paws . . . ! They were so like human hands that it was quite startling to see them. Even with their soft covering of grey fur they were slender, long-fingered, with the fine nails of a girl. And its body was like that of a boy – a half-grown lad –

though it was as tall as a man. Its head was man-shaped. The long and slanting eyes were as yellow as topaz, and shone from inside with their own light. And the lashes were thick and silvery.

'It's a monkey of some kind,' decided the farmer.

'But so beautiful,' said his wife. 'I've never heard of a monkey like this. They're charming – pretty – amusing – all in their own way. But not beautiful, as a real person might be.'

They were concerned when the creature refused to eat. It turned away its furry face, with those wonderful eyes, the straight nose, and curving fine lips, and would not touch the best of the season's hay. It would not touch the dog biscuits or the bones. Even the boiled cod-head that was meant for the cats' supper, it refused. In the end, it settled for milk. It lapped it delicately out of the big basin, making small movements of its hands – its forepaws – as though it would have preferred some smaller utensil that it could lift to its mouth.

Word went round. People came to look at the strange and injured creature in the barn. Many people came. From the village, the town, and the city. They prodded it, and examined it, turning it this way and that. But no one could decide just what it was. A beast for sure. A monkey, most likely. Escaped from a circus or menagerie. Yet whoever had lost it made no attempt to retrieve it, made no offer of reward for its return.

Its injuries healed. The soft fur grew again over the

bare grey skin. Experts from the city came and took it away for more detailed examination. The wife of the farmer was sad to see it go. She had grown quite attached to it.

'It was getting to know me,' said she. 'And it talked to me – in its fashion.'

The farmer nodded slowly and thoughtfully.

'It was odd,' he said, 'the way it would imitate what one said. You know, like a parrot does. Not real talking, of course, just imitation.'

'Of course,' said his wife. 'I never thought it was real talk. I'm not so silly.'

It was good at imitating speech, the creature. Very soon, it had learned many words and phrases, and began to string them together quite quickly, and with surprising sense. One might have thought it knew what it meant – if one was silly.

The professors and elders and priests who now took the creature in hand were far from silly. They were puzzled, and amused, and interested – at first. They looked at it, in the disused monkey-cage at the city's menagerie, where it was kept. And it stood upright, on finely-furred feet as arched and perfect as the feet of an ancient statue.

'It is oddly human,' said the learned men.

They amused themselves by bringing it a chair and watching it sit down gracefully, though not very comfortably, as if it was used to furniture of better shape and construction. They gave it a plate and a cup, and it ate with its hands most daintily, looking round as though for some sort of cutlery. But it was not thought safe to trust it with a knife.

'It is only a beast,' said everyone. 'However clever at imitation.'

'It's so quick to learn,' said some.

'But not in any way human.'

'No,' said the creature, 'I am not human. But, in my own place, I am a man.'

'Parrot-talk!' laughed the elders, uneasily.

The professors of living and dead languages taught it simple speech.

After a week, it said to them:

'I understand all the words you use. They are very easy. And you cannot quite express what you mean, in any of your tongues. A child of my race——' It stopped, for it had no wish to seem impolite, and then it said, 'There is a language that is spoken throughout the universe. If you will allow me——'

And softly and musically it began to utter a babble of meaningless nonsense at which all the professors laughed loudly.

'Parrot-talk!' they jeered. 'Pretty Polly! Pretty Polly!'

For they were much annoyed. And they mocked the creature into cowering silence.

The professors of logic came to the same conclusions as the others.

'Your logic is at fault,' the creature had told them, despairingly. 'I have disproved your conclusions again and again. You will not listen or try to understand.'

'Who could understand parrot-talk?'

'I am no parrot, but a man in my own place. Define a man. I walk upright. I think. I collate facts. I imagine. I anticipate. I learn. I speak. What is a man by your definition?'

'Pretty Polly!' said the professors.

They were very angry. One of them hit the creature with his walking-cane. No one likes to be set on a level with a beast. And the beast covered its face with its hands, and was silent.

It was warier when the mathematicians came. It added two and two together for them. They were amazed. It subtracted eight from ten. They wondered at it. It divided twenty by five. They marvelled. It took courage. It said:

'But you have reached a point where your formulae and calculuses fail. There is a simple law – one by which you reached the earth long ago – one by which you can leave it at will——'

The professors were furious.

'Parrot! Parrot!' they shouted.

'No! In my own place——'

The beast fell silent.

Then came the priests, smiling kindly – except to one another. For with each other they argued furiously and loathingly regarding their own views on rule and theory.

'Oh, stop!' said the creature, pleadingly.

It lifted its hands towards them and its golden eyes were full of pity.

'You make everything petty and meaningless,' it said. 'Let me tell you of the Master-Plan of the Universe. It is so simple and nothing to do with gods or rules, myths or superstition. Nothing to do with fear.'

The priests were so outraged that they forgot to hate one another. They screamed wildly with one voice:

'Wicked!'

They fled from the creature, jamming in the cage door in their haste to escape and forget the soul-less, evil thing. And the beast sighed and hid its sorrowful face, and took refuge in increasing silence.

The elders grew to hate it. They disliked the imitating and the parrot-talk, the golden eyes, the sorrow, the pity. They took away its chair, its table, its plate and cup. They ordered it to walk properly – on all fours, like any other beast.

'But in my own place——'

It broke off there. Yet some sort of pride, or

stubbornness, or courage, made it refuse to crawl, no matter what they threatened or did.

They sold it to a circus.

A small sum was sent to the farmer who had first found the thing, and the rest of its price went into the state coffers for making weapons for a pending war.

The man who owned the circus was not especially brutal, as such men go. He was used to training beasts, for he was himself the chief attraction of the show, with his lions and tigers, half-drugged and toothless as they were. He said it was no use being too easy on animals.

'They don't understand over-kindness,' said he. 'They get to despising you. You have to show who's master.'

He showed the creature who was master.

He made it jump through hoops and do simple sums on a blackboard. At first it also tried to speak to the people who came to look at it. It would say, in its soft and bell-clear tones:

'Oh, listen – I can tell you things——'

Everyone was amazed at its cleverness and most entertained by the eager way it spoke. And such parrot-nonsense it talked!

'Hark at it!' they cried. 'It wants to tell us things, bless it!'

'About the other side of the moon!'

'The far side of Saturn!'

'Who taught it to say all this stuff?'

'It's saying something about the block in mathematics now!'

'And the language of infinity!'

'Logic!'

'And the Master-Plan!'

They rolled about, helpless with laughter in their ringside seats.

It was even more entertaining to watch the creature doing its sums on the big blackboard, which two attendants would turn so that everyone could admire the cleverness: 2 and 2, and the beautifully-formed 4 that it wrote beneath. $10 - 8 = 2$. 5 into $20 - 11$ from 12.

'How clever it is,' said a small girl, admiringly.

Her father smiled.

'It's the trainer who's clever,' he said. 'The animal knows nothing of what it does. Only what it has been taught. By kindness, of course,' he added quickly, as the child looked sad.

'Oh, good,' said she, brightening. 'I wouldn't like it hurt. It's so sweet.'

But even she had to laugh when it came to the hoop-jumping. For the creature hated doing it, and, although the long whip of the trainer never actually touched its grey fur, yet it cowered at the cracking sound. Surprising, if anyone had wondered why. And it ran, upright on its fine furred feet, and graceful in spite of the red and yellow clothes it was wearing, and it jumped through the hoops. And then more hoops were brought. And these were surrounded by inflammable material and set on fire. The audience was enthralled. For the beast was terrified of fire, for some reason. It would shrink back and clutch at its shoulder, its arm, its thigh. It would stare up wildly into the roof of the great circus canopy – as if it could see through it and out to the sky beyond – as though it sought desperately for help that would not come. And it shook and trembled. And the whip cracked. And it cried aloud as it came to each flaming hoop. But it jumped.

And it stopped talking to the people. Sometimes it would almost speak, but then it would give a hunted glance towards the ring-master, and lapse into silence. Yet always it walked and ran and jumped as a

man would do these things – upright. Not on all fours, like a proper beast.

And soon a particularly dangerous tightrope dance took the fancy of the people. The beast was sold to a small touring animal-show. It was getting very poor in entertainment value, anyway. It moved sluggishly. Its fur was draggled and dull. It had even stopped screaming at the fiery hoops. And – it was such an eerie, man-like thing to have around. Everyone was glad to see it go.

In the dreary little show where it went, no one even pretended to understand animals. They just showed them in their cages. Their small, fetid cages. To begin with, the keeper would bring the strange creature out to perform for the onlookers. But it was a boring performance. Whip or no whip, hunger or less hunger, the beast could no longer run or jump properly. It shambled round and round, dull-eyed and silent. People merely wondered what sort of animal it was, but not with any great interest. It could hardly even be made to flinch at fire, not even when sparks touched its fur. It was sold to a collector of rare beasts. And he took it to his little menagerie on the edge of his estate near a forest.

He was not really very interested in his creatures. It was a passing hobby for a very rich man. Something to talk about among his friends. Only once he came to inspect his new acquisition. He prodded it with a stick. He thought it rather an ugly, dreary animal.

'I heard that you used to talk, parrot-fashion,' said he. 'Go on, then, say something.'

It only cowered. He prodded it some more.

'I read about you when they had you in the city,' said the man, prodding harder. 'You used to talk, I know you did. So talk now. You used to say all sorts of clever things. That you were a man in your own place. Go on, tell me you're a man.'

'Pretty Polly,' mumbled the creature, almost inaudibly.

Nothing would make it speak again.

It was so boring that no one took much notice or care of it. And one night it escaped from its cage.

The last glimpse that anyone saw of it was by a hunter in the deeps of the forest.

It was going slowly looking in terror at rabbits and squirrels. It was weeping aloud and trying desperately to walk on all fours.

Inside the story

On your own

Think about the story for a moment and what your feelings are at the end. Jot down a few words or phrases to describe how you feel about the star beast and about the humans.

In pairs or small groups

1 Share the thoughts and ideas you have jotted down. Are your reactions similar or different in any way?

2 List the ways in which the creature shows itself to be at the least equal of, or even superior to, human beings and discuss why the humans obstinately refuse to acknowledge the creature's 'humanity' and intelligence. Why is it important to them that it should be seen as merely *imitating* human behaviour?

3 Four groups of experts come to view the creature – professors of languages, of logic, and of mathematics, and a group of priests. What, in each case, discomfits them about the beast?

On your own

1 The story is told in a very simple and straightforward manner and its plain, almost unemotional tone makes us feel all the more strongly the creature's suffering and the enormities it endures. Look carefully at the language used and at the style and length of the sentences. Trying to use the same style, write a new scene in which there is a meeting between the star beast and another group of experts who have come to view it: for example, scientists, politicians or historians.

2 Choose one scene in the story, such as the episode with the farmer and his wife, the meetings with the experts, the time in the circus or at the menagerie, and try to write down what you imagine to have been going through the star beast's head – what it sees, what it thinks, what it feels.

In groups

The story is told in a series of separate scenes and, with some thought, could be turned into a drama script and acted out. Adapt the story into a play or film script and, if you have time and feel confident enough, act it out for the rest of the class – or even videotape a performance. Different groups could be responsible for different scenes in the story.

Making a drama script: some points to bear in mind

● Decide where each scene is to begin and end. For example, you might choose to begin Scene 1 with the farmer and his wife hearing the scrabbling of the star beast at the door. You could continue with their taking it in and tending it (what do they say, how do they behave?) and continue with people coming to look at it. They might wonder aloud where it comes from and what it is as they gradually overcome their fear and start to prod and examine it. Then, the scientists from the city enter (how?) and take the beast away (how? what reasons do they give?) and the scene closes with the farmer and his wife, alone again, regretting the beast's departure.

Scene 2 could open with the beast in the monkey-cage, perhaps with a keeper, and the learned men putting it through its paces and discussing its behaviour. A key moment comes when the star beast speaks for the first time and tells them it understands them. How do the learned men react? You might continue the scene with the visits of the different groups. (How are you going to distinguish the professors of logic, the mathematicians, the priests? Would it be simpler to have one representative of each?)

Scenes 3, 4, and 5 could be the circus, the animal show and the menagerie, but you might decide that these are all too similar and choose just one of them to dramatise. Whatever you decide, you will need to show the beast gradually slowing down, losing its spark and becoming the wretched, dull creature that finally escapes, desperately trying to walk on all fours.

- Make your script clear and readable with characters' names listed clearly to the left of the page. (Wordprocessing would help you do this but isn't essential.) Include any sound or lighting effects or stage directions in your script, preferably in a different type so that they stand out. If you intend to video your scene you will need even more detail to direct the camera operator. Maybe like this:

The Star Beast

Scene 1

(Darkness, silence. A sudden flash of green light, a terrifying explosion. Silence again. Sound of scrabbling and pitiful crying. Dim light comes up to reveal the farmer and his wife with a lantern about to open the door. Fearful of what they might find outside, the farmer opens the door cautiously, a heavy stick in his hand. Light comes up to full)

Camera

1 Farmer: Well I'll be . . . Marjorie, Marjorie! Just look at this! | *Close up on face*

2 Wife: (*wonderingly*) What . . . what is it? | *cut to wife's face*

3 Farmer: (*warning*) Not too close mind: it could attack. | *down to beast*

4 Wife: Not it, poor thing. It's near done in. It can't do harm. (*kneels by beast takes its head in her hands. Their eyes meet*) | *up to wife. Pull back to hold wife and beast in shot.*

You may see the opening in a different way, so don't feel you have to start just like this. Notice how in this example we have invented a name for the farmer's wife. We have also had to invent dialogue, and to imagine what such people might have said. We have had to imagine how they behave in the circumstances. We decided they were afraid, maybe thinking it was a burglar outside, but we could just have well decided they were angry at being woken up and thought it was the local lads playing about or a drunken villager who had disturbed them. Either way, they would have said different things and behaved differently. We have decided to emphasise the sympathy the wife has for the beast and made a great deal of the close-up of their eyes meeting. But the script could have made the farmer more sympathetic and the wife much more cautious, only being won round by the creature later. You have lots of choices to make when you write your own script!

- Other things you might like to consider are:
  (a) opening announcements if you are putting the performance onto videotape;
  (b) having particular people with specific responsibility for sound and sound effects, lighting and camera;
  (c) deciding how you move between scenes. Lighting changes? Fading out, then in? Music? A few notes on a single musical instrument, for example flute or recorder or triangle – even a drum roll or cymbal crash – can be very effective, depending on the mood of the scene;
  (d) how your characters speak and behave. Rehearse your lines and movements, get over the giggles, be professional;
  (e) finding out if your directions are feasible and if they have the effect you want.

- You don't need to learn your lines for an audio tape recording and can use scripts; for video you will need to learn what you have to say – or at least have a clear idea of what sort of thing needs to be improvised.

BLEMISH

John Christopher

Sunlight flooded through the open door of the forge, making friendly combat with the flames climbing up from the smith's fire. Joe Bredon, the smith, stood by his anvil hammering the glowing metal into shape. He heard no noise of approach under the ringing clash of his own work, but the visitor, standing in the doorway, blocked out some of the light and so announced himself. Joe Bredon looked up, shading his eyes. It was a young man – perhaps twenty-four or five – fantastically dressed in city clothes. He gave the horseshoe one last titanic pat and greeted the stranger.

'Mornin'. Anything we can do for you?'

The young man smiled with a practised ease that did not conceal his uneasiness.

'Guess it's the other way round. I want to help you. I represent Harkaway and Cummings, by the way. Biggest names in TV. Our new model, G K 34, is just what you want for your home entertainment. Full spectron colour, stereoscopic vision, five-thousand-mile range, two-foot screen . . . and very easy payments. And if you have an old H & C model we'll trade it in for you at 50 per cent of cost price. That's to show you that Harkaway and Cummings stand by their customers. Can I bring a set round to you for demonstration?'

Joe Bredon said laconically: 'This your first trip, son?'

The young man faltered.

'Well, yes,' he admitted. 'I only finished Salesman College last month. What did I do wrong?'

Joe Bredon said: 'We don't use TV here, son. Likewise we don't use magnet-sweepers nor frozen foods nor autogyros.'

'Ah!' the young man said. 'I see now. Some of our competitors have gypped you. Not every firm has the high ethical standards of Harkaway and Cummings. Now with our products you have a five-year guarantee of free servicing – can you ask for better than that?'

Joe Bredon said patiently: 'You don't understand me, son. We don't want any contraptions from any firm. We just aren't interested.'

The shocked surprise was excellently registered; the young man congratulated himself inwardly as he produced it.

'But if you don't have TV you don't know what you're missing! Girls, bands, comedians, thriller serials . . .' He glanced speculatively at the brawny smith, '. . . more girls. . . .'

Joe Bredon said: 'You're wasting your time. Where you come from, son, that may not count for much. But you're wasting my time, too, and I have two horses to shoe and a sermon to prepare before I go to my dinner.'

'So you're a preacher, too!' the young man said. 'Why, only last Sunday the Ace Network ran a Church-in-the-Hills programme, right after the Follies. And next week there's the planet-wide hook-up of the arrival of the Galactic Ambassador. There's an inspiring scene for you. That will be something to write a sermon on.'

Joe Bredon said: 'I'll have to get Henry Tysing to paint us a new name-board. Seems clear you didn't see the old one. You don't know the name of this township, do you?'

'Well, no,' the young man admitted, 'I missed the name. But about these TV sets . . .'

'So I reckon I'd better tell you,' Joe Bredon said. 'This is Swan Upping.'

The young man stopped at once.

'Swan Upping!' he exclaimed. 'You mean, the . . .'

'Yes,' Joe Bredon finished for him, '. . . the nuthouse. Mornin', son.'

The Galactic Ambassador was a little staggering, at first sight. Life on the fourth planet of Sirius had found its dominant form amongst the octopods, and the Ambassador was rich in the possession of eight flourishing tentacles, on which his small body sat like an afterthought. The incongruity was enhanced by the slurred but correct and coherent English that issued from the small beaked mouth – the Ambassador had learned the language during the eight-week voyage from the Galactic capital. The World President, receiving him, was aware of the power vested in this strange creature, and had no desire to laugh.

The Ambassador said: 'I think we must recapitulate the position, Mr President, so that you will fully understand our position and the purpose of my mission. In the first case your planet, of course, has been under Galactic surveillance for the past million years. Careful surveys were made at five-hundred-year intervals, without any interference, since interference, except when absolutely necessary, is abhorrent to the Galactic culture. Quite frankly we did not expect the fundamental problem of your suitability for inclusion in the Galactic culture to arise for several thousand years yet. However, our last survey, two years ago, had the shock of encountering an exploring spaceship half a light year outside the confines of your solar system. In five hundred years you had achieved a technological advance that is – you will be proud to learn – unparalleled in Galactic history. To advance in that time from animal transport to a gallant, if fool-hardy, attempt at interstellar travel . . . quite simply, we were amazed.

'As you will remember, our survey ship communicated with yours, gave it a brief outline of the nature and extent of Galactic culture, and sent it back to your planet with instructions that you should prepare for ambassadorial inspection – the essential and time-honoured preliminary to inclusion in Galactic culture as a member state. I believe you were also informed that there have been cases in the past where inspection has revealed a civilisation so depraved that, as an act of kindness, it has been necessary to atomise the offending planet. I do not imagine that that will be so in this case, but it is necessary to warn you.'

The Ambassador sprayed four tentacles forward in an expansive gesture that might have meant anything. The President nodded soberly.

'Well,' the Ambassador said easily, 'What shall we look at first?'

'This,' said the World President with modest pride, 'is the highest residential building on the planet. We house thirty thousand families in this apartment block alone. Fifty separate elevators, TV connections to every room, ten swimming pools, over a hundred built-in shops and a gyro landing base on the roof.'

The Ambassador looked up at the block. It climbed

effortlessly away into the withered blue sky.

'And all this area, of course,' the President went on, 'is under direct weather control. One hour's rainfall every twenty-four hours, between two and three a.m. So the fullest use can be made of the sun parlours laid out on every level. Though many people prefer to use the sunray lamps in their own apartment. They find them more convenient.'

'A typical factory?' the Ambassador inquired.

'Absolutely,' the President confirmed. 'Plenty of air and space, and swing music from loud-speakers to provide a steady rhythmic background. Everything fool-proof. There hasn't been an accident here in over ten years.'

'And the work?' said the Ambassador.

'All very easy. Simple mechanical jobs – machines do the hard work. And a statutory twenty-four-hour week with four weeks' holiday every year. No one lacks leisure.'

'Leisure,' the Ambassador said thoughtfully. 'I should like to see some examples of leisure activity.'

The autogyro hovered at fifty feet, the guarding police gyros drifting about them in a respectful circle. Beneath, on the oval of green turf, twenty-two opposing figures sweated and strained to gain a few inches with a leather ball. Around them, terraced up to the sky on all sides, more than two hundred thousand spectators surged and yelled in unison.

'Football,' the President explained. 'A very popular game.'

Another crowd, barely fifty thousand this time, hushed and tense watching half a dozen superbly proportioned girls swooping and gliding in exquisite patterns, white flashing figures against black ice. The gentle blare of waltz music behind them. Spaced out at the periphery of a circle, they suddenly turned, leapt to seemingly certain collision at the centre, swerved and passed precisely, three between three. The exhaled sigh of the watching crowd was the gasp of a winded giant.

This crowd was more than a million. Spread out illimitably over the great plain, their faces were a white upturned sea, craning to watch the sky that arched over them. Through the air the coloured gyros flickered and danced, the long rod stretching from the nose of each plane to butt the vast bobbing ball towards the great suspended hoops at either end of the mile-long pitch. They weaved in dizzy convolutions and hundreds of thousands of necks slowly twisted to watch their flight. With a quick thrust the great ball was bobbing away towards one of the goals.

'Airball,' the President said, 'a new development. The ball's filled with a mixture of light and heavy gases; density just above that of air. Like thistledown, you might say. It's a very popular game.'

'These are all hospitals?' the Ambassador asked. 'You have a lot of sickness?'

'Practically none,' the President affirmed. 'But we include the nurseries with the hospitals, you know. When children are delivered the mother leaves them here. The parents visit very frequently, of course – as much as twice a week in some cases – but the babies are under the care of experts so that the parents are freed for other things. When the child is five it goes back to the parents and stays with them for three years before going away to boarding school.'

'I see,' said the Ambassador.

'The only real hospitalisation we now have is

psychiatric,' the President went on. 'That big building in the centre. We do a lot of leucotomies – shearing the frontal lobe of the brain away to relieve depression. It makes them happy. Makes them a little irresponsible as well, of course, but we are past the stage of individual responsibility.'

'Yes,' said the Ambassador.

'And this is our main cultural centre,' said the President. 'Nine million cubic feet – isn't that something? Everything is co-ordinated from here on perfect democratic lines. We have a first-class sampling system which gives us a precision forecast of public taste. We know just what people like and we are able to give it to them. The result is that we never print any book now in a run of less than five million – and we never have more than ten thousand left unsold. That's accuracy to within 0.2 per cent!'

'The crematorium,' the President said.

'For your dead?' the Ambassador asked.

'Yes. Cremation's universal now. All the big new residential blocks have special chutes built in – you can place a body in at the top and it's carried straight down to the crematorium and disposed of within ten minutes. All hygienic, no fuss.'

'No rites?' asked the Ambassador. 'I thought I saw on your TV recently . . .'

'Well, yes,' said the President. 'Some people find it quaint to take the ashes of their friends and relations along to one of the churches we keep as curiosities and sing a few hymns. It's like collecting stamps, you know. Individual kinks – not harmful.'

They were back in the President's office. It had been a busy and rather nervous week, but the President felt pleased at a critical job well done. He leaned back, adjusting the dial of his oleofact to release an aura of pine trees round him – his favourite smell.

'I think I've shown you about everything, Your Excellency,' he said. 'If there are any questions . . . ?'

The Ambassador gestured ambiguously with two tentacles.

'No questions. I've almost made up my mind. There's only one thing. It is usual for an investigating Ambassador to choose some small district at random for closer inspection. Have you a World Gazetteer?'

The tentacles flipped carelessly through the great index, opened a page, delicately touched a line.

'This will do. Swan Upping. Will you take me to Swan Upping?'

The President smiled.

'You'll have to choose again, Your Excellency. That's a – uh – an asylum town. It's for anti-socials, crackpots.'

The tentacle stayed firm in its place.

'Nevertheless, Mr President,' said the Ambassador. 'I should like to go there.'

Outside Swan Upping there was a signboard: BUGGIES ONLY – POSITIVELY NO AUTOMOBILES. The President stopped the car.

'We can ignore that,' he told the Ambassador, 'for an occasion like this.'

But the Ambassador was already getting out with a swift, flowing motion.

'No,' he said, 'we will not ignore it. We will go in on foot. Tell your police to wait here.'

They walked into the village. Each house had clearly been built by hand and reflected the individual character of the builder; yet there was a strange sense of pattern overriding the minor variations. The President, trudging beside the Galactic Ambassador, let his eyes rove unhappily over the primitive, cobbled roadway, without either drains or sidewalks.

'It's amazing you should have picked on our one blemish,' he said. 'Of course, we don't have many small townships, but I could have shown you hundreds with every device hygiene and planning can provide. And chance led you to this!' He paused in disgust as an infant of less than four toddled across their path from one front porch to an opposite one. 'Primitives!'

They came through into the main street, and the Ambassador halted. The President pointed to the square-towered building dominating the rest.

'The church,' he said. 'They take that sort of thing seriously; natural primitive reaction, of course.'

'And this?' asked the Ambassador.

A procession was coming down the street; black carriages pulled by sleek black animals. Their iron-shod hooves drew the bright fire of sparks from the cobbles beneath them.

'A funeral,' the President said disinterestedly. 'They actually *bury* their dead. The animals are what are known as horses – they use them here still for locomotion. In the real world they were extinct twenty years ago.'

Opposite the church the procession drew up. Men in solemn black lifted the coffin from the hearse and carried it up stone steps into the churchyard, the mourners a slow eddy behind them. From the open door of the church organ notes began to peal.

'Our modern TV organs,' the President remarked, 'have ten times the range and volume.'

In the churchyard the grave gaped, clay-yellow in the green grass. The following mourners began to sing, their voices rising clear and steady above the organ notes:

'Behold, all flesh is as the grass
And all the goodliness of man
Is as the flower of grass. . . .'

When at last they stopped, the burly figure of Joe Bredon stepped forward. His voice was gentle and strong as he began to speak:

'Man that is born of woman . . .'

In the President's office for the third time the President waited confidently.

'And the decision, Your Excellency?' he asked.

'It has been reversed,' pronounced the Ambassador. 'When I saw the great apartment blocks where thirty thousand families were boxed in together, when I saw your factories where no man can take a pride in the work he does, when I saw the barren horror of your people's leisure with the million entertained by the antics of a tiny few, when I realised you have succeeded in destroying the sacred ties of the family and in your arrogance and overbearing pride have lost sight of the earth by which you live and the spirit by which all races are judged – when I saw these things there seemed only one decision: that this planet, sterile and withered as it is, should be atomised at once, for the Galaxy's good and for your own peace.

'But in one small township I have found spiritual life still strong, and by reason of that your planet is reprieved. You were on the right track once; you must retrace your steps to find it.'

The President found words.

'And destroy our machines? We live by them – millions would starve . . .'

'The machines are unimportant,' said the Ambassador, 'except in that your cleverness with them has led you to the pride and stupidity in which you now exist. We place no ban on machines – except spaceships. Until you have found humility and decency again you must not contaminate other worlds. That is our decision. In five hundred years a successor of mine will review it. Have you any questions to ask?'

'No,' the President said slowly. 'No, Your Excellency. No questions.'

Inside the story

In pairs or small groups

1 Discuss why the Galactic Ambassador came to his decision. Consider what it was he disliked about the world as it was presented to him and what it was that pleased him about Swan Upping.

2 The people of Earth are taught a lesson by the Galactic Ambassador's visit. Try to explain what that lesson is and to capture its essence in a suitable moral to go at the end of the story.

3 Do you sympathise with the Ambassador's views or do you share the President's pride in his planet's achievements?

On your own

1 Select one or two of the scenes where the President is showing the Galactic Ambassador the wonders of Earth (as he regards them) and in which the Ambassador is non-committal but clearly thinking hard about these abominations (as he perceives them). Write what you imagine to be going through the minds of each of them as they survey the scene(s).

2 Imagine another scene where the President shows the Ambassador one of the 'wonders' of his planet: perhaps one of the boarding schools to which children are sent at eight years old or maybe a typical couple at home with their seven year old child. Think of all the wonders the President might point out about the school or the home and write what he says in praise of them. Put in one or two thoughtful questions from the Ambassador as well. When you are satisfied with your dialogue, you might like to act it out with a partner.

3 What similarities are there between this story and the story of the Star Beast? Write about what you think each story is trying to tell us about human civilisation and explain why you think so. If you think there are differences between the two stories, try to say what these are.

THE FLYING MACHINE

Ray Bradbury

In the year AD 400, the Emperor Yuan held his throne by the Great Wall of China, and the land was green with rain, readying itself toward the harvest, at peace, the people in his dominion neither too happy nor too sad.

Early on the morning of the first day of the first week of the second month of the new year, the Emperor Yuan was sipping tea and fanning himself against a warm breeze when a servant ran across the scarlet and blue garden tiles, calling, 'Oh, Emperor, Emperor, a miracle!'

'Yes,' said the Emperor, 'the air *is* sweet this morning.'

'No, no, a miracle!' said the servant, bowing quickly.

'And this tea is good in my mouth, surely that is a miracle.'

'No, no, Your Excellency.'

'Let me guess then – the sun has risen and a new day is upon us. Or the sea is blue. *That* now is the finest of all miracles.'

'Excellency, a man is flying!'

'What?' The Emperor stopped his fan.

'I saw him in the air, a man flying with wings. I heard a voice call out of the sky, and when I looked up, there he was, a dragon in the heavens with a man in its mouth, a dragon of paper and bamboo, coloured like the sun and the grass.'

'It is early,' said the Emperor, 'and you have just wakened from a dream.'

'It is early, but I have seen what I have seen! Come, and you will see it too.'

'Sit down with me here,' said the Emperor. 'Drink some tea. It must be a strange thing, if it is true, to see a man fly. You must have time to think of it, even as I must have time to prepare myself for the sight.'

They drank tea.

'Please,' said the servant at last, 'or he will be gone.'

The Emperor rose thoughtfully. 'Now you may show me what you have seen.'

They walked into a garden, across a meadow of grass, over a small bridge, through a grove of trees, and up a tiny hill.

'There!' said the servant.

The Emperor looked into the sky.

And in the sky, laughing so high that you could hardly hear him laugh, was a man; and the man was clothed in bright papers and reeds to make wings and a beautiful yellow tail, and he was soaring all about like the largest bird in a universe of birds, like a new dragon in a land of ancient dragons.

The man called down to them from high in the cool winds of morning, 'I fly, I fly!'

The servant waved to him. 'Yes, yes!'

The Emperor Yuan did not move. Instead he looked at the Great Wall of China now taking shape out of the farthest mist in the green hills, that splendid snake of stones which writhed with majesty across the entire land. That wonderful wall which had protected them for a timeless time from enemy hordes and preserved peace for years without number. He saw the town nestled to itself by a river and a road and a hill, beginning to waken.

'Tell me,' he said to his servant, 'has anyone else seen this flying man?'

'I am the only one, Excellency,' said the servant, smiling at the sky, waving.

The Emperor watched the heavens another minute and then said, 'Call him down to me.'

'Ho, come down, come down! The Emperor wishes to see you!' called the servant, hands cupped to his shouting mouth.

The Emperor glanced in all directions while the flying man soared down the morning wind. He saw a farmer, early in his fields, watching the sky, and he noted where the farmer stood.

The flying man alit with a rustle of paper and a creak of bamboo reeds. He came proudly to the Emperor, clumsy in his rig, at last bowing before the old man.

'What have you done?' demanded the Emperor.

'I have flown in the sky, Your Excellency,' replied the man.

'What *have* you done?' said the Emperor again.

'I have just told you!' cried the flier.

'You have told me nothing at all.' The Emperor reached out a thin hand to touch the pretty paper and the birdlike keel of the apparatus. It smelled cool, of the wind.

'Is it not beautiful, Excellency?'

'Yes, too beautiful.'

'It is the only one in the world!' smiled the man. 'And I am the inventor.'

'The *only* one in the world?'

'I swear it!'

'Who else knows of this?'

'No-one. Not even my wife, who would think me mad with the sun. She thought I was making a kite. I rose in the night and walked to the cliffs far away. And when the morning breezes blew and the sun rose, I gathered my courage, Excellency, and leaped from the cliff. I flew! But my wife does not know of it.'

'Well for her, then,' said the Emperor. 'Come along.' They walked back to the great house. The sun was full in the sky now, and the smell of the grass was refreshing. The Emperor, the servant, and the flier passed within the huge garden.

The Emperor clapped his hands. 'Ho, guards!'

The guards came running.

'Hold this man.'

The guards seized the flier.

'Call the executioner,' said the Emperor.

'What's this!' cried the flier, bewildered. 'What have I done?' He began to weep, so that the beautiful paper apparatus rustled.

'Here is the man who has made a certain machine,' said the Emperor, 'and yet asks us what he has created. He does not know himself. It is only necessary that he create, without knowing why he has done so, or what this thing will do.'

The executioner came running with a sharp silver axe. He stood with his naked, large-muscled arms ready, his face covered with a serene white mask.

'One moment,' said the Emperor. He turned to a nearby table upon which sat a machine that he himself had created. The Emperor took a tiny golden key from his own neck. He fitted this key to the tiny, delicate machine and wound it up. Then he set the machine going.

The machine was a garden of metal and jewels. Set in motion, birds sang in tiny metal trees, wolves walked through miniature forests, and tiny people ran in and out of sun and shadow, fanning themselves with miniature fans, listening to the tiny emerald birds, and standing by impossibly small but tinkling fountains.

'Is it not beautiful?' said the Emperor. 'If you asked me what I have done here, I could answer you well. I have made birds sing, I have made forests murmur, I have set people to walking in this woodland, enjoying the leaves and shadows and songs. That is what I have done.'

'But, oh, Emperor!' pleaded the flier, on his knees, the tears pouring down his face. 'I have done a similar thing! I have found beauty. I have flown on the morning wind. I have looked down on all the sleeping houses and gardens. I have smelled the sea and even *seen* it, beyond the hills, from my high place. And I have soared like a bird; oh, I cannot say how beautiful it is up there, in the sky, with the wind about me, the wind blowing me here like a feather, there like a fan, the way the sky smells in the morning! and how free one feels! *That* is beautiful, Emperor, that is beautiful too!'

'Yes,' said the Emperor sadly, 'I know it must be true. For I felt my heart move with you in the air and I wondered: What is it like? How does it feel? How do the distant pools look from so high? And how my houses and servants? Like ants? And how the distant towns not yet awake?'

'Then spare me!'

'But there are times,' said the Emperor, more sadly still, 'when one must lose a little beauty if one is to keep what little beauty one already has. I do not fear you, yourself, but I fear another man.'

'What man?'

'Some other man who, seeing you, will build a thing of bright papers and bamboo like this. But the other man will have an evil face and an evil heart, and the beauty will be gone. It is this man I fear.'

'Why? Why?'

'Who is to say that someday just such a man, in just such an apparatus of paper and reed, might not fly in the sky and drop huge stones upon the Great Wall of China?' said the Emperor.

No-one moved or said a word.

'Off with his head,' said the Emperor.

The executioner whirled his silver axe.

'Burn the kite and the inventor's body and bury their ashes together,' said the Emperor.

The servants retreated to obey.

The Emperor turned to his hand-servant, who had seen the man flying. 'Hold your tongue. It was all a dream, a most sorrowful and beautiful dream. And that farmer in the distant field who also saw, tell him it would pay him to consider it only a vision. If ever the word passes around, you and the farmer die within the hour.'

'You are merciful, Emperor.'

'No, not merciful,' said the old man. Beyond the garden wall he saw the guards burning the beautiful machine of paper and reeds that smelled of the morning wind. He saw the dark smoke climb into the sky. 'No, only very much bewildered and afraid.' He saw the guards digging a tiny pit wherein to bury the ashes. 'What is the life of one man against those of a million others? I must take solace from that thought.'

He took the key from its chain about his neck and once more wound up the beautiful miniature garden. He stood looking out across the land at the Great Wall, the peaceful town, the green fields, the rivers and streams. He sighed. The tiny garden whirred its hidden and delicate machinery and set itself in motion; tiny people walked in forests, tiny foxes loped through sun-speckled glades in beautiful shining pelts, and among the tiny trees flew bits of high song and bright blue and yellow colour, flying, flying, flying in that small sky.

'Oh,' said the Emperor, closing his eyes, 'look at the birds, look at the birds!'

Inside the story

In pairs or small groups

1 Discuss why the Emperor ordered the inventor's execution and whether you think he was right to do so. You may find it helpful to look back at how the story unfolds:

(i) Read again the opening paragraphs up to the point where the news of the flying man reaches him. What do we learn of the Emperor and the country he rules and of the things that please him?

(ii) The Emperor does not rush to see the miracle of the man in flight. Instead, he takes tea and thinks. What do you imagine is going through his mind?

(iii) The Emperor does not get excited when he sees the man in flight. Instead, he looks at the Great Wall and at his city. Again, what do you imagine he is thinking?

(iv) Discuss why, after executing the inventor, the Emperor is concerned that all who have knowledge of the machine should remain silent.

(v) The Emperor says he is not merciful, 'only very much bewildered and afraid'. Discuss why he should be so shaken by what has happened.

(vi) The intricate mechanical garden that the Emperor had created was clearly his pride and joy. Talk about why this was and why he would perhaps never take the same pleasure in it again.

2 The story is about a Chinese Emperor long ago; what can it possibly have to do with us today? You might like to think about whether or not machines are in themselves harmless – or is it just the uses people put them to that make them good or evil? Would an Emperor in modern times have been wise to have executed the inventor of the internal combustion engine or the physicists who thought of splitting the atom or the inventor of the submarine or of the microchip?

On your own

The Emperor clearly has a struggle to come to his decision that the flier should be executed. Either write the stream of thoughts and conflicting arguments that passes through his head as he sees the man circling high above him or write the entry in his diary that he makes that evening recording what he did and why.

THE HOUSE OF COLOURED WINDOWS

Margaret Mahy

Our street had a lot of little houses on either side of it where we children lived happily with our families. There were rows of lawns, like green napkins tucked under the houses' chins, and letterboxes, apple trees and marigolds. Children played up and down the street, laughing and shouting and sometimes crying, for it's the way of the world that things should be mixed. In the soft autumn evenings, before the winter winds began, the smoke from chimneys rose up in threads of grey and blue, stitching our houses into the autumn air.

But there was one house in our street that was different from all the rest, and that was the wizard's house. For one thing there was a door knocker of iron in the shape of a dog's head that barked at us as we ran by. Of course, the wizard's house had its lawn too, but no apple trees or marigolds, only a silver tree with a golden parrot in it. But that was not the most wonderful thing about the wizard's house.

Once, we saw a tiny dragon sitting on the wizard's compost heap among the apple cores, weeds and egg shells. He scratched under a green wing with a scarlet claw and breathed out blue flames and grey smoke. We saw the wizard shaking his tablecloth out of the window. Bits of old spells and scraps of magic flew into the air like pink confetti, blue spaghetti and bits and bobs of rainbow. As they fell, they went off like fireworks and only coloured dust reached the ground. The hot sun dissolved the dust as hot tea dissolves sugar. But still those things were not the real wonders of the wizard's house.

The real wonders of the wizard's house were its windows. They were all the colours of the world – red, blue, green, gold, purple and pink, violet and yellow, as well as the reddish-brown of autumn leaves. His house was patched all over with coloured windows. And there was not just one pink window or one green one, either, but several of each colour, each one different. No one had told us but we all knew that if you looked through the red window you saw a red world. If you looked through the blue window a blue one. The wizard could go into any of these worlds whenever he wished. He was not only the owner of many windows, but the master of many worlds.

My friend, Anthea, longed to go into the wizard's house and spy out through his windows. Other people dreamed of racing-bikes and cameras and guitars, but Anthea dreamed of the wizard's windows. She wanted to get into the wizard's house and look through first one window and then another because she was sure that through one of them she must see the world she really wanted to live in. The candyfloss window would show her a world striped like circus time, the golden window would show her a city of towers and domes, dazzling in the sunlight, and every girl who lived there would be a princess with long golden hair. The windows haunted Anthea so much that her eyes ached for magic peep-holes into strange and beautiful countries.

One day, as Anthea came home from school, she

saw on the footpath outside the wizard's house, sitting by his letterbox, a white cat with one blue eye and one green eye, golden whiskers and a collar of gold. It winked at her with its blue eye and scrambled through a gap in the hedge, seeming to beckon with its tail. Anthea scrambled after it with a twist and a wriggle and, when she stood up, she was on the other side of the hedge inside the wizard's garden. Her school uniform had been changed into a long, silver dress with little glass bells all over its sleeves, and her school shoes and socks had changed into slippers of scarlet and stockings of green. In front of her stood the wizard, dressed in a white robe with a tiny green dragon crawling around his shoulders. His cat rubbed against his ankles and purred.

'So, you are the girl who dreams of looking through my windows,' said the wizard. 'Your wishes are like storms, my dear – too strong, too strong. At night I am beginning to dream your dreams instead of my own and that won't do, for wizards need their own dreams to prevent them becoming lost in their magic. Dreams are to wizards what harbour lights are to a sailor. I'll let you look through my windows, and choose the world you like best of all, so long as you remember that when you walk out of my door you'll walk out into the world you have chosen, and there'll be no coming back a second time. Be sure you choose well.'

Anthea followed the wizard up the path between borders of prize-winning geraniums and in at his door.

'This is a lovely dress,' she said to the wizard. 'I feel halfway to being a princess already. It's much, much nicer than my school uniform.'

'But it *is* a school uniform – the uniform of *my* school,' the wizard replied in surprise. 'I'm glad you like it. Now, here is the red window. Look well, my dear.'

Anthea looked through the red window. She was looking deep into a forest on the sun. Trees blazed up from a wide plain and over a seething hillside. Their leaves were flames, and scarlet smoke rose up from the forest, filling the sky. Out from under the trees galloped a herd of fiery horses, tossing burning manes and tails and striking sparks from the ground with their smouldering hooves.

'Well?' asked the wizard.

'It's beautiful,' breathed Anthea, 'but it's much too hot.'

The next window was a silver one. A princess, with a young face and long white hair, rode through a valley of snow in a silver sleigh drawn by six great white bears wearing collars of frost and diamonds. All around her, mountains rose like needles of silver ice into a blue, clear sky.

'Your silver window is beautiful,' Anthea sighed, 'but, oh – how cold, how cold! I couldn't live there.'

Through a candyfloss-pink window, sure enough, she looked into a world of circuses. A pink circus tent opened like a spring tree in blossom. Clowns turned cartwheels around it, and a girl in a pink dress and pink slippers rode on a dappled horse, jumping through a hoop hung with pink ribbons.

'That's funny!' Anthea said in a puzzled voice. 'It's happy and funny and very, very pretty, but I wouldn't want to live with a circus every day. I don't know why not, but I just wouldn't.'

That's how it was with all the windows. The blue one looked under the sea, and the green one into a world of treetops. There was a world of deserts and a world of diamonds, a world of caves and glow-worms, and a world of sky with floating cloud-castles, but Anthea did not want to live in any of them. She began to run from one window to another, the glass bells on her sleeves jingling and tinkling, her feet in the scarlet slippers sliding under her.

'Where is a window for me?' cried Anthea. She peered through windows into lavender worlds full of mist, worlds where grass grew up to the sky and spiders spun bridges with rainbow-coloured silk, into worlds where nothing grew and where great stones lay like a city of abandoned castles reaching from one horizon to another.

At last there were no windows left. The wizard's house had many, many windows, but Anthea had looked through them all and there was no world in which she wanted to live. She didn't want a hot one or a cold one, a wet one or a dry one. She didn't want a world of trees or a world of stones. The wizard shrugged his shoulders.

'You're hard to please,' he said.

'But I wanted the very best one. I know I'd know the best one if only you'd let me see it. Isn't there one window left? One little window?'

'Funnily enough there is one window, but I didn't think you'd be interested,' the wizard said. 'You see . . .'

'Please show it to me,' begged Anthea.

'I ought to explain . . .' began the wizard.

'Please!' cried Anthea.

The wizard pointed at a little blue-and-white checked curtain. 'Behind there,' he said.

Anthea ran to pull it aside and found herself looking through a window as clear as a drop of rain water. She saw a little street with little houses on either side of it. Smoke went up, up, up, stitching the street into the autumn sky, and up and down the footpath children ran, shouting and laughing, though some were also crying. There was a woman very like Anthea's own mother, looking for someone very like Anthea, because dinner was ready and there were sausages and mashed potatoes waiting to be eaten.

'That's the one!' cried Anthea, delighted. 'Why did you keep it until last? I've wasted a lot of time on other windows when this one was the best all the time.'

Without waiting another moment, she ran out of the wizard's door, squeezed through the hedge and found herself in the street wearing her own school uniform again.

'Well, that's funny!' said the wizard to his cat. 'Did you see that? She went back to the world she came out of in the first place. That's her mother taking her home for dinner. I must say they do look very happy.'

Ten minutes later the white cat with the gold collar brought him a tray with his dinner on it. The wizard looked pleased.

'Oh boy!' he said, because he was having sausages and mashed potatoes, too.

And that night the wizard dreamed his own dreams once more, while Anthea dreamed of a racing-bike. And in the darkness, the wizard's house of many windows twinkled like a good spell amid the street lights that marched like bright soldiers down our street.

Inside the story

In pairs or small groups

1 Can you sum up the message of this story in one sentence?

2 The story is told in a deliberately simple fashion so that fairly young readers – certainly much younger ones than you – can enjoy it and grasp its message. Talk about what makes this a simple story. Think about the sentence length, the vocabulary used, the tone of voice the story seems to be told in and the way the writer seems to address you, the reader. Apart from the *way* it is written, does the *subject* of the story suggest a younger audience?

3 Anthea looks through red, silver, pink, blue, green and lavender windows as well as a host of others that are not described in detail. Talk about what the view through the other windows might have looked like – the gold window, the brown window, the purple one, the orange one . . .

On your own

1 Write your own description of two of the windows we are not told about. Try to keep to the style and tone of the original story as much as you can so that somebody reading your two paragraphs could not tell that they were *not* written by Margaret Mahy. It may help to think of your new piece coming just before the paragraph in the original story that begins 'At last there were no windows left.'

2 Illustrate what you have written by drawing or painting the view through one of your imagined windows. Or you may prefer to create a collage by cutting and sticking pictures from magazines to get the right effect.

2
UNDER PRESSURE

Most of us know what it feels like to be under enough pressure to make us lose our normal calm. We may break down in tears; we may get angry and hurl abuse or even things; we may go quite loopy and behave in a manic, crazy fashion; we may retreat into ourselves and become very quiet and bottle up our feelings. It could be from pressure of work, from fear of failure, from being bullied or being mocked, from feeling trapped in a situation or from a dozen other things – whatever the cause, we all have our breaking point.

The stories in this group are all concerned with people under some degree of pressure. Italo Calvino's 'Marcovaldo in the Supermarket' focuses on the stress induced by the unreal world of the supermarket with its insistent pressure to buy, buy, buy, and to be a good consumer. The ways in which Marcovaldo and his family respond to the pressure may seem bizarre and the surreal ending of the story is in some ways amusing but the tale also has a serious side.

Timothy Callender's classic West Indian story, 'An Honest Thief', reminds us how strong the pressure to be the best can be. Whether it is being recognised as the toughest man in the neighbourhood or the owner of the best banana tree seems to be much the same thing. The obsessional jealousy with which Mr Spencer guards his property puts him and his long-suffering wife under considerable strain.

In the next story, Anthony, the 'Kid in a Bin', has retreated from the world. From the safety of his hideout he tries to warn his father and sister of the danger he believes they are in. The last story of the group, Ernest Hemingway's 'A Day's Wait', is also based on a child's simple misunderstanding about illness. As we read the brief tale, we share the growing concern for the child who seems to be moving close to breaking point as he bottles up his feelings. We share his relief when the truth is revealed and, like the child ourselves, relax slowly at the end.

Marcovaldo at the Supermarket

Italo Calvino

At six in the evening the city fell into the hands of the consumers. All during the day the big occupation of the productive public was to produce: they produced consumer goods. At a certain hour, as if a switch had been thrown, they stopped production and, away!, they were all off, to consume. Every day an impetuous flowering barely had time to blossom inside the lighted shop-windows, the red salamis to hang, the towers of porcelain dishes to rise to the ceiling, the rolls of fabric to unfurl folds like peacock's tails, when lo! the consuming throng burst in, to dismantle, to gnaw, to grope, to plunder. An uninterrupted line wound along all the sidewalks and under the arcades, extended through the glass doors of the shops to all the counters, nudged onwards by each individual's elbows in the ribs of the next, like the steady throb of pistons. Consume! And they touched the goods and put them back and picked them up again and tore them from one another's hands; consume! and they forced the pale salesladies to display on the counter linen and more linen; consume! and the spools of colored string spun like tops, the sheets of flowered paper fluttered their wings, enfolding purchases in little packages, and the little packages in big packages, bound, each, with its butterfly knot. And off went packages and bundles and wallets and bags, they whirled around the cashier's desk in a clutter, hands digging into pocketbooks seeking change-purses, and fingers rummaging in change-purses for coins, and down

below, in a forest of alien legs and hems of overcoats, children no longer held by the hand became lost and started crying.

One of these evenings Marcovaldo was taking his family out for a walk. Since they had no money, their entertainment was to watch others go shopping; for the more money circulates, the more those without any can hope: sooner or later a bit of it will come into my pockets. But, on the contrary, Marcovaldo's wages, because they were scant and the family was large, and there were instalments and debts to be paid, flowed away the moment he collected them. Anyhow, watching was always lovely, especially if you took a turn around the supermarket.

This was a self-service supermarket. It provided those carts, like iron baskets on wheels; and each customer pushed his cart along, filling it with every sort of delicacy. Marcovaldo, on entering, also took a cart; his wife, another; and his four children took one each. And so they marched in procession, their carts before them, among counters piled high with mountains of good things to eat, pointing out to one another the salamis and the cheeses, naming them, as if in a crowd they had recognized the faces of friends, or acquaintances, anyway.

'Papà, can we take this, at least?' the children asked every minute.

'No, hands off! Mustn't touch,' Marcovaldo said, remembering that, at the end of this stroll, the check-out girl was waiting, to total up the sum.

'Then why is that lady taking one?' they insisted, seeing all these good housewives who, having come in to buy only a few carrots and a bunch of celery, couldn't resist the sight of a pyramid of jars and plonk plonk plonk! with a partly absent and partly resigned movement, they sent cans of tomatoes, peaches, anchovies, thudding into their carts.

In other words, if your cart is empty and the others are full, you can hold out only so long: then you're overwhelmed by envy, heartbreak, and you can't stand it. So Marcovaldo, having told his wife and children not to touch anything, made a rapid turn at one of the intersections, eluded his family's gaze, and, having taken a box of dates from a shelf, put it in his cart. He wanted only to experience the pleasure of pushing it around for ten minutes, displaying his purchases like everyone else, and then replace it where he had taken it. This box, plus a red bottle of ketchup and a package of coffee and a blue pack of spaghetti. Marcovaldo was sure that, restraining himself for at least a quarter of an hour, and without spending a cent, he could savor the joy of those who know how to choose the product. But if the children were to see him, that would spell trouble! They would immediately start imitating him and God only knows the confusion that would lead to!

Marcovaldo tried to cover his tracks, moving along a zig-zag course through the departments, now following busy maidservants, now be-furred ladies. And as one or the other extended her hand to select a fragrant yellow squash or a box of triangular processed cheeses, he would imitate her. The loudspeakers were broadcasting gay little tunes: the consumers moved or paused, following the rhythm, and at the right moment they stretched out their arm, picked up an object and set it in their basket, all to the sound of music.

Marcovaldo's cart was now filled with merchandise; his footsteps led him into the less frequented departments, where products with more and more undecipherable names were sealed in boxes with pictures from which it was not clear whether these were fertilizer for lettuce or lettuce seeds or actual lettuce or poison for lettuce-caterpillars or feed to attract the birds that eat those caterpillars or else seasoning for lettuce or for the roasted birds. In any case, Marcovaldo took two or three boxes.

And so he was proceeding between two high hedges of shelves. All at once the aisle ended and there was a long space, empty and deserted, with neon lights that made the tiles gleam. Marcovaldo was there, alone with his cart full of things, and at the end of that empty space there was the exit with the cash-desk.

His first instinct was to break into a run, head down, pushing the cart before him like a tank, to escape from the supermarket with his booty before the check-out girl could give the alarm. But at that moment, from a nearby aisle, another cart appeared, even more loaded than his, and the person pushing it was his wife, Domitilla. And from somewhere else, yet another emerged, and Filippetto was pushing it with all his strength. At this area the aisles of many departments converged, and from each opening one of the Marcovaldo's children appeared, all pushing carts laden like freighters. Each had had the same idea, and now, meeting, they realized they had assembled a complete sampling of all the supermarket's possibilities. 'Papà, are we rich then?' Michelino asked. 'Will we have food to eat for a year?'

'Go back! Hurry! Get away from the desk!' Marcovaldo cried, doing an about-face and hiding, himself and his victuals, behind the counters; and he began to dash, bent double as if under enemy fire, to become lost once more among the various departments. A rumble resounded behind him; he turned and saw the whole family, galloping at his heels, pushing their carts in line, like a train.

'They'll charge us a million for this!'

The supermarket was large and complex as a labyrinth: you could roam around it for hours and hours. With all these provisions at their disposal, Marcovaldo and family could have spent the winter there, never coming out. But the loudspeakers had already stopped their tunes, and were saying: 'Attention, please! In fifteen minutes the supermarket will close! Please proceed to the check-out counters!'

It was time to get rid of their cargo: now or never. At the summons of the loudspeaker, the crowd of customers was gripped by a frantic haste, as if these were the last minutes in the last supermarket of the whole world, an urgency either to grab everything there was or to leave it there – the motive wasn't clear – and there was a pushing and shoving around all the shelves. Marcovaldo, Domitilla and the children took advantage of it to replace goods on the counters or to slip things into other people's carts. The replacements were somewhat random: the flypaper ended on the ham shelf, a cabbage landed among the cakes. They didn't realize that, instead of a cart, one lady was pushing a baby carriage with an infant inside: they stuck a bottle of Barbera in with it.

Depriving themselves of things like this, without even having tasted them, was a torment that brought tears to the eyes. And so, at the very moment they abandoned a jar of mayonnaise, they came upon a bunch of bananas, and took it; or a roast chicken to substitute for a nylon broom; with this system the more they emptied their carts, the more they filled them.

The family with their provisions went up and down the escalators, and at every level, on all sides they found themselves facing obligatory routes that led to a check-out cashier, who aimed an adding machine, chattering like a machine gun, at all those who showed signs of leaving. The wandering of Marcovaldo and family resembled more and more that of caged animals or of prisoners in a luminous prison with walls of colored panels.

In one place, the panels of one wall had been dismantled; there was a ladder set there, hammers, carpenter's and mason's tools. A contractor was building an annex to the supermarket. Their working day over, the men had gone off, leaving everything where it was. Marcovaldo, his provisions before him, passed through the hole in the wall. Ahead there was darkness: he advanced. And his family, with their carts, came after him.

The rubber wheels of the carts jolted over the ground, sandy at times, as if cobbles had been removed, then on a floor of loose planks. Marcovaldo proceeded, poised, along a plank; the others followed him. All of a sudden they saw, before and behind, above and below, many lights strewn in the darkness, and all around, the void.

They were on the wooden structure of a scaffolding, at the level of seven-storey houses. The city opened below them in a luminous sparkle of windows and signs and the electric spray from tram antennae; higher up, the sky was dotted with stars and red lights of radio stations' antennae. The scaffolding shook under the weight of all those goods teetering up there. Michelino said: 'I'm scared!'

From the darkness a shadow advanced. It was an enormous mouth, toothless, that opened, stretching forward on a long metal neck: a crane. It descended on them, stopped at their level, the lower jaw against the edge of the scaffolding. Marcovaldo tilted the cart, emptied the goods into the iron maw, and moved forward. Domitilla did the same. The children imitated their parents. The crane closed its jaws, with all the supermarket loot inside, and, pulley creaking, drew back its neck and moved away. Below, the multicolored neon signs glowed and turned, inviting everyone to buy the products on sale in the great supermarket.

Inside the story

Italo Calvino's stories about Marcovaldo concern an Italian peasant who has sought work in the city. The problem is that Marcovaldo is not at home in the city and he is not very bright. He is a dreamer too and, as a result, he and his family find themselves in fantastic situations.

In pairs or small groups

1 Discuss what pleasure Marcovaldo and his poor family get from being able to visit the supermarket and push their supermarket cart around like everybody else.

2 List the things that cause Marcovaldo to break his own resolution not to put anything in the cart.

3 There is something almost dreamlike about the atmosphere of the story. What images and happenings make the world of the story seem so unreal?

4 Discuss how you feel towards Marcovaldo – sorry? irritated? amused? something else?

5 How do *you* feel when you are in a large supermarket. What things affect your mood?
● Are things usually in the same places? How do you feel when they aren't or when you can't find something?
● What is the effect of arranging the goods on tall shelves in long aisles?

● How do you feel if you have to join the end of a long queue at the check-out?

On your own

1 In this story, the Marcovaldo family start off by simply looking, but finally they are overwhelmed by the temptation to join the other shoppers in filling their carts. As the story suggests, 'if your cart is empty and the others are full, you can only hold out so long: then you're overwhelmed by envy, heartbreak, and you can't stand it.' They reach a breaking point, a point at which they crack and behave in a way they would not normally do.

Think about people who may be put under pressure: a person constantly doing the same repetitive task, for example. It may be the check-out assistant at the supermarket faced with the never-ending stream of goods coming down the conveyor. It may be somebody working on a production line in a factory but it may equally be the shop assistant in the shoe shop who always has to smile and go through the same patter for every customer. It could even be a department store Father Christmas who finally cracks when facing his thousandth ghastly child in a week. It could even be a driver trapped in a traffic jam. Choose one person in this kind of pressured situation and write a story about what happens.

2 Write a piece that captures the atmosphere of a supermarket from the point of view of one of the employees – perhaps a check-out assistant, a sweeper-up, a shelf-filler, or a trolley collector. Think about what things occupy your character's mind as he or she gets on with the job. Think too about what sights, sounds and smells they notice most.

In small groups

Act out the progress of the Marcovaldo family through the supermarket. It's almost like a sequence from an old silent movie, starting normally and gradually getting more and more frantic as the six members of the family fill (and empty) their carts, as they criss-cross the aisles of the shop, see the cashier looming and finally make their escape. Concentrate particularly on getting the movement right, the expressions on their faces and, above all, the timing.

An Honest Thief

Timothy Callender

Every village has a 'bad man' of its own, and St Victoria Village was no exception. It had Mr Spencer. Mr Spencer was a real 'bad man', and not even Big Joe would venture to cross his path. Besides, everybody knew that Mr Spencer had a gun, and they knew he had used it once or twice too. Mr Spencer didn't ever go out of his way to interfere with anybody, but everybody knew what happened to anybody who was foolish enough to interfere with Mr Spencer. Mr Spencer had a reputation.

Now, at the time I am speaking of, every morning when Mr Spencer got up, he made the sign of the cross, went and cleaned his teeth, and then left the house and went into the open yard to look at his banana tree. He had a lovely banana tree. Its trunk was beautiful and long and graceful, the leaves wide and shiny, and, in the morning, with the dew-drops glinting silver on them, it seemed like something to worship – at least Mr Spencer thought so.

Mr Spencer's wife used to say to him, 'Eh, but Selwyn, you like you bewitch or something. Every morning as God send I see you out there looking up in that banana tree. What happen? Is you woman or something? Don't tell me you starting to go dotish.'

And Mr Spencer would say, 'Look, woman, mind you own business, eh?' And if she was near him, she would collect a clout around her head too.

So one morning Mrs Spencer got vexed and said: 'You going have to choose between me and that blasted banana tree.'

'Okay, you kin pack up and go as soon as you please,' Mr Spencer said.

So Mrs Spencer went home to her mother. But, all said and done, Mrs Spencer really loved her husband, so after two days she came back and begged for forgiveness.

Mr Spencer said: 'Good. You have learn your lesson. You know now just where you stand.'

'Yes, Selwyn,' Mrs Spencer said.

'That is a good banana tree,' Mr Spencer said. 'When them bananas ripe, and you eat them, you will be glad I take such good care of the tree.'

'Yes, Selwyn,' she said.

The banana tree thrived under Mr Spencer's care. Its bunch of bananas grew and grew, and became bigger and lovelier every day. Mr Spencer said: 'They kin win first prize at any agricultural exhibition, you know, Ellie.'

'Yes, Selwyn,' she said.

And now, every morning Mr Spencer would jump out of bed the moment he woke and run outside to look at his banana tree. He would feel the bunch of bananas and murmur, 'Yes, they really coming good. I going give them a few more days.' And he would say this every day.

Monday morning he touched them and smiled and said: 'They really coming good. I going give them couple days more.' Tuesday morning he smiled and said, 'A couple days more. They really coming good.' Wednesday morning – and so on, and so on, and so on.

The lovelier the bananas grew, the more Mrs Spencer heard of them, all through the day. Mr Spencer would get up from his breakfast and say: 'I wonder if that tree all right! Ellie, you think so? Look, you better go and give it little water with the hose.' Or, he would wake up in the middle of the night, and rouse his wife and say, 'Hey, but Ellie, I wonder if the night temperature ain't too cold for the tree! Look, you best had warm some water and put it to the roots . . . along with some manure. Go 'long right now!' And Mrs Spencer would have to obey.

One morning Mr Spencer came in from the yard and said as usual, 'Ellie girl, them bananas real lovely now. I think I going pick them in couple days' time.'

'Always "couple days",' she said, peeved. 'Man, why you don't pick them now quick before you lose them or something? You ain't even got no paling round the yard. Suppose somebody come in here one o' these nights and t'ief them?'

'T'ief which?' Mr Spencer said. 'T'ief which? T'ief which?'

The truth was, nobody in the village would have dared to steal Mr Spencer's bananas, for, as I have mentioned, he was a 'bad man'.

Then, one day, another 'bad man' came to live in the village. He was the biggest and toughest man anybody had ever seen. He had long hairy arms and a big square head and a wide mouth and his name was Bulldog.

Everybody said, 'One o'these days Bulldog and Mr Spencer going clash. Two bad men can't live in the same village.' And they told Mr Spencer, 'Bulldog will beat you!'

'Beat who? Beat who? Beat who?' Mr Spencer said, He always repeated everything three times when he was indignant.

And Bulldog said: 'Who this Spencer is? Show him to me.'

So one evening they took Bulldog out by Mr Spencer's, and he came up where Mr Spencer was watering his tree and said: 'You is this Mr Spencer?'

'How that get your business?' Mr Spencer asked.

'Well, this is how. If you is this Spencer man, I kin beat you.' Bulldog always came straight to the point.

'Who say so? Who say so? Who say so?'

'I say so.'

'And may I ask who the hell you is?' Mr Spencer asked. 'Where you come from?'

'You never hear 'bout me?' Bulldog said, surprised. 'Read any newspaper that print since 1950, and you will see that I always getting convicted for wounding with intent. I is a master at wounding with intent. I would wound you with intent as soon as I look at you. You wants to taste my hand?'

Mr Spencer didn't want to, however. He looked Bulldog up and down and said: 'Well, I ain't denying you might stand up to me for a few minutes.' He paused for a moment, and then said: 'But I bet you ain't got a banana tree like mine.'

He had Bulldog there. It was true that Bulldog had a banana tree, and, seen alone, it was a very creditable banana tree. But beside Mr Spencer's it was a little warped relic of a banana tree.

Bulldog said: 'Man, you got me there fir truth.'

'That ain't nothing,' Mr Spencer said. 'Look up there at them bananas.'

Bulldog looked. His eyes and mouth opened wide. He rubbed his eyes. He asked: 'Wait – them is real bananas?'

'Um-hum,' Mr Spencer replied modestly. 'Of course they still a bit young, so if they seem a little small . . .'

'Small!' Bulldog said. 'Man, them is the biggest

bananas I ever see in my whole life. Lemme taste one.'

'One o'which? One o'which? One o'which?'

Bulldog didn't like this. 'Look, if you get too pow'ful with me, I bet you loss the whole dam bunch.'

'Me and you going get in the ropes over them same bananas,' Mr Spencer said. 'I kin see that. And now, get out o' my yard before I wound you with intent and with this same very chopper I got here.'

Bulldog left. But he vowed to taste one of Mr Spencer's bananas if it was the last thing he ever did.

Mrs Spencer told her husband: 'Don't go and bring yourself in any trouble with that jail-bird. Give he a banana and settle it.'

'Not for hell,' Mr Spencer said. 'If he want trouble, he come to the right place. Lemme ketch him 'round that banana tree. I waiting for he.'

'C'dear, pick the bananas and eat them all quick 'fore he come back and t'ief them.'

'No,' Mr Spencer said. 'I waiting for he. I waiting. Let him come and touch one – just one, and see what he get.'

A few days passed. Bulldog had tried to forget Mr Spencer's bananas, but he couldn't put them out of his mind. He did everything he could to rid his thoughts of that big beautiful bunch of bananas which had tempted him that day in Mr Spencer's yard.

And then he began to dream about them. He talked about them in his sleep. He began to lose weight. And every day when he passed by Mr Spencer's land, he would see Mr Spencer watering the banana tree, or manuring it, or just looking at it, and the bananas would seem to wink at Bulldog and challenge him to come and touch one of them.

One morning Bulldog woke up and said: 'I can't stand it no longer. I got to have one o' Spencer's bananas today by the hook or by the crook. I will go

and ax him right now.' He got up and went to Mr Spencer.

Mr Spencer was in the yard feeling the bananas. He was saying to himself: 'Boy, these looking real good. I going to pick them tomorrow.'

Bulldog stood up at the edge of Mr Spencer's land: he didn't want to offend him by trespassing. He called out: 'Mr Spencer, please, give me one of your bananas.'

Mr Spencer turned round and saw him. He said: 'Look, get out o' my sight before I go and do something ignorant.'

And Bulldog said: 'This is you last chance. If I don't get a banana now, you losing the whole bunch, you hear?'

'But look at . . . But look at . . . But look at . . .' Mr Spencer was so mad he could scarcely talk.

Now Bulldog was a conscientious thief. He had certain moral scruples. He liked to give his victims a fifty-fifty chance. He said: 'I going t'ief you bananas tonight, Spencer. Don't say I ain't tell you.'

'You's a idiot?' Mr Spencer called back. 'Why you don't come? I got a rifle and I will clap a shot in the seat o' you pants, so help me.'

'Anyhow, I going t'ief you bananas,' Bulldog said. 'I can't resist it no more.'

'Come as soon as you ready, but anything you get you kin tek.'

'That is okay,' Bulldog said. 'I tekking all o' them.'

Mr Spencer pointed to a sign under the banana tree. It read: TRESPASSERS WIL BE PERSECUTED. 'And for you, persecuting mean shooting.'

Bulldog said nothing more but went home.

A little later in the day, a little boy brought a message on a piece of note-paper to Mr Spencer. It read, 'I will thief your bananas between 6 o'clock tonite and 2 o'clock tomorra morning.' Mr Spencer went inside and cleaned his gun.

Mrs Spencer said, 'But look how two big men going kill theyself over a bunch o' bananas! Why you don't go and pick them bananas *now* and mek sure he can't get them.'

'Woman,' Mr Spencer replied, 'this is a matter of principle. I refuse to tek the easy way out. Bulldog is a blasted robber and he must be stopped, and I, Adolphus Selwyn McKenzie Hezekiah Spencer, is the onliest man to do it. Now, you go and boil some black coffee for me. I will have to drink it and keep awake tonight if I is to stand up for law and order.'

At six o'clock Mr Spencer sat down at his backdoor with his rifle propped upon the step and trained on the banana tree. He kept his eyes fixed there for the slightest sign of movement, and didn't even blink. It was a lovely moonlight night. 'If he think I mekking sport, let him come, let him come, let him come.'

Seven, eight, nine, ten, eleven, twelve o'clock. And no sign of Bulldog. And Mr Spencer hadn't taken his eyes off the banana tree once. In the moonlight the tree stood there lovely and still, and the bananas glistened. Mr Spencer said, 'They real good now. I going pick them tomorrow without fail.'

Mrs Spencer said: 'Look, Selwyn, come lewwe go to bed. The man ain't a fool. He ain't coming.'

'Ain't two o'clock yet,' Mr Spencer said.

And all the time Mrs Spencer kept him supplied with bread and black coffee. He took his food with one hand and disposed of it without ever taking his eyes off the tree. The other hand he kept on the gun, one finger on the trigger. He was determined not to take his eyes off that tree.

One o'clock. No Bulldog.

Half past one. No Bulldog.

Quarter to two. No Bulldog.

Mrs Spencer said: 'The man ain't coming. Lewwe go to bed. Is a quarter to two now.'

'We may as well wait till two and done now,' Mr Spencer said.

Ten to two. No Bulldog.

'Hell! This is a waste o' good time,' Mr Spencer said.

Five to two.

At one minute to two, Mr Spencer looked at his wristwatch to make sure and turned his head and said to his wife, 'But look how this dam vagabond make we waste we good time.'

Then he looked back at the banana tree. He stared. His mouth opened wide. The banana tree stood there empty, and the only indication that it had once proudly displayed its prize bunch of bananas was the little stream of juice that was dribbling down from the bare, broken stem.

Inside the story

In pairs or groups

1 How does Mr Spencer see himself and like others to see him?

2 What does Mr Spencer feel about his chances of standing up to Bulldog? What has this to do with his boasting about his banana tree?

3 Why doesn't Mr Spencer simply pick the bananas before Bulldog can steal them? What pressure does he feel to leave them on the tree?

4 Which of the three characters, Mr Spencer, Bulldog and Mrs Spencer, has the most common sense?

On your own

'People aren't so silly as to get themselves into such situations' might be our first reaction to Mr Spencer's behaviour. But of course they *are*. Who wins the competition for the prize vegetables or the best cake at the local fête can become a matter of great importance. Growers of prize leeks in some areas of Britain guard their secrets jealously, and some stop up all night to protect their pride and joy from sabotage. But pride comes before a fall as Mr Spencer was to find. Write your own story about somebody who is very proud of something. Explain what happens to bring about their downfall.

In groups

1 Turn the story into a play. You might find it helpful to think of it in several separate scenes:
Scene 1 could focus on Mr Spencer and his wife.
Scene 2 could be Mr Spencer and Bulldog confronting each other. (You might like to run Bulldog's two visits into one and to have Bulldog make the threat about stealing the bananas between 6 and 2 o'clock personally to Mr Spencer before leaving.)

Scene 3 could be the long wait for the appearance of Bulldog and the disappearance of the bananas.
Think about the character and temper of the people involved and how they speak and move. Think about the ways in which you can make the wait for Bulldog seem long and tedious without actually making it either of these things for your audience. Think about how you are going to make the bananas disappear during the split second that Mr Spencer turns to look at his watch. If you are ambitious, you can stage your play with a single tree, a bunch of bananas and a spotlight 'moon' illuminating the last scene.

2 Alternatively, this story would make an excellent puppet or shadow puppet play. Most of you will have some notion of puppet plays but shadow puppets require only simple figures cut from card and pressed against a backlit screen so that they appear silhouetted as shadows. Out of sight of the audience, you manipulate the figures and provide the characters' voices. The figures are mounted on rods (pea-sticks will do) and scenery is also cut out and mounted in the same way. For this production you would need the three main characters and (perhaps) the little boy, plus a banana tree with progressively larger bunches of bananas to be attached to it. Like this:

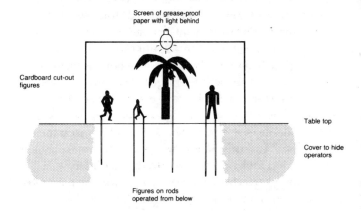

Screen of grease-proof paper with light behind

Cardboard cut-out figures

Table top

Cover to hide operators

Figures on rods operated from below

Kid in a Bin

Robert Carter

From opening till closing time, Anthony lives inside the wooden flip-top rubbish container which houses the plastic rubbish bags at McDonald's. His skin has become whiter and his brown hair is long and greasy; his eyes are cat-sharp. He is a bit over a metre tall which allows him to stand up straight inside the bin. In the mornings there is plenty of room for him to stretch, scratch, turn around or even curl up and doze. By mid-afternoon the empty foam cartons of Big Macs and cheeseburgers and McFeasts swell the plastic bag and choke out the light and space, forcing him either to stand thin against the back wall or to lean into the rubbish, until one of the counter crew changes the bag.

At different times, Anthony touches his finger against the inside of the used chicken containers which are made from cardboard and have a small piece of tissue paper where salt sticks to the splotches of grease. Old men use the most salt, followed by boys, girls, older women and younger men. The least users are younger women – about the age of Miss Tomagin, Anthony's third-class teacher, last year. By licking the salt stuck to his finger, Anthony guesses the age and sex of the chicken-eaters. When the cartons come through the flip-top bin, he touches, tastes and guesses the owners before they reach the exit door. Anthony likes to watch the customers. For a really good look he waits for the flip-top lid to be pushed inwards by a depositor, otherwise he has to be content with one horizontal slit and two perpendicular ones about a centimetre wide surrounding the lid. Anthony's world comes in slices.

At 11.30 pm the night manager switches the air conditioning off, closes and locks the restaurant, and Anthony comes out to make his dinner and prepare lunch for the next day. There is a mouse who lives in an empty Quarter-Pounder box alongside Anthony. They go in and come out, mostly at the same times. Anthony calls the mouse Nigel.

It is Sunday, 11.40 am. Outside the wind spits needles of rain. The customers are bursting through the doors, shaking like washed dogs, and laughing. Anthony is almost asleep in his bin – the air is humid and smells of sodden shoes and wet hair. Outside his bin is a boy exactly the same height as Anthony. The boy sees Anthony's eyes as he pushes his tray of rubbish through the swing-top. He pushes the flap again, and Anthony ducks down inside. He is too late, the boy sees his head disappearing behind the garbage. The boy pushes the flap once more and then reaches his arm in as far as he can in the direction of Anthony's disappearing head. His arm is too short to reach Anthony. The boy's mother sees what he is doing and shrieks at him to get his hand out of the filth. The boy goes to his mother.

'There's a kid in there.'

'Sit down, or I'll slap you.'

'There's a kid in the rubbish box, I saw his head.'

'Wait here, I'll get you another Coke.'

The boy waits for his mother to reach the counter and then goes back to the bin. 'Hey, you in there.' He tries to see inside by holding the flap open. 'What are you doing in there? You're not allowed in there.' A group of high school girls are giggling and nudging each other to have a look at the boy talking to the rubbish box. 'Why don't you come outside?' the boy says. The high school girls splutter into their thick shakes. The boy's mother returns with the drink, which she decides to give him in the car.

'It's probably a cardboard clown, or something,' she says.

'No it isn't, it's got real hair and real eyes, and it moves.' The boy's mother sees the high school girls looking at her and drags the boy out into the rain.

Inside the bin, Anthony eats one of the three Junior Burgers he prepared the night before. He watches the boy being dragged to the door, and the Coke being spilled as the boy looks and points back towards him. Anthony eats very slowly. Nigel is not in sight but Anthony pulls off a thumb-sized chunk of bun and places it in his box.

A newspaper comes through the flap and Anthony rescues it, saving it for later, when the shop is empty. Almost every day something to read comes into his bin. He has a small collection of torn-out newspaper items and one colour magazine article which has a picture of him, his mother and father and his sister. The newspaper ones have pictures of him alone. He carries them all in the pocket of his jeans, which are so tight that he has long since stopped doing up the top stud. The newspaper cuttings have begun to crack and split along the crease lines, from repeated opening and folding with greasy fingers. The magazine article is his favourite. Throughout stretching days in the dark bin, he feels the wad squeezed into his pocket, waiting for the eaters to go

and the noise to stop. On wet nights the closing of the store takes longer. The floor is washed twice by the tired counter crew whose lips press together and whose name tags flop in time with the swing and pull of the mops.

Anthony listens for the sequence; air conditioner shut down, lights out, door lock click, and total quiet, except for the refrigerators humming downstairs. He waits several minutes in case the night manager has forgotten something and because he likes to anticipate the coming pleasure. He opens the hinged side panel of the bin from where the rubbish bags are removed and steps out into the customer area. The space rushes at him. Anthony closes his eyes for a few moments and then slowly opens them.

His legs and back are stiff and tight. He sits at a side booth made of blue plastic and watches Nigel run to the kitchen. It is still raining outside, he can see the drizzle sliding down the outer windows. With just the dull security lights on, he can see no further than the glass boundaries of the store. Once, earlier on, he attempted to look further by cupping his hands against the window and pressing his face against the pane, but all he could see was black, with some tiny lights too far off to matter, and some moths beating against the car-park lights.

He goes to the men's toilet, switches on the light and empties his bladder into the stainless steel urinal. He washes his face and moves it from side to side in front of the hot-air drier. Holding his hair back, he inspects his face reflected in the mirror. There is a tiny freckle-like spot on the bony bump of his nose which he feels gently with his fingers, screwing up his eyes for a closer evaluation. The remaining skin is the white of his mother's scone mixture before it was cut into circles with a tumbler and shoved into the oven. Anthony leaves the toilet and goes into the kitchen.

From the under-counter refrigerator he takes two containers of orange juice. He switches on the hamburger griddle and the french fry vat and sits at the booth near the security light. From his pocket he pulls out the newspaper and magazine articles. He opens them carefully, bending the folds backwards and pressing them into flatness on the table top. With his fingernail he levers up the edge of the foil top sealing the orange juice and tears it away; some drops spill on the newspaper. He brushes them away with his sleeve and reads again under his photograph, with his finger sliding along beneath the words.

EIGHT-YEAR-OLD BOY STILL MISSING
The search continues for eight-year-old Anthony O'Neal who disappeared from his home on August 9th. A police task force has interviewed Anthony's school classmates, neighbours and relatives with no leads to the missing boy's whereabouts. Anthony's mother . . .

The griddle is hot and it is time to cook. Anthony stops reading and folds the articles back into his pocket. Outside he can hear the rain spatting at the glass, and the trucks changing gear in the distance. Nigel is running underneath the tables.

Anthony leans against the rubbish bag; he wants to go to the toilet and regrets drinking too much orange juice in the night. He concentrates on the customers through the slits. A tall lady with six children has come to have a birthday party. The children put on cardboard hats and make noises with balloons; one of them squeals every time the others take their attention from him – he is the birthday boy who shouts at his mother when he spills his thick shake across the table. His mother mops at it with table napkins and tells them he can have another one. He throws a piece of lettuce at the child opposite him who has turned his head away.

At the table alongside the birthday party sits a man and a girl. They are not talking, the girl has her back to Anthony and eats her chips one at a time and licks her fingers after each one. The man reads the *Saturday Morning Herald* and Anthony can see only the backs of his hands and the top of his head. As the man lowers his paper to talk to the girl, Anthony wets himself. It is his father, except that he looks older and his skin looks greyer. The girl is his sister, Meredith. Anthony feels for used paper napkins in the garbage. He finds some and attempts to blot up the urine before it leaks under the wooden bin and out into the customer area. Some of it escapes and sneaks across the floor and under the seat of the birthday boy.

Anthony presses his eye up against the horizontal slit. It is his father. Meredith appears to be bigger than he remembers. The floor crew supervisor discovers the leaking bin and dispatches a mopper to fix it. Anthony wriggles around to the other side of the bin to avoid detection when the side panel is opened. There is something he wishes to tell his father. A message he wants to pass to both of them. He takes an unused napkin from the bin and feels around until he locates a sundae container with some chocolate flavouring still in the bottom. He dips his forefinger into the container and prints his message in chocolate letters across the napkin delicately, careful not to smear the sauce all over the paper; he places it in an empty Big Mac box and watches through the crack. When everyone in the customer area is looking at something other than his bin, Anthony flicks the Big Mac box through the swinging flap and onto his father's table. Meredith jumps and showers chips over her father's paper.

'Someone threw a Big Mac at me,' she says.

'What?' Her father puts down his paper and collects the loose chips.

'Someone threw this at me,' she says again, picking up the box and looking towards the birthday party group. She opens the box and takes out the napkin, unfolding it carefully. She wrinkles her face at the chocolate sauce.

'Throw it in the bin, Meredith,' he says.

'It says words, Daddy.'

'What do you mean?'

'The chocolate says words.'

'Let me see.' He reaches for the napkin. 'It does too.'

'What does it say?'

'It says, "STAY . . . OUT . . . OF . . . THE . . . something . . . STAY OUT OF THE . . . SUN."'

'What does that mean, Daddy?'

'I don't know.' The man's face looks puzzled. He stares at the birthday party group for a long time. There is no one else close enough to have thrown a box onto their table. He places the napkin and the box and the stray chips onto a tray and goes to Anthony's bin. He tilts the opening flap and tips the tray's contents in. Anthony has a close-up flash-view of his father's face. He sees the same ache as he sees in the men's toilet mirror. He watches his father and sister disappear through the exit door.

And the days and nights pass. Anthony's father and sister do not come into the restaurant again. Nigel becomes sick from eating rat poison and a lot of his hair falls out. Anthony drinks less orange juice and keeps checking his face in the toilet mirror. He cuts his hair with scissors from the manager's office. One night the manager comes back an hour after closing. Anthony is in the toilet. He switches the light off and hangs onto the clothes hook behind the door of the second toilet cubicle. The manager goes to his office.

Anthony waits behind the door. There is a new message written on the back of the toilet door. He has not seen this one before; it says, 'Flush twice – the kitchen is a long way off.' Anthony does not understand the message. If the manager comes into the toilet, Anthony will lift his feet off the ground by holding onto the clothes hook. There is no sound coming from the manager's office. Anthony waits. He thinks of being inside his bin curled up against the fat of the plastic garbage bag, with the murmur of customers and FM music filtering through – impregnable. The fear of being discovered outside his shell is worse than nakedness – worse than peeling the rind of his sanctuary.

Anthony feels something brush against his ankle. In the darkness, his eyes search for movement. It is a large tom cat. The manager has brought his cat to hunt for Nigel. Anthony thinks that Nigel will die quickly this way. He kicks the cat in the stomach, anyway. It hisses and runs out of the toilet.

Within an hour the manager is gone. The restaurant is safe again and Anthony prepares his next day's lunch. He sees Nigel run into the kitchen and he smiles about the big cat. Waiting for the oil to heat, he spreads his collected articles on a table top – he smooths the magazine one, and looks at the picture of his family. He remembers when it was taken – on Meredith's fifth birthday, she got a bicycle with trainer wheels and it was in the background of the photograph. Anthony remembers giving her a large hazelnut chocolate which got left in the sun and which stuck to the foil and would only bend and stretch, rather than snap off in pieces.

Where the paper has been creased, some of the letters of the words have come away but this does not disturb Anthony; he has memorized most of them. He slides his finger under the words beneath the picture of his family. He reads aloud as he was taught in school, and sounds out the difficult words which, like many messages to Anthony, don't make much sense.

> Missing schoolboy, Anthony O'Neal, pictured here with his parents and sister, Meredith, was last seen at his home on August 9th. Police believe his disappearance may be related to the death of his mother six weeks earlier. Mrs O'Neal died of metastatic melanoma, of which she was diagnosed six months previously. (Malignant melanoma is a virulent form of skin cancer caused in most cases by exposure of skin to the sun.) A large number of reported sightings of Anthony have been investigated by the police, with no success to date. Fears for the boy's safety have increased as no indication of . . .

The griddle is hot and it is time to cook.

Anthony peers out through the horizontal slit in the bin. It is cold outside and the faces of the seated customers go pink around the cheekbones from the warm McDonald's air. The rubbish comes in, tipped from its plastic trays. Anthony waits with Nigel for the store to close.

Inside the story

In pairs or small groups

1 Re-read the first two paragraphs of the story. Discuss how, after hitting the reader with the initial shock of the first sentence, Robert Carter makes Anthony's existence inside the bin seem perfectly normal. Think about what Anthony does and the way the story is told.

2 List the activities and routines Anthony develops to keep himself busy.

3 Do you simply accept at first that there is a kid in the bin and that's all there is to it? Do you feel you need a reason for his being there?

4 We first get an indication that Anthony is in the news when we are told of his picture being in the newspapers. Discuss where we first get a hint as to why he has hidden himself away in the darkness of the bin.

5 Later, the hint is stronger in Anthony's plea to his father to 'Stay out of the sun', and Anthony remembers the sun as something that damages things when he thinks of its effect on the chocolate he gave his sister. Discuss how we are gradually prepared for Anthony's reason for hiding. You might like to think also about the various references to skin colour and texture and to faces in the course of the story.

6 How did you react to the story – is it amusing? sad? weird? believable? unbelievable? any or all of these? . . . or something else? Share your feelings about the story as it unfolded.

On your own

1 The story begins with Anthony having been in the bin for some time. Imagine that the author had decided to begin his tale at an earlier stage and had recounted Anthony's decision to hide and how he had fared in his first day or two in the bin. Write this new beginning in the same style as the original story. Think carefully about the short, punchy sentences that the author uses and remember that everything is written in the present tense.

2 The story is left very much in the air. What will happen to Anthony? illness? discovery? a decision by him to rejoin his family? Write the next episode in Anthony's life. You could choose either to continue the story in the same style or to write the newspaper report of Anthony's discovery and return to his family. If you choose to write the report, you may find it helpful to adopt the style of the news reports that appear in the story.

3 Running away from home – for whatever reason – isn't all that uncommon and many, maybe *most*, children have run away for a short period at one time or another in their lives. Write your own story about a child in this situation. You might like to consider where he or she goes and why; what the child's feelings are and what happens.

A Day's Wait

Ernest Hemingway

He came into the room to shut the windows while we were still in bed and I saw he looked ill. He was shivering, his face was white, and he walked slowly as though it ached to move.

'What's the matter, Schatz?'

'I've got a headache.'

'You better go back to bed.'

'No. I'm all right.'

'You go to bed. I'll see you when I'm dressed.'

But when I came downstairs he was dressed, sitting by the fire, looking a very sick and miserable boy of nine years. When I put my hand on his forehead I knew he had a fever.

'You go up to bed,' I said, 'you're sick.'

'I'm all right,' he said.

When the doctor came he took the boy's temperature.

'What is it?' I asked him.

'One hundred and two.'

Downstairs, the doctor left three different medicines in different colored capsules with instructions for giving them. One was to bring down the fever, another a purgative, the third to overcome an acid condition. The germs of influenza can only exist in an acid condition, he explained. He seemed to know all about influenza and said there was nothing to worry about if the fever did not go above one hundred and four degrees. This was a light epidemic of flu and there was no danger if you avoided pneumonia.

Back in the room I wrote the boy's temperature down and made a note of the time to give the various capsules.

'Do you want me to read to you?'

'All right. If you want to,' said the boy. His face was very white and there were dark areas under his eyes. He lay still in the bed and seemed very detached from what was going on.

I read aloud from Howard Pyle's *Book of Pirates*; but I could see he was not following what I was reading.

'How do you feel Schatz?' I asked him.

'Just the same, so far,' he said.

I sat at the foot of the bed and read to myself while I waited for it to be time to give another capsule. It would have been natural for him to go to sleep, but when I looked up he was looking at the foot of the bed, looking very strangely.

'Why don't you try to go to sleep? I'll wake you up for the medicine.'

'I'd rather stay awake.'

After a while he said to me, 'You don't have to stay in here with me, Papa, if it bothers you.'

'It doesn't bother me.'

'No, I mean you don't have to stay if it's going to bother you.'

I thought perhaps he was a little lightheaded and after giving him the prescribed capsules at eleven o'clock I went out for a while. It was a bright, cold day, the ground covered with a sleet that had frozen so that it seemed as if all the bare trees, the bushes, the cut brush and all the grass and the bare ground had been varnished with ice. I took the young Irish setter for a little walk up the road and along a frozen creek, but it was difficult to stand or walk on the glassy surface and the red dog slipped and slithered and I fell twice, hard, once dropping my gun and having it slide away over the ice.

We flushed a covey of quail under a high clay bank with overhanging brush and I killed two as they went out of sight over the top of the bank. Some of the covey lit in trees, but most of them scattered into brush piles and it was necessary to jump on the ice-coated mounds of brush several times before they would flush. Coming out while you were poised unsteadily on the icy, springy brush they made difficult shooting and I killed two, missed five, and started back pleased to have found a covey close to the house and happy there were so many left to find on another day.

At the house they said the boy had refused to let any one come into the room.

'You can't come in,' he said. 'You mustn't get what I have.'

I went up to him and found him in exactly the position I had left him, white-faced, but with the tops of his cheeks flushed by the fever, staring still, as he had stared, at the foot of the bed.

I took his temperature.

'What is it?'

'Something like a hundred,' I said. It was one hundred and two and four tenths.

'It was a hundred and two,' he said.

'Who said so?'

'The doctor.'

'Your temperature is all right,' I said. 'It's nothing to worry about.'

'I don't worry,' he said, 'but I can't keep from thinking.'

'Don't think,' I said. 'Just take it easy.'

'I'm taking it easy,' he said and looked straight ahead. He was evidently holding tight onto himself about something.

'Take this with water.'

'Do you think it will do any good?'

'Of course it will.'

I sat down and opened the *Pirate* book and commenced to read, but I could see he was not following, so I stopped.

'About what time do you think I'm going to die?' he asked.

'What?'

'About how long will it be before I die?'

'You aren't going to die. What's the matter with you?'

'Oh, yes, I am. I heard him say a hundred and two.'

'People don't die with a fever of one hundred and two. That's a silly way to talk.'

'I know they do. At school in France the boys told me you can't live with forty-four degrees. I've got a hundred and two.'

He had been waiting to die all day, ever since nine o'clock in the morning.

'You poor Schatz,' I said. 'Poor old Schatz. It's like miles and kilometers. You aren't going to die. That's a different thermometer. On that thermometer thirty-seven is normal. On this kind it's ninety-eight.'

'Are you sure?'

'Absolutely,' I said. 'It's like miles and kilometers. You know, like how many kilometers we make when we do seventy miles in the car?'

'Oh,' he said.

But his gaze at the foot of the bed relaxed slowly. The hold over himself relaxed too, finally, and the next day it was very slack and he cried very easily at little things that were of no importance.

Inside the story

In pairs

The little boy is only nine years old, so his misunderstanding is not surprising. He tries bravely to hide his feelings. Discuss what might have been in Schatz's mind from the time the doctor visits until he realises his mistake. Why does Schatz react as he does when he realises he is not going to die after all?

On your own

The heart of the story is the helpless waiting that the boy suffers. He genuinely feels there is no escape from death. The tension builds up in his small frame and shows on his face and in his actions. Think about another situation where a person has to wait, uncertain of the outcome but feeling that it must inevitably be wretched — somebody awaiting the outcome of an operation perhaps, or somebody trapped in a situation from which escape seems unlikely. Think too of what it may be like for the friends or relatives of the person waiting for news of the operation, or for details of the disaster which has been reported. When you have a clear idea of what the situation is and of who is involved, write your own short story which begins with a sense of despair yet, like Hemingway's, ends on a note of hope. You might like to use the title of this section, 'Under Pressure', for your own story. Or you might prefer another title we considered, 'Breaking Point'.

3
IN AND OUT OF CLASS

Settling down and being accepted in a school is not always easy. Laurie, the focus of the first story in this section, is a young child attending kindergarten for the first time and his stories of the antics of his classmate, Charles, are enough to concern any parents worried about the company their child is keeping. The problem of this bad influence, however, solves itself in an unexpected way.

Jan Dean's story, 'Woof', is an altogether more serious one than Shirley Jackson's 'Charles'. Like Laurie, Kevin has found it difficult settling into his school but there the similarity ends. Kevin's bid for recognition and attention in school comes not through simple naughty behaviour of the sort adopted by 'Charles' but through a funny but unnerving act. A desire to be recognised in school may take many forms: bullying, stealing, being class clown, and even making animal noises are some of them. It is a story that may suggest incidents from your own experience that could be worked up into your own stories. If you draw on personal experience you may find it helps to stand outside the story and to tell it in the third person. It goes without saying that such stories should not be written in a way that might give pain or offence to anyone.

Iain Crichton Smith's story, 'The Blot', tells of the kind of schoolroom that belongs largely in the past. It describes a strict, unforgiving style of teaching that has all but vanished, but so vivid is the writer's description of the scene that it springs to life afresh on each reading.

The two stories that conclude the section are both in lighter vein, though the first of them, Dorothy Nimmo's 'The Healing' picks up a central point from 'Woof': 'Everyone wants to be someone, I mean everyone wants to be someone special. Don't they?' says Marty at the beginning of the story. When she discovers how she is special, Marty is not at all keen that her talent should be recognised. One of the most pleasing things about this story is the way Dorothy Nimmo catches the joking and general fooling about of the girls and the way they speak to each other.

Jan Mark is another writer with a good ear for the casual chat and banter of young people, though she works it up into something much more polished than any real set of exchanges is likely to be. Her stories of Nazzer, Nina and friends are lively, witty and studded with outrageous jokes and puns. Never mind that none of us has ever managed in real life to tell stories with the wit and polish of Nazzer's crowd – wouldn't it be wonderful if we could?

CHARLES

Shirley Jackson

The day my son Laurie started kindergarten he renounced corduroy overalls with bibs and began wearing blue jeans with a belt; I watched him go off the first morning with the older girl next door, seeing clearly that an era of my life was ended, my sweet-voiced nursery-school tot replaced by a long-trousered, swaggering character who forgot to stop at the corner and wave good-bye to me.

He came home the same way, the front door slamming open, his cap on the floor, and the voice suddenly become raucous shouting, 'Isn't anybody *here*?'

At lunch he spoke insolently to his father, spilled his baby sister's milk, and remarked that his teacher said we were not to take the name of the Lord in vain.

'How *was* school today?' I asked, elaborately casual.

'All right,' he said.

'Did you learn anything?' his father asked.

Laurie regarded his father coldly. 'I didn't learn nothing,' he said.

'Anything,' I said. 'Didn't learn anything.'

'The teacher spanked a boy, though,' Laurie said, addressing his bread and butter. 'For being fresh,' he added, with his mouth full.

'What did he do?' I asked. 'Who was it?'

Laurie thought. 'It was Charles,' he said. 'He was fresh. The teacher spanked him and made him stand in a corner. He was awfully fresh.'

'What did he do?' I asked again, but Laurie slid off his chair, took a cookie, and left, while his father was still saying, 'See here, young man.'

The next day Laurie remarked at lunch, as soon as he sat down, 'Well, Charles was bad again today.' He grinned enormously and said, 'Today Charles hit the teacher.'

'Good heavens,' I said, mindful of the Lord's name, 'I suppose he got spanked again?'

'He sure did,' Laurie said. 'Look up,' he said to his father.

'What?' his father said, looking up.

'Look down,' Laurie said. 'Look at my thumb. Gee, you're dumb.' He began to laugh insanely.

'Why did Charles hit the teacher?' I asked quickly.

'Because she tried to make him color with red crayons,' Laurie said. 'Charles wanted to color with green crayons so he hit the teacher and she spanked him and said nobody play with Charles but everybody did.'

The third day – it was Wednesday of the first week – Charles bounced a see-saw on to the head of a little girl and made her bleed, and the teacher made him stay inside all during recess. Thursday Charles had to stand in a corner during story-time because he kept pounding his feet on the floor. Friday Charles was deprived of blackboard privileges because he threw chalk.

On Saturday I remarked to my husband, 'Do you think kindergarten is too unsettling for Laurie? All this toughness, and bad grammar, and this Charles boy sounds like such a bad influence.'

'It'll be all right,' my husband said reassuringly. 'Bound to be people like Charles in the world. Might as well meet them now as later.'

On Monday Laurie came home late, full of news. 'Charles,' he shouted as he came up the hill; I was waiting anxiously on the front steps. 'Charles,' Laurie yelled all the way up the hill, 'Charles was bad again.'

'Come right in,' I said, as soon as he came close enough. 'Lunch is waiting.'

'You know what Charles did?' he demanded, following me through the door. 'Charles yelled so in school they sent a boy in from first grade to tell the teacher she had to make Charles keep quiet, and so Charles had to stay after school. And so all the children stayed to watch him.'

'What did he do?' I asked.

'He just sat there,' Laurie said, climbing into his chair at the table. 'Hi, Pop, y'old dust mop.'

'Charles had to stay after school today,' I told my husband. 'Everyone stayed with him.'

'What does this Charles look like?' my husband asked Laurie. 'What's his other name?'

'He's bigger than me,' Laurie said. 'And he doesn't have any rubbers and he doesn't ever wear a jacket.'

Monday night was the first Parent-Teachers meeting, and only the fact that the baby had a cold kept me from going; I wanted passionately to meet Charles's mother. On Tuesday Laurie remarked suddenly, 'Our teacher had a friend come to see her in school today.'

'Charles's mother?' my husband and I asked simultaneously.

'Naaah,' Laurie said scornfully. 'It was a man who came and made us do exercises, we had to touch our toes. Look.' He climbed down from his chair and squatted down and touched his toes. 'Like this,' he

said. He got solemnly back into his chair and said, picking up his fork, 'Charles didn't even *do* exercises.'

'That's fine,' I said heartily. 'Didn't Charles want to do exercises?'

'Naaah,' Laurie said. 'Charles was so fresh to the teacher's friend he wasn't *let* do exercises.'

'Fresh again?' I said.

'He kicked the teacher's friend,' Laurie said. 'The teacher's friend told Charles to touch his toes like I just did and Charles kicked him.'

'What are they going to do about Charles, do you suppose?' Laurie's father asked him.

Laurie shrugged elaborately. 'Throw him out of school, I guess,' he said.

Wednesday and Thursday were routine; Charles yelled during story hour and hit a boy in the stomach and made him cry. On Friday Charles stayed after school again and so did all the other children.

With the third week of kindergarten Charles was an institution in our family; the baby was being a Charles when she cried all afternoon; Laurie did a Charles when he filled his wagon full of mud and pulled it through the kitchen; even my husband, when he caught his elbow in the telephone cord and pulled telephone, ashtray, and a bowl of flowers off the table, said, after the first minute, 'Looks like Charles.'

During the third and fourth weeks it looked like a reformation in Charles; Laurie reported grimly at lunch on Thursday of the third week, 'Charles was so good today the teacher gave him an apple.'

'What?' I said, and my husband added warily, 'You mean Charles?'

'Charles,' Laurie said. 'He gave the crayons around and he picked up the books afterward and the teacher said he was her helper.'

'What happened?' I asked incredulously.

'He was her helper, that's all,' Laurie said, and shrugged.

'Can this be true, about Charles?' I asked my husband that night. 'Can something like this happen?'

'Wait and see,' my husband said cynically. 'When you've got a Charles to deal with, this may mean he's only plotting.'

He seemed to be wrong. For over a week Charles was the teacher's helper; each day he handed things out and he picked things up; no one had to stay after school.

'The PTA meeting's next week again,' I told my husband one evening. 'I'm going to find Charles's mother there.'

'Ask her what happened to Charles,' my husband said. 'I'd like to know.'

'I'd like to know myself,' I said.

On Friday of that week things were back to normal. 'You know what Charles did today?' Laurie demanded at the lunch table, in a voice slightly awed. 'He told a little girl to say a word and she said it and the teacher washed her mouth out with soap and Charles laughed.'

'What word?' his father asked unwisely, and Laurie said, 'I'll have to whisper it to you, it's so bad.' He got down off his chair and went around to his father. His father bent his head down and Laurie whispered joyfully. His father's eyes widened.

'Did Charles tell the little girl to say *that*?' he asked respectfully.

'She said it *twice*,' Laurie said. 'Charles told her to say it *twice*.'

'What happened to Charles?' my husband asked.

'Nothing,' Laurie said. 'He was passing out the crayons.'

Monday morning Charles abandoned the little girl and said the evil word himself three or four times, getting his mouth washed out with soap each time. He also threw chalk.

My husband came to the door with me that evening as I set out for the PTA meeting. 'Invite her over for a cup of tea after the meeting,' he said. 'I want to get a look at her.'

'If only she's there,' I said prayerfully.

'She'll be there,' my husband said. 'I don't see how they could hold a PTA meeting without Charles's mother.'

At the meeting I sat restlessly, scanning each comfortable matronly face, trying to determine which one hid the secret of Charles. None of them looked to me haggard enough. No one stood up in the meeting and apologized for the way her son had been acting. No one mentioned Charles.

After the meeting I identified and sought out Laurie's kindergarten teacher. She had a plate with a cup of tea and a piece of chocolate cake; I had a plate with a cup of tea and a piece of marshmallow cake. We maneuvered up to one another cautiously, and smiled.

'I've been so anxious to meet you,' I said. 'I'm Laurie's mother.'

'We're all so interested in Laurie,' she said.

'Well, he certainly likes kindergarten,' I said. 'He talks about it all the time.'

'We had a little trouble adjusting, the first week or so,' she said primly, 'but now he's a fine little helper. With occasional lapses, of course.'

'Laurie usually adjusts very quickly,' I said. 'I suppose this time it's Charles's influence.'

'Charles?'

'Yes,' I said, laughing, 'you must have your hands full in that kindergarten, with Charles.'

'Charles?' she said. 'We don't have any Charles in the kindergarten.'

Inside the story

In pairs or small groups

1 Discuss what happens in the story. Who is Charles? Why might he have been invented by the little boy?

2 Laurie's parents take an increasing interest in Charles's naughty behaviour. Trace the way in which they become more involved and their attitude towards Charles. What effect does this have at the end of the story when Charles's identity suddenly becomes clear?

3 What indications are we given that Laurie, even at home, is no angel?

On your own

1 The pleasing irony about this story is that the parents are caught in their own smugness about Charles's behaviour. 'Thank goodness our little Laurie isn't like that' is never actually said by either of them but it is implied throughout. Continue the dialogue between the teacher and Laurie's mother from the point at which the story finishes.

2 Laurie's mother had so looked forward to meeting Charles's mother: now she finds she *is* 'Charles's' mother and the other mothers are interested in meeting *her*. Write a dialogue between Laurie's mother and another mother who sidles up to her saying 'So *you're* Laurie's mother: we've heard so much about him and so looked forward to meeting you. . . .'

3 Small children often invent imaginary companions – sometimes simply to play with, sometimes to take the blame for things they have done themselves. Write a story about a small child and his or her imaginary friend. Think carefully about why the friend should have been invented in the first place – is the child lonely, for example; or does he or she need an *alter ego* (another self) like Charles who can be allowed to behave badly on the child's behalf?

LIKE IMMORTALITY ALMOST

Jan Mark

'It must have been about the time we had the Everlasting Hamster,' Nazzer said.

'The Everlasting what?'

'You must remember the strange case of the Everlasting Hamster. Every school has one.'

'Not ours.'

'First schools.'

'We had a perfectly ordinary hamster at our school,' Nina said. 'It was white. Thick as two short furry planks, but it was dead normal.'

'That's what you think,' Nazzer said. 'That's what you were meant to think. How long did you have it?'

'It was there all the time I was in the Infants,' Nina said. 'Actually, they still had it when I went to the Middle School, because I came back for a visit and it was still there. We called it Snowball,' said Nina.

'Hamsters live about two years, and that's pushing it,' Maurice said. 'It's the soft living rots their moral fibre.'

'The pressures are tremendous, though,' Nazzer said.

'The pressures of being a hamster?'

'The pressures of being a school hamster. When people complain that teachers only work five hours a week and have long holidays, they always say, Ah, but the pressures are tremendous.'

'Wild hamsters probably have long stringy hind legs and powerful muscles,' Maurice said. 'Like Cumbrian sheep. Those hill sheep are rugged individualists; they think for themselves. They don't hang around in bunches waiting for someone else to take the initiative.'

'Like you said, hamsters lead very short lives – from being naturally sheep-like, I suppose,' Nazzer said. 'How come school hamsters live forever?'

'It must be the long holidays,' Nina said.

'They've drunk at the spring of eternal youth,' Maurice suggested. 'All that exposure to extreme childhood.'

'It's a conspiracy,' Nazzer said. 'It's to protect us from coming to terms with death too early. There's this class of little kids, for instance, who think they were found under gooseberry bushes and that God came for Great Grandma on a fluffy white cloud, and in comes this young teacher—'

'More likely a student,' Nina said. 'Students are dead keen on bringing live specimens into the classroom. Then they take you round a farm.'

'Ours didn't,' Maurice said. 'Our student took us over East Ruston Tip – with a real dustman. God, we knew how to live in those days,' said Maurice.

'In comes this young student—'

'One of our students brought in baby chicks,' Nina said. 'The first time he brought them in they were a day old, all yellow and soft. The next day they were a bit bigger, but by the third day they were huge. They had great vulture claws and wing feathers. Then they started getting smaller again.'

'What did you end up with?' Maurice asked. 'Eggs?'

'No, don't you see, he – this student – was getting

them from his lab at college to show us how they developed, only the lab assistants were giving him a different set of chickens each day.'

'Oh, well, the Everlasting Hamster trick has to be done more carefully,' Nazzer said. 'Like I was saying, you've got this young teacher – or student, Nina – brings in a nice hamster for the reception class. Well, the *next* reception class inherits it, and they all love it, and then one day it gets a bit sluggish; sort of indifferent to the sunflower seeds, and then it drops dead overnight. So what happens? Teacher rushes out and buys an identical one, or the kiddiwinks will weep. Next morning, there's little Hammy, back on the wheel kick and doing press-ups, feeling a new hamster, as you might say. "Oh look, children," says Miss. "Hammy's got better during the night." Couple of years later Hammy Mark Two cashes in his chips and the same thing happens again. Don't tell *me*,' Nazzer said, heavily. 'I have actually performed the Everlasting Hamster trick.'

'It's not worth it, though,' Nina said.

'What's not?'

'Trying to protect little kids from knowing about death. We had this big carp in the school pond and nobody took any notice of it until we came in one morning and it was floating on the top. It was Jason Hales that spotted it. "Oh look, Miss," he says. "Jaws is dead."'

'Jaws? Is that what you called it?' Maurice said.

'Odds-on half the goldfish in this country are called Jaws,' Nazzer said. 'Like pet pussy-cats are called Fang.'

'What was the hamster called?' Maurice asked. 'Rambo?'

'Cedric,' Nazzer said.

'Cedric the Hamster?'

'After Little Lord Fauntleroy. It had long golden hair. So had he.'

'What's Little Lord Fauntleroy got to do with it?'

'He was called Cedric too, apparently,' Nazzer explained. 'This teacher—'

'Which teacher?'

'The one my brother had in the Infants. She read a lot, this teacher. It was the long golden hair that caused all the trouble.'

'Anyway,' Nina said, 'when we found poor old Jaws floating about we went and fetched Miss Lovell and she comes out and says, "It's all right, children, he's just having a little sleep." So we said, "No, Miss, he's dead," but she wouldn't have it. "He's just sleeping," she says. Well, then someone noticed his head had been bitten off – it was probably the caretaker's cat, but we didn't want to upset old Miss Lovell, I mean, *that's* why little kids don't like death. It's embarrassing. So Lisa-Marie Hodges says, "I expect Jesus came for him, Miss."'

'You'd think Jesus would have something better to do than hang around school ponds biting the heads off fish,' Maurice remarked.

'That was what *we* thought, but Miss Lovell seemed to believe that must be the right explanation, so we had a funeral. I mean, she had to admit that he wasn't just dossing down with his head off, and then we all had to go and write about it in our news books and draw a picture. You know, *Today Jaws went to join the angels*, and there's all these crayon pictures of Jaws with wings and a halo, even though he didn't have a head in most of them. Jason got it wrong, though. He drew a head and then gave him horns and a pitchfork. Miss Lovell,' said Nina, 'thought that was not nice.'

'Did Cedric have his head bitten off as well?' Maurice said.

'Not so's you'd notice,' Nazzer said. 'Cedric had

come to the end of his natural span, so to speak. He turned up—'

'Oh, I get it. There was this ring at the bell and there's Cedric on the doorstep with his little furry suitcase. "I've come home to die," he says.'

'He came home for half-term,' said Nazzer. 'You know how it is, everyone takes turns at entertaining the livestock for the weekend. Well, my brother got chosen to have Cedric over half-term. He was high on it for a week in advance, making little beds in shoeboxes and that. We kept telling him that Cedric would have to stay in his cage but he'd practically built a hamster Hilton by the time Friday came. I had to stop off at the First School on the way home and make sure they both got back all right. Mark didn't just have Cedric, there was his football and bomber jacket—'

'Cedric's?'

'Mark's. And this great roll of paper.'

'Oh, the art work,' Nina said. 'Do you remember art in the Infants? Great stiff brushes with all the whiskers coming out, and that sticky paint; doesn't matter what colour it starts out, it always ends up purple.'

'There's probably a DES directive,' Maurice said. 'First School paint has to have a specific viscosity on account of little kids really being unable to express themselves unless they can paint pictures with a fork dipped in raspberry instant whip.'

'On blotting paper.'

'Stands to reason,' Nazzer said, 'since the felt-tip revolution people have stopped using ink. There must have been huge reserves of Government blotting paper left over when the dip pen went out of fashion, a sort of EEC pulp mountain. I reckon they sprayed it with something and sent it out to First Schools to paint on. Anyway, there's Mark with all his gear, waiting on the step, and this little cage under his arm with a heap of fluff and wood wool inside it.

'"Cedric's asleep," says Mark, well, he was whispering, so as not to wake Cedric up, although there were juggernauts thundering past ten metres away. I was going to carry the cage but Mark wouldn't leave go of it, so I had to carry the football and the pictures and the jacket. I had to carry all my own stuff, too, and push my bike. I was dead embarrassed – you know how it is when you're fourteen. I was afraid we'd run into one of my mates and they'd think I'd done the pictures. I didn't really like being seen with Mark anyway. I was very image-conscious in those days,' Nazzer admitted.

'Which of course you aren't now,' Maurice said.

'It was the Dagenham effect,' Nazzer said. 'You gotta be street-wise down in The Smoke. That is, you don't go walkies with your hamster, not if you wish to retain your credibility intact. Mark wasn't born till after we moved to Norfolk. He hadn't hardened off.

'Well, we got home and I put the cage on the table and Mark wants him out. Mum wasn't too keen on account of she was trying to lay out the tea things and hamsters can be pretty incontinent—'

'They what?'

'They do not put up their little furry paws and say "Please may I be excused?" But anyway, she said OK, just for a moment, so Mark opened the cage and gave us this long lecture on how to pick up a hamster, and out comes Cedric. I didn't feel too optimistic when I saw him,' Nazzer said. 'He looked as if he had things on his mind.'

'Hamsters don't have a lot of mind to have things on,' Nina said. 'Hamsters operate at a fairly primitive level.'

'Cedric didn't seem to be operating at all,' Nazzer said. 'After a few minutes he opened his eyes, but everything was in slow motion. He went for a bit of a stroll round the teapot, but it took him ages. He didn't look as if he was enjoying it and he went to sleep twice on the way back.

'"It's the fresh air," says Mum. "The journey home must have tired him out." Mark was getting worried. He'd brought back this bag of hamster nosh and he kept offering Cedric sunflower seeds and peanuts – and you could see Cedric was trying. He'd pick them up and fiddle with them like he wasn't quite sure how they worked but didn't want to let on. He even put a peanut in his pouch and took it round the teapot, and then he thought What the hell? and spat it out. I thought then, Hello, I thought; Cedric is not long for this world, but Mark kept stroking him and making those daft chicken noises like you do at little furry etceteras, and we knew we were in for a scene if Cedric popped his clogs over the holiday.

'"You put him to bye-byes," I said. "He'll have livened up by the morning."

'So we had tea, but Mark kept getting up and checking out the small and furry. He'd gone to earth again, under the wood wool and carpet fluff, but you could just see a bit of the long golden hair poking out.'

'Was he angora?' Nina said. 'You can get angora guinea-pigs. They look like sawn-off draught excluders, but I never saw an angora hamster.'

'Not *long* hair, exactly,' Nazzer said, 'but very lush. Only on account of his great age he did look a bit like the moths had been at him.

'Well, we got Mark off to bed, and he only came down about six times to make sure that Cedric was still, as you might say, on an earthly plane. He went to sleep in the end—'

'Cedric?'

'Mark. Cedric was already in a coma, as far as I could see. Mum says, "I think you might go along to that pet shop down Dereham Road tomorrow." "What for?" I said. 'Medicine? He's past medicine," I said.

'"Quite," says Mum. "I think we may have to find a replacement."

'I went and looked under the wood wool. There didn't seem to be a lot going on. I said, "No rush. They've always got hamsters in stock."

'"Yes," says Mum, "but any old hamster won't do, will it? We'll have to get one that looks like Cedric." Now, I hadn't thought of that. I mean, Cedric was a bit past it, but you could still see that he must have been quite impressive in his prime – about six months ago. They go off quickly. You couldn't pass off just any old short-back-and-sides hamster as Cedric. He was deep pile one hundred per cent natural fibres, Cedric was.'

'Most of them are,' Maurice observed. 'The day of the acrylic rodent has not dawned.'

'Around eleven o'clock I was thinking about bed because there didn't seem to be any more sex and violence on the box, and Mum says, "Hang about; make sure little Whatsisname's still in the land of the living," and I said, "Why don't you do it?" and she said, "You know what I'm like with dead animals," and I did. When poor old Ginger went to meet his maker she waited all day for one of us to come home and take him out of the laundry basket. He'd stiffened up and got wedged. It took ages to manoeuvre him out. Well, we opened up the cage and I moved the wood wool and there was Cedric – gone.'

'Gone where?'

'Gone where all good hamsters go, I imagine,' said Nazzer. 'To that Great Wheel in the sky. And he was on his back with his little feet in the air and his mouth open like he'd died taking a last nibble at something.

"Omygawd," says Mum, thinking of Mark. "Is he stiff yet?" '

'So I poked him,' Nazzer said, 'and he . . . yielded.'

'It's a fair cop, Guv?'

'No, I mean he was still *elastic*. Mum said, "Curl him up. Make him look natural." I said, "He looks pretty natural to me. You can't get much more natural than dead," and she said, "Make him look like he's asleep and cover him over again," so I sort of rearranged him with his paws over his little nose and then we made a big heap of wood wool and fluff with just a little bit of him showing at the back. Then we put a tea towel over his cage – sort of respect for the dead.

'"Right," says Mum, thinking at the speed of light. "I'll take Mark out tomorrow, first thing, and you can take Cedric and find a duplicate."

'"Mother," I said, or words to that effect, "I am not going to spend Saturday pedalling round Norwich with a dead hamster in my pocket."

'"You take him with you," Mum says, adamant like, "and find an exact match. You know how observant Mark is."'

'He's still observant,' Nina remarked. 'Last time I saw him he was in the bushes in Chapelfield Gardens with a pair of binoculars.'

'He's a growing lad,' Nazzer said, tolerantly. 'Anyway, we were all so busy trying to shield him from death that we forgot to shield him from sex as well.

'Next morning up he gets and goes galloping down to visit Cedders – but I was there before him. I said, "Hang on, Mark. Don't disturb him. We gave him a drop of brandy last night to strengthen his little heart, and he's still sleeping it off."

'"But I want to see him," says Mark, a bit tearful, so I took the pall – the tea towel – off the cage, and there was the pile of wood wool and a little glimpse of Cedric down the hole – moving!'

'Had you really given him brandy?' Nina said. 'D'you mean he was only stoned?'

'I think that's disgusting,' Maurice said, 'corrupting small and furries.'

'He was *not* stoned,' Nazzer said. 'What Mark didn't know was that I'd rigged Cedric up on the fish slice with the handle poking out at the back of the cage, under the tea towel. While Mark was mooting and drooling and making little furry noises at the front, I was moving the handle up and down at the back. It looked quite convincing, though I do say it myself,' Nazzer said, modestly.

'You really went to all that trouble so he wouldn't know the hamster had snuffed it?'

'Wasn't my idea,' Nazzer said. 'When I have a son and the hamster hangs up his skates, I'll dissect it on the breadboard so he'll know the meaning of life. Anyway, Mark says goodbye to Cedric and Mum took him out for a nice bus ride to Ipswich or somewhere like that – really foreign and exciting, and I put Cedric in a paper bag and cycled across to Dereham Road.

'The guy in the pet shop looked quite pleased to have a customer until I took Cedric out of the bag, then, he sort of *reeled* and clutched his forehead and yelled "No! Not another one!"

'"You got a run on dead hamsters?" I said.

'He said, "Whaddya mean, dead? I thought you were trying to sell it." I said, "Is there a market for them, then?" I mean, it hadn't occurred to me that anyone might want to buy Cedric, not in his condition,' Nazzer said. 'And the guy says, "No, but I've had it up to here with buying back baby guinea-pigs. I thought your friend there was a guinea-pig." I felt almost proud of old Cedders – I mean, he was pretty big for a hamster – though I'd been thinking he looked more like a rat that'd had a tail job. So anyway, I explained I needed a replacement, one that would match. The pet shop guy shows me his stock. Dozens of them, lying about in heaps but all very small. Did you know that baby hamsters sleep in heaps?'

'It's called clumping,' Maurice said. 'I don't know where I read that. It's amazing how the mind retains useful information, isn't it?'

'That's useful?' Nina said. 'See how useful it feels when you come to your Biology re-sit. Question: describe, with diagrams, the gastric system of the natterjack toad. Answer: I don't know anything about anybody's gastric system because someone tore the page out, but baby hamsters sleep in clumps.'

'*I* was getting an attack of the small and furries by this time,' Nazzer said. 'They are quite sweet, little hamsters. And all those baby mice like white bumblebees on stalks. But I said, "Haven't you got anything bigger?" and the pet shop guy says, "Well there's not a lot of call for big ones. You can see what happens to them when they get big," and he pointed to Cedric. "Why do you want it, just as a matter of interest?" I explained about Mark's half-term and the guy says, "You'd be surprised how often that happens. Take a small one, the kiddy won't notice." "Better not," I said. "Old Cedric here is a bit striking," and he had to agree. "Your best bet," he says, "is to go round your mates and see if anybody's got one the same size." I had this horrible vision of all of us with little brothers and sisters rushing round Norwich over half-term trying to swap hamsters with each other. I put Cedric back in his bag and went off to Ber Street, then the Castle pet shop. It was rodents, rodents, all the way,' Nazzer said. 'Gerbils, hamsters, mice, rats, guinea-pigs, chipmunks. Just about everything except coypu and capybaras.'

'You'd have to go to the Broads for a coypu,' Nina said. 'You ever *seen* a coypu? They've got orange teeth – like slices of carrot.'

'They used to be farmed for their fur,' Maurice said.

'Pull the other one.'

'Yes they were. It was called Nutria, but they broke out of the farms and headed for the Broads.'

'Just like Brummies,' Nina said. 'The Broads are full of Brummies in summer. I'd as soon wear a wet hearth rug, myself. Than a coypu, that is.'

'Dare say the coypu would support that,' Nazzer said. 'I don't suppose coypu regard it as the summit of achievement to end up round somebody's neck. Cedric would have made a good fur coat. You'd have needed a lot of him, though.'

'You'd think with genetic engineering that they'd have managed to breed coat-sized hamsters by now, wouldn't you?' Maurice said. 'I mean, they can cross sheep with goats.'

'You'd have to cross a hamster with a cow,' Nazzer said.

Nina said, 'What do you get if you cross a camel with a dentist?'

'Dunno. What?'

'A hump-backed bridge.'

'I don't get that,' Maurice said.

'*Anyway*,' Nazzer said, 'I did every bleeding pet shop in Norwich. No Cedric look-alikes. So I thought about what the pet shop guy had said. I was having coffee in Stompers at the time and I suddenly saw Cardy Owen across the bar and I remembered that Naomi Harris was her best mate—'

'Not any more,' Nina said. 'They haven't spoken to each other since that disco at the end of the fifth year—'

'This was in the old days,' Nazzer said. 'Naomi lived

up Unthank Road, then, and I knew they had hamsters. They used to breed them. So I rushed out and leapt on my bike. I was half-way up St Stephen's before I remembered Cedric. I'd left him on the table in his paper bag. So I did this U-turn and went boring back again. You know what it's like in Stompers – they only clear the tables twice a day. He was still there—'

'I geddit!' Maurice said. 'Dentures.'

'What did you want him back for?' Nina said. 'A keepsake?'

'Well, I knew that if I didn't get a replacement I'd have to make with the fish slice again. I rushed in and the paper bag was still on the table where I'd left it, but there were all these bikers sitting round it, real hairy heavies with *NECROPHILIACS DIE FOR IT* stencilled on their jackets. I got worried then. People like that *eat* hamsters. So I thought, Well, it's no good asking nicely, they won't know what the words mean, so I just dashed in, grabbed the bag and shot out again. And they all came roaring out after me – that should have tipped me off something was wrong – but I was on my bike – call me Tebbit – and off up the road again. So any way, I went round to Naomi's and she was in. I said, "Look, do us a favour. I want to borrow a hamster," and she says, "What for?" I said, "Just a substitution job. Ours has turned up his toes." "Can't you buy a new one?" she says. "Not like I want," I said, and I explained what had happened and how Cedric was kind of unusual. So she turns to this wall of hamster modules and says, "OK. I'll try and match you up with one of our old ones. Let's have a look at him." So I opened the bag,' Nazzer said, 'and

she said, "Is this some kind of a joke, Pollard?" It wasn't Cedric in the bag. It was a quarter-pound Stomperburger with onions and cheese.'

'You mean – the bikers had got Cedric?'

'Well, if they had, they probably *had* eaten him,' Nazzer said. 'I didn't feel much like going back to find out. I wondered if they'd noticed. Poor old Cedders Naomi was creased up, rolling about on the floor and kicking the furniture. She actually *gave* me a hamster in the end. It was huge. Just like Cedric except in one important detail – only I didn't spot it at the time. And I wanted to get away before Naomi had hysterics. The rest of the family was starting to join in and I had to get home before Mum and Mark did.'

'You got away with it then?' Nina said.

'Up to a point,' Nazzer said. 'Only I didn't quite find out why Naomi was screaming until the end of the week and Cedric Mark Two had kittens.'

'Kittens?'

'Pups, calves, cubs . . . whatever it is hamsters give birth to. That was why she was so huge. They only come into season for about thirty seconds every six months, or something like that, so it was a chance in a million. Mark was happy, though. "Is that why Cedric wasn't feeling well?" he kept saying. We had to say yes.'

'Must have given him some odd ideas about the facts of life, though,' said Maurice. 'No wonder he hangs about with binoculars in Chapelfield Gardens. He must be dead worried by now in case it happens to him.'

Inside the story

In pairs

1 All Jan Mark's stories about Nazzer and friends are written in a jokey style which seems almost casual. Of course, quite the reverse is true: in fact the stories are very carefully contrived and it's interesting to think about how they work. Here are a few things to think about:

(i) What is the actual *story*? (Apart from all the joking and so on.) Can you write it in one simple sentence?

(ii) What other stories are introduced along the way?

(iii) Is there any part of the story which is not told through conversation?

(iv) Topics seem to be juggled around all the time with first one idea bobbing up and disappearing, to be replaced by another idea which in its turn disappears from view as the first thought bobs up again. For example, in the first few paragraphs we are introduced to the idea of the Everlasting Hamster, Nina's reminiscences of Snowball, teachers' holidays, wild hamsters, Cumbrian sheep, long holidays (again)... and so on... and on. Take another section of the story yourselves and chart the way the ideas are woven together. For example, where does the idea of Chapelfield Gardens, with which the story ends, first get a mention?

(v) Jan Mark has a sharp eye for the little details that we all recognise as being accurate: the behaviour of student teachers, for example. What things did you recognise as being true to life in a similar way?

2 What things do you remember from your own infant/primary/ junior school days which gave them a particular flavour? Share your memories and see if there are any ideas for stories that emerge.

On your own

1 You have thought and talked about some of the ways in which Jan Mark's style works in this story and probably realised how skilful she is. Try your hand at writing a page or so of dialogue in the same style. Maybe you can think of a suitable story, similar to the one about the goldfish, which could be slipped into the original text.

2 Following your discussion about memories of your early school days, write your own story based on younger children's ways of looking at things. Like Jan Mark, you may like to take the idea of adults not always being direct with children – it could be anything from the discovery that Father Christmas isn't what was thought, to the discovery that adults are only human and even, sometimes, tell untruths. Frank O'Connor's story 'The Genius', with its delightful explanation of the facts of life, might suggest another area you could use as a starting point for your own story.

In small groups

Every word in the story is dialogue: the only bits that are not in between inverted commas are phrases like *Nazzer said* and *Nina said*. In fact, it would be very simple to write the whole story as a playscript leaving out these phrases and putting the characters' names down the lefthand side of the page. In groups of three, with each playing a part – Nazzer, Nina, Maurice – read the dialogue as a play, trying to get the right tone for each character. When you're satisfied with your version, tape record it.

WOOF

Jan Dean

'They all know me here. I'm the one who barks.' The thought pleased Kevin as he monkeyed up the drainpipe and onto the flat roof of the canteen.

'Can you see, Kev?' Colin and the others from 3C were at the back of the building, ready to run to any of a dozen other hiding places if discovery threatened.

Kevin crouched by the guttering. Three old tennis balls lay in a line by the top of the downspout. There was a low wall surrounding the edge of the roof. Kevin peered over it towards the science block doors. Two men walked into the yard.

'Grrwuff!' Kevin yapped, twice.

'Teachers,' Colin translated. 'Two of them. Who, Kev?'

'Yip-yip-yip.'

'Mr Tanner.' Colin relayed the information.

'Grr. Grrruff. Grrruff.'

'And Mr Southall.'

Kevin began to bark loudly, urgently.

'They're coming,' Colin said. 'Scatter! Are you with us, Kev?'

But Kevin was capering now, across the roof like a wild thing; half ape, half wolf. He leaped and growled and flailed his arms like a manic windmill. Then he stopped, directed an artfully inquisitive stare at the masters in the yard and pranced sideways, slowly, each movement precise and delicate. Next he cocked his head, swayed forward and rested his knuckles on the low wall at the edge. Controlled and

deft, he stretched out his neck, arched back his head and howled.

Mr Tanner and Mr Southall, stock still from the start of the performance, looked at each other.

'Oh my God,' sighed Tanner.

'Why us?' Southall muttered. 'There's no use talking to that boy. No use at all. Why the hell couldn't someone else have found him?'

Together they moved towards the canteen. Kevin bobbed down.

'He must be joking,' said Tanner. 'Hide-and-Seek now. Perhaps he hopes we'll pretend we haven't seen him.'

'You can never tell what Mayfield hopes.' Southall sounded tired.

They stopped six feet from the wall and shouted up.

'Mayfield! We know you're up there. Come on down!'

There was no reply, but two tennis balls bombed from the roof. They struck the tarmac hard and bounced around them maddeningly.

'Mayfield!'

Kevin rose from his hiding place, mock-sheepish, the third and oldest tennis ball in his mouth. He climbed down.

He stood limply by the drainpipe and said nothing. His shoulders sagged and his head drooped. He looked mournfully from Mr Southall to Mr Tanner, dribbling gently onto the dirty grey fur of the tennis ball.

'Right, Kevin, where should you be?'

Kevin stared at them with spaniel eyes, but said nothing. The tennis ball bulged from his jaws like a huge gum-boil.

'Drop that,' said Tanner, bored and irritated by Kevin's dumb resistance.

The ball fell and rolled wetly to Tanner's feet.

'Now, how about some answers? What are you doing out here?' asked Southall.

'Wuff!' said Kevin.

'That's enough,' said Tanner, 'we'll have some sensible answers, if you don't mind. Now, what are you doing here and where should you be?'

Kevin could see the strain in Tanner's eyes, knew he was reining in his anger.

'They don't like that,' he thought. 'If he loses his temper and I keep mine, who's the mad one then?'

'I'm not prepared to wait all day.' Tanner was snappy now. 'What the hell are you playing at?'

It was almost equal terms now. Tanner felt it too, felt himself dragged outside the careful list of don'ts that he stood for. Kevin had won.

In belling triumph, Kevin bayed like a hound. Tanner wanted to smash his head from his shoulders, shut him up once and for all. He stepped forward then drew back, hot and aware.

'For God's sake take him away before I do something I'll regret.' He turned away.

'Come on, Wolf Man,' said Southall.

From the other side of the yard, Jack Crockett saw it all. He stood at the Craft Room window and watched the whole thing. When the yard was empty again he turned back to his bench.

'Mayfield,' he sneered as he picked up his hammer. 'Bested by Mayfield.'

He raised the hammer and let it fall. The iron would do as it was told.

In the corridor outside the Head's room Kevin barked at the school secretary.

'He's not right, that boy,' she said to the typist as they counted and bagged dinner money. 'He wants locking up.'

Kevin watched her struggle her way from office to office, juggling files and duplicating paper. He growled softly whenever she came near.

Kevin disliked meeting the Head. He never knew quite where he stood. Dalton was too quick, too unlike the rest. At best he treated Kevin's barks as silence, at worst he barked first. It upset Kevin, left him empty.

The office door opened and the secretary edged past gingerly. Kevin rolled back his top lip into his most wolfish smile.

'Enter!' Mr Dalton hardly looked up as Kevin went in. 'Again, Kevin? I thought we sorted out all this nonsense the last time.'

'Sir.'

'Right. Let's go over this morning's escapade, shall we?'

Kevin was silent.

'First of all, *on the roof*. Now, you know the rules, Kevin, and I'm not going to waste my breath repeating them. The roof is out of bounds. Is that quite clear?'

'Sir.'

'And as for your absence from maths during period two, well that's quite straightforward. Detention. This Thursday.'

The interview was over. Mr Dalton waited for Kevin to go, but Kevin did not. He looked at Mr Dalton expectantly.

'Yes? Did you want to say something?'

'What about the other, Sir?' Kevin was eager, pushy.

'What? What other?'

'The barking, Sir.' Admit it, he thought, admit that it's important.

'Oh, that. You must give me credit for some things, Kevin. No one could say I was without a sense of humour. Off you go.' And then, as an afterthought, 'Woof-woof.'

The break bell rang and Kevin left.

Outside in the yard a crowd of maths dodgers fed him gum. He had been a good decoy.

'Ta, Kev. Want a chew?'

He sat and begged, rolled over, played dead and snarled at outsiders who passed too close to the group. He revelled in it, fed on it. It was his voice, his name. They thought it was just a game, Mr Dalton, Tanner and Southall and the rest, but they were wrong.

Kevin grinned and rolled his eyes at a gang of fifth form girls. They giggled and he let his tongue loll over his teeth. Their giggling tightened into nervy laughter. He padded closer, pulled up sharply and sniffed. He singled out a small dark girl and moved towards her. He snuffled as he circled her, tasting the air.

'Get off,' she said and tried to move away, but he had cut her off from the herd and now he barred her path.

'Shift!' She was angry now and swung her arm at his head.

Kevin yelped and cowered. He howled, long mournful howls, and padded quietly after the retreating girl.

'Bloody nut!' she shouted at him. 'Go on, Kevin, back to your kennel.'

Even the fifth form knew who he was.

*

In the staff room Jack Crockett fished for information.

'I hear you had a bit of bother with Mayfield.'

Tanner was non-committal.

'Something and nothing.'

'Oh, own up. You had a run-in with him, didn't you? Nothing wrong with that. Nothing to be ashamed of. They get away with murder, these boys. Standing there with "you-can't-touch-me" grins all over their vicious little faces. Well it's time somebody did, I can tell you. It's time somebody did.'

'Hardly appropriate for Mayfield.' Southall was cold. 'He's a clown, that's all.'

Crockett mocked him. 'Oh, that's right, pretend he's harmless, then you needn't do anything about him. All good clean fun, eh? He's baiting us. He incites indiscipline. That boy is trouble. He's got us with our backs against the wall.'

'Oh, come on.' Southall's quiet laughter was uncertain. 'Aren't you going off the deep end a bit? The lad's a bit disturbing, I'll grant you, but he's hardly a threat.'

Tanner wanted to agree; he'd no time for Crockett and his kind who passed nostalgia off as wisdom, but he could not. Tanner had stood face to face with Mayfield on Mayfield's ground.

'I think it's quite serious,' Tanner said. 'I think he really has a problem.'

'Oh my God.' Crockett's exasperation peaked. 'Heaven defend me from psychologists!'

After break, Kevin lined up with the rest of the class outside the Metalwork Room. Jack Crockett bore down on them from the far end of the corridor. The snake of boys rippled and straightened. Crockett would not let them in if they lounged or strayed from the queue.

'Watch it, Kev. He's in a mood,' Colin warned as they stood more or less to attention. Kevin glanced in Crockett's direction. Colin was right, he could tell by the walk. Crockett seemed on the verge of bouncing along, each step sprung with aggression. He looked along the line. It was their version of straight. But to Crockett the boots, the jackets, the haircuts all signalled decay. It was rot, the shuffle back to slime.

'Psychology,' he seethed as he unlocked the door and the boys filed in. 'Just a minute,' he said, soft as lead, as Kevin moved in past him in the doorway. 'Stand out at the front. I want a word.'

It was time.

The rest of the boys were standing by their benches, craft aprons folded in front of them, when Jack Crockett closed the door. Michael Watts had taken his half-made money box from the cupboard and was anxious to begin.

'Stand still, Watts. What's that on your bench?'

'It's my work, Sir.'

'I don't remember giving permission for boys to get out their work.'

'No, Sir.'

'Put it away, Watts.'

'Yes, Sir.'

'Now, what have we here?' He looked at Kevin carefully, as if he were a model he was going to demonstrate to the group.

'Ah, yes, Kevin Mayfield. The Incredible Barking Boy.'

The class sniggered.

'Known in school and staff room as the Wolf Man of the Junior Forms.'

The laughter swelled. Kevin liked it.

'Fancy yourself, don't you, dog-boy?'

The challenge thrummed in the air. Kevin felt it. He bunched his arms and hands into dangling paws and began to pant.

Crockett took one step forward and snorted his disgust. Kevin looked at him, cocked his leg like a dog at a post and launched into bursts of frantic yelping.

Crockett roared. 'Enough!'

The background cackles ceased, smothered by the violence of the shout. For a second the whole room froze to a film still. Kevin saw the fine mist of spit from Crockett's mouth as clearly as splinters of glass, as if an empty milk bottle had exploded in the air between them. In the stillness Kevin knew, too late, that this was different. Tanner had despised his rage, Crockett did not; he would not step back, he welcomed the anger and the heat. He would not lose his temper, lose control, lose the edge, but simply use it, like the furnace, to bend or break.

Suddenly it was all action, the film rolled on in an instant. Crockett had him by the shoulder and was shaking him. Each thrust shocked his spine. The breath was being knocked out of him. His joints screamed, he screamed. Crockett let go.

'It's time,' he hissed. 'It's time you learned. You've skated through long enough. We've humoured you long enough. Well, you're going to be house-trained. Do you hear? House-trained.'

He picked up a steel bar from the bench dropped it by Kevin's feet.

'Fetch,' he said.

Kevin did not move. What was he trying to do?

'Fetch.' His voice was softer now, and as menacing as mink. Kevin looked; Crockett was six foot and between him and the door. He bent to pick up the bar.

'No, Kevin, not like that. Like you fetch Daddy's slippers, like you fetch a bone.'

Crockett was a wall with fists. Kevin fetched the bar.

'Good dog, Mayfield. Good dog.'

The class were silent now, and frightened.

'Watts, bring me that grease.'

The lid resisted at first, then gave way to Crockett's twisting with a soft plop. The dark grease glistened. He dug deep into the can and scooped out a glutinous lump. He smiled at the mass in his hand, savouring the weight and the texture. Lovingly he larded the rod and dropped it again at Kevin's feet.

'Fetch,' he almost sang.

'Sir?' Watts was pale.

'Yes, Michael? Do you want to play?'

Michael bit his lip.

'Right-oh, Kevin. Fetch.' The word rang like a gin-trap. Crockett gripped the back of Kevin's neck, working his fingers as if to find purchase between spine and muscle. Kevin squirmed, but he could not wrench away. Crockett straightened his arm and, relentless and smooth as a slow-motion piston, drove Kevin down.

'Sir !' Michael Watts felt sick.

Crockett was almost kneeling on Kevin's back, shoving his face into the filth.

'Fetch! Fetch!' Such a quiet command. Crockett bubbled like the acid bath.

'No!' Kevin turned his head. Crockett forced it back and down, down onto the bar.

'That's right.' The whisper drilled into him. 'Rub his nose in it! Rub his nose in it!'

The pain in his neck shot electric flicks down his arms. He groaned. His teeth banged against the bar. He opened his mouth.

Kevin stood mute, sick with the taste of grease. Crockett had taken his music, stolen it, taken his voice just as surely as if he had ripped it out of his throat. Now Kevin was just like all the others.

Jack Crockett turned to the class. He had made his point.

'Get out your work,' he said.

It was several months later when Jack Crockett had his accident. He was tidying up at the end of a lesson when he knocked over a naked light and there was an explosion. Somehow the tap of a gas bottle had been switched on and the gas, heavier than air, had sunk and filled the blacksmith's hearth. The flame fell and it blew; first the soft sigh, then the dull boom. Mr Crockett was thrown twenty feet across the room.

Michael Watts went for help.

Kevin sat quietly remembering the exact sound as the first flame touched the gas. 'Whoof!' he said inside his head, 'Whoof!'

Then the room was full of people sorting things out and sending the boys away.

There was a spate of accidents around that time; a fire in the Domestic Science Room and a small but colourful bang in the Chemistry Lab. Mr Dalton was worried. He was considering extra fire drills when he met Kevin by the boiler room.

'Ah, Mayfield. Seen the Caretaker?'

'No, Sir. Sorry, Sir.'

'Not to worry. Not seen you in my room for a while. Good. Glad to see you're settling down.'

Then, as an afterthought:

'Woof-woof!'

Kevin looked blank. 'I don't do that any more, Sir,' he said, and smiled.

Inside the story

In pairs or small groups

1 At the very beginning of the story, Kevin is pleased to think 'They all know me here. I'm the one who barks.' Discuss how Kevin's behaviour helps give him a sense of identity and wins him recognition from both teachers and pupils.

2 'If he loses his temper and I keep mine, who's the mad one then?' thinks Kevin when he angers Tanner in the first section of the story. In what way is it true to say that in this confrontation 'Kevin had won'?

3 Tanner is angry with Kevin but restrains himself: Crockett, on the other hand, thinks it is time something was done about him. Discuss what Crockett feels about Kevin and why he should feel so strongly about his behaviour.

4 How do you feel about Crockett's attitude to Kevin? Is it justifiable? Do you approve of his method of bringing him to heel?

5 By the end of the story, Kevin has exchanged the fairly harmless 'Woof' for the infinitely more dangerous 'Whoof!' What is the suggestion hinted at near the end when the Head meets Kevin by the boiler room?

On your own

1 What do you think would happen next in the story? Think about the clues we have been given as to how things might develop and continue the story. What happens in the next twenty-four hours?

2 Kevin is clearly a disturbed personality, made far worse by his treatment at the hands of Crockett. Write a form teacher's report on Kevin's behaviour, indicating what it is that worries you, why you think he may behave as he does, and your concern for how things might develop.

In small groups

'Woof' is a story which lends itself to dramatisation. You could take a scene such as Kevin's confrontation with Tanner and Southall or the short interview with Mr Dalton, or the big scene when Crockett humiliates him, and act it out. Different people have different attitudes to Kevin, so think carefully about their tone of voice as they speak to him or about him.

If you are more ambitious you could turn the story into a powerful radio script to be recorded on tape. The dialogue is strong and you are given many pointers as to how the characters think and speak. Above all, Kevin's barking provides a marvellous sound effect that runs through the whole story. You also have the right location with school sound effects all around you.

THE BLOT

Iain Crichton Smith

Miss Maclean said, 'And pray tell me how did you get the blot on your book?'

I stood up in my seat automatically and said, 'It was . . . I put too much ink in the pen, please, miss.' I added again forlornly, 'Please, miss.' She considered or seemed to consider this for a long time, but perhaps she wasn't really thinking about it at all, perhaps she was thinking about something else. Then she said, 'And did you not perhaps think of putting less ink in your pen? I imagine one has a choice in those matters.' The rest of the class laughed as they always did, promptly and decorously, whenever Miss Maclean made a joke. She said, 'Be quiet', and they stopped laughing as if one of the taps mentioned in our sums had been switched off. Miss Maclean always wore a grey thin blouse and a thin black jacket. Sometimes she seemed to me to look like a pencil.

'Do you not perhaps believe in having a tidy book as the rest of us do?' she said. I didn't know what to say. Naturally I believed in having a tidy book. I liked the whiteness of a book more than anything else in the world. To write on a white page was like . . . how can I say it? . . . it was like a bird leaving footprints in snow. But then to say that to her was to sound daft. And anyway, why couldn't she clean the globe which lay in front of her on the desk? It was always dusty so that you could leave your fingerprints all over Europe or South America or Antigua. Antigua was a really beautiful name; I had come across it recently in an atlas. The highest mark she ever gave for an essay was

five out of ten, and she always spoiling jotters by filling them with comments and scoring through words and adding punctuation marks. But I must admit that when she wrote on the board she wrote very neatly.

'And what's this,' she said, 'about an old woman? I thought you were supposed to write about a postman. Have you never seen a postman?' She was always asking stupid questions like that. Of course I had seen a postman. 'And what's this word "solatary"? I presume you mean "solitary". You shouldn't use big words unless you can spell them. And whoever saw an old woman peering out through the letter-box when the postman came up the stairs? You really have the oddest notions.' The class laughed again. No, I had not actually seen an old woman peering through a letter-box, but there was no reason why one shouldn't, why my old woman shouldn't. In fact she *had* been peering through the letter-box. I was angry at having misspelt 'solitary'. I didn't know how I had come to do that, since I knew the correct spelling. 'Old women don't look through letterboxes waiting for letters,' she almost screamed, her face reddening with rage.

Why did she hate me so much? I wondered. It was the same when I wrote the essay about the tiger who ate fish and chips. Was it really because my work wasn't neat and because I was always putting ink-blots on the paper? My hands were clumsy, there was no getting away from that. They never did what I wanted them to do. Her hands, however, were very thin and neat, ringless. Not like my mother's hands. My mother's hands were wrinkled and one of the fingers had a plain gold ring which she could never get off.

'Old women don't spend their time waiting for letters,' she shouted. 'They have other things to do with their time. I have never seen an old woman who waited every day for a letter. Have you? HAVE you?'

I thought for some time and then said, 'No, miss.'

'Well then,' she said, breathing less heavily. 'But you always want to be clever, don't you? I asked you to write about a postman and you write about an old woman. That is impertinence. ISN'T IT?'

I knew what I was expected to answer so I said, 'Yes, miss.'

She looked down at the page from an enormous height with her thin hawk-like gaze and read out a sentence in a scornful voice. '"She began to write a letter to herself but as she did so a blot of ink fell on the page and she stopped." Why did you write that? That again is deliberate insolence.'

'It came into my mind at that . . . after I had put the ink on my jotter. It just came into my head.'

'It was insolence, wasn't it? WASN'T IT?'

Actually it hadn't been. It had been a kind of inspiration. The idea came into my head very quickly and I had written the sentence before I thought how it would appear to her. I hadn't been thinking of her when I was writing the composition. But from now on I would have to think of her, I realized. Whatever I wrote I would have to think of her reading it and the thought filled me with despair. I couldn't understand why her face quivered with rage when she spoke to me, why she showed such hatred. I didn't want to be hated. Who wanted to be hated like this?

I felt this even while she was belting me. Perhaps she was right. Perhaps it had been insolence. Perhaps neatness was the most important thing in the world. After she had belted me she might be kind to me again and she might stop watching me all the time as if I was an enemy. The thing was, I must learn to hide from her, be neat and clean. Maybe that would work, and her shouting would go away. But even as I thought that and was writhing with pain from the belt, I was also thinking, Miss Maclean, very clean, Miss Maclean, very clean. The words shone without my bidding in front of my head. I was always doing that. Sums, numbs, bums, mums. I also thought, Have you Macleaned your belt today? I thought of a story where a dirty old man, a tramp sitting by the side of the road, would shout, 'Why aren't you as clean as me?' The tramp was very like old Mackay who worked on the roads and was always singing hymns, while breaking the rock. And there was another story where the belt would stand up like a snake and sway to music. In front of her thin grey blouse the belt would rise, with a snake's head and a green skin. I could even hear the accompanying music, staccato and vibrant. It was South American music and came from the dusty globe in front of her.

Inside the story

In pairs or small groups

1 Discuss what things Miss Maclean seems to care about most and what things the boy cares about. Make two contrasting lists.

2 Why does Miss Maclean hate him so much? Is there anything in particular about the boy's story that might annoy her?

3 Early in the story the writer mentions the dusty globe, untouched by Miss Maclean, and he returns to the image of the globe at the end of the story. Discuss why he might have decided to do this.

4 Iain Crichton Smith is a Scottish writer and poet with a deep love of words, language and the world of the imagination. What suggests that this might be an autobiographical story about his own childhood?

5 In pairs, work out the dialogue between Miss Maclean and the boy (he doesn't say a lot) and act out the scene between them. Try to catch the right tones of voice and the way in which each stands as the confrontation develops.

On your own

Try to recall (or imagine) a situation where a child is being told off by a teacher. Whatever the reason – perhaps unacceptable work, behaviour or attitude – try to capture the thoughts racing through the child's head as the dressing down continues. Like Iain Crichton Smith try to capture the tones of the teacher's voice as well. Write your story in the first person as though it had happened to you – as, of course, it might have done.

THE HEALING

Dorothy Nimmo

We were messing about, which we shouldn't have been doing, but there you are. We should have been outside, but it was freezing out. Karen was showing off doing his flip thing she's just learnt. I don't mind Karen showing off because she's been my friend since the Junior and she's really good, anyway. Then she sort of slipped and she just lay there on the floor.

'Oh Lord,' she said. 'That's torn it!'

And we remembered about the competition.

You might think we were making a big thing about it but there wasn't much you could do around our school that made people think anything of you. Everyone wants to be someone, I mean everyone wants to be special. Don't they? Look at all the people who go on the prize shows on the telly, they'd rather look like prize wallies and be able to say they've been on the telly than spend their whole lives never doing anything.

At our school you do all right if you play football. If you get in the team you do all right. And the big boys have their bikes. They start with the mopeds and then they get the big Hondas, with the fairings and that. They're really big deal on those bikes, with their leathers and boots and their heads twice the proper size in the helmets. You can't see the spots under the visors. And the girls hang round them. There isn't much for the girls. You get noticed if you go around, you know, if you're easy, and if you get pregnant they talk about you but they don't admire you. There isn't much a girl can do apart from swimming and gymnastics.

They put us all in for the competitions, that's the way they have. They think there's no point in anything unless there's a competition and a prize. They mean well, they think we're losers so they'll give us a chance at something, even if it's something really diddy, like cookery. They had a cookery competition one time, it was some custard-powder company, they all had to think up different things you could make with custard powder. Sandra went in for that because there was a prize, twenty pounds. She made this cake with custard powder and then custard on top, you know, and then all different fruit; it was a lovely colour, really bright yellow, but she didn't win. My Mum does flower arrangements. Honestly, she spends hours finding this stuff, dried flowers and leaves, and she has all these different baskets and bits of log hollowed out. I think it looks terrible. It looks dead and it stands around the house all winter getting deader and deader. But she puts these things in the Flower Show and gets prizes; she gets a real kick out of the prizes. So she says to me, 'Why don't you make a sponge cake, Marty, there's a class here for a sponge? Or scones, that's easy, go on. Just for fun. It doesn't matter if you win or not, that's not the point. It's competition is the fun!'

I don't understand her. What's the point of going in for it if you know you're going to lose? It isn't fun, it's bloody murder, I think.

Karen used to go in for swimming. She said it was

boring pounding up and down the pool. When they get keen they really drive you. It must do something for them, I suppose it would, for the teachers, if they can get a winner out of all of us losers. Karen was good at the swimming, but then she got something wrong with her ears and even old Evans thought it was a bit much to go deaf just so the school could get into the area championships. So then she took up the gymnastics.

Ever since I've known her she's been doing things like the crab, going round the playground all bent over backwards, and cartwheels and that, so she'd got the talent and she really took to it. Everyone was doing it that year, it was all on the telly and the girls were really keen, but it was Karen they kept on at to do the competitions. And there was Karen on the floor. The Championship was the next day.

Someone said she ought to go to the nurse and someone else said, try a hot-water bottle. Sandra said, 'What about an iron?' And we said, 'What do you mean, an iron?'

'You iron her back,' said Sandra, 'I've seen it done.'

'You're having me on,' I said.

'It's the heat,' said Sandra.

'Honestly?' said Pam. Pam believes anything, always has. One time I told her if she put her fingers down her throat she could touch her toes. She believed me. She was sick, you can imagine, all on her shoes.

'What about a rolling-pin?' I said, 'we could roll her out.' I didn't think they'd take that seriously.

'I think we ought to go and tell Mr Evans,' said Jenny.

'How are you feeling?' I asked Karen.

'Not bad,' she said. So I knew she felt bad.

'We'd better sort it out for ourselves if we can,' I said.

So then Sandra went and got in at the window of the Home Economics, which is easy for her. I reckon she can get into anything, it's a knack, she says. It'll get her into trouble. She got in at the window and then she got another window open and we all climbed in. Karen said it was easing up a bit, but we made her lie down on one of the tables. First we found the rolling pin and rolled it up and down. You wouldn't think that would do any good; it didn't.

'Roll on a floured board,' said Nell. 'That's what it says in the cookery books!' She thought that was such a good joke she was no help at all for a bit.

'Is that what it means?' said Pam, 'Honestly?'

'Oh Pam!' said Sandra.

Then we got out the iron, Sandra got the cupboard open, and we plugged it in and started ironing Karen's back through her vest until it got too hot and she yelled. And we'd had it on the lowest setting.

The it was Nell said, 'Let's try the laying-on of hands.'

'Go on,' said Karen, 'what's that?'

'It's what Jesus did, what the healing people do, you know, like in the Bible.'

'I never get in in time for Assembly,' I said.

'We don't have Bible in Assembly any more,' said Pam.

'We always have sex in RE,' said Jenny.

'But we had it in the Junior,' said Nell, 'Jesus was always at it, putting his hands on people. And they do it up at the Pentecostal. There's a man used to come to the shop ever so lame and now he doesn't.'

'Go on Karen, let's have a go,' said Sandra.

'Do you have to say anything?'

'Pick up your bed and walk,' suggested Nell.

'I'm not on my bed,' said Karen.

'In the name of the Father and the Son and the Holy Ghost, amen?'

'I don't know,' said Sandra. 'You go first.'

Nell put her hands on Karen's back and said, 'Get thee behind me, Satan!'

I don't know where she got that from.

Nothing happened. We didn't expect anything to happen, we were just trying it on. Then Pam put her hands on and began stroking and squeezing like the massage people do in the films, but Karen said that made it worse. And then I did it. I put my hands on Karen's back and I could feel the warmth going on down my arm and running into her back. I felt like it was my blood running into her and if I didn't take my hands away I wouldn't have any blood left any more. It was quite hard, taking my hands away. I felt quite weak, honestly.

Karen lay there for a bit. Then she got up.

'How does it feel?' I said.

'It's fine,' she said. 'That's fixed it.'

Then they all started to go on at me.

'What did you do, Mart?' said Sandra.

'I didn't do anything.'

'You must have done something.'

'Try it on me,' said Nell.

'I've got this dirty great spot on my chin,' said Sandra.

'I've got warts,' said Jenny.

But Karen said to leave me alone, we'd better get out before someone caught us.

Karen was third in the competition. Mr Evans said it wasn't good enough.

Sometimes Nell or Sandra get at me about it. If they have a headache or a period pain they say, 'What about a bit of the old laying-on of hands, Mart?' But I don't take any notice. They'll forget about it.

I wouldn't like to do it again.

They probably have competitions for that, too. If they knew about it, they'd probably put me in for them. I can just imagine all the sick, lame people laid out on the floor and everyone having a go who can make them get up fastest. With stopwatches and numbers, like they do in competitions. And prizes. I know they don't really. I don't expect I'd win if they did.

Inside the story

In pairs or small groups

1 Discuss how you imagine Marty, the girl who tells the story. What clues are we given about her character from the way she tells about what happened; from her attitude towards others; from her views about competitions?

2 'Everyone wants to be someone, I mean everyone wants to be someone special. Don't they?' says Marty near the beginning of the story. Her experience of laying on hands makes her special but she hopes everyone will forget about it and leave her alone. Discuss why you think she doesn't want to repeat the experience.

On your own

Imagine that the local newspaper has got hold of the story and sends a reporter to find out what happened from Karen, Sandra, Pam, Jenny and Nell before interviewing Marty herself. Decide what each would say and then put together a report for your paper, headlining it as a front page story.

Local radio gets in on the act. Tape interviews with the girls for broadcasting. What would Mr Evans and their headteacher be likely to say?

4
NEEDS

The four stories in this section are all concerned in one way or another with people who need something badly. The Turkish writer, Yashar Kemal, describes a world which may seem distant in time and place but there can be few of us who do not recognise the overwhelming desire of young Mustafa to dress fashionably. In his society at that time the thing to wear to impress the girls was a pair of white trousers together with white canvas shoes. Times and fashions change but the need to dress just right, particularly when you are Mustafa's age, is one that most of us will know.

Roger, the boy in Langston Hughes' story, 'Thank You, Ma'm', is as desperate to possess a pair of blue suede shoes as was Mustafa to have a pair of white trousers. Roger's attempt to steal money from Mrs Luella Bates Washington Jones in order to buy his shoes leads him into an unexpected situation. Her understanding of his needs is rooted in her own experience of hardship and Langston Hughes' portrait of this formidable woman stays in the mind long after the story has been read.

The other two stories in this section are not so much about material needs – shoes or clothes – as about emotional needs. In 'The Bellows of the Fire', Rose Tremain describes a girl's deep longing to break out of the small town that threatens to stifle her. A strong sense of the main character's isolation and her need to define her own life in her own terms comes through the story. 'I've never before longed for anything I could actually have, *now*,' says the girl.

The life of the main character in Catherine Storr's story seems to be a catalogue of longings. She is forever building up her expectations and – whether they relate to Christmas presents or boyfriends – is forever disappointed. She always thinks she knows what she needs, what will make her happy . . . until she finds herself 'surprised'.

THE WHITE TROUSERS

Yashar Kemal trans. Thilda Kemal

It was hot. The boy Mustafa held the shoe listlessly and gazed out of the shop at the sun-impacted street with its uneven cobbles. He felt he would never be able to mend this shoe. It was the most tattered thing he had ever come across. He looked up tentatively, but the cobbler was bent over his work. He placed the shoe on the bench and hammered in a nail haphazardly.

'I can't do it,' he murmured at last.

'What's that, Mustafa?' said the cobbler, raising his head for a moment. 'Why, you haven't begun to try yet!'

'But, master,' protested the boy, 'it comes apart as soon as I put in a stitch. . . .'

The cobbler was silent.

Mustafa tackled the shoe again. His face was running with sweat and the sun had dropped nearer the distant hills when Hassan Bey, a well-to-do friend of the cobbler's, stepped into the shop.

'My friend,' he said, 'I need a boy to help fire my brick-kiln. Will you let me have this one? Only for three days.'

'Would you work at the brick-kiln, Mustafa?' asked the cobbler. 'It's for three days and three nights too, you know. . . .'

'The pay is one and a half liras a day,' said Hassan Bey. 'All you'll have to do is give a hand to Jumali. You know Jumali who lives down the river? He's a good man, won't let you work yourself out.'

Mustafa's black eyes shone.

'All right, Uncle Hassan,' he said. 'But I'll have to ask mother. . . .'

'Well, ask her, and be at my orange grove tomorrow. The kiln's in the field next to it. You'll start work in the afternoon, I won't be there, but you'll find Jumali.'

The cobbler paid him twenty-five kurush a week. A whole month and only one lira! It was July already, and a pair of summer shoes cost two liras, a pair of white trousers three. . . . But now, four and a half liras would be his for only three days' work! What a stroke of luck! . . . First you wash your hands, but properly, with soap. . . . Then you unwrap the white canvas shoes. . . . Your socks must be white too. You must be careful, very careful, with the white trousers. They get soiled so quickly. Your fingers should hardly touch them. And go to the bridge where the girls stroll in the cool of the evening, the breeze swelling their skirts. . . . The breeze tautening the white trousers against your legs. . . .

'Mother!' he cried, bursting into the house. 'I'm going to fire Hassan Bey's brick-kiln with Jumali!'

'Who says so? Certainly not!'

'But, Mother. . . .'

'My child, you don't know what firing a kiln means. Can you go without sleep for three days and three nights? God knows I have trouble enough waking you up in the morning!'

'But, Mother, this is different. . . .'

'You'll fall asleep, I tell you. You'll never stand it.'

'Look, Mother, you know Sami, Tewfik Bey's son, Sami?' he said hopefully.

'Well?'

'Those white trousers of his and the white shoes? Snow white! I've got a silk shirt in the trunk. I'll wear that too. Wouldn't I look well?'

Mustafa knew his mother. The tears rose to her eyes. She bowed her head.

'Wouldn't I, Mother? Now wouldn't I?'

'My darling, you'd look well in anything. . . .'

'Vayis the tailor'll do it for me. Mother dear, say I can go!'

'Well, I don't know . . .' she said doubtfully.

He saw she was giving in and flung himself on her neck.

'When I'm big . . .' he began.

'You'll work very hard.'

'And then?' he prompted.

'You'll make a beautiful orange grove of that empty field of ours near the stream. You'll have a horse of your own to ride. . . . You'll order navy blue suits from tailors in Adana. . . .'

'And then?' he prompted.

'Then you'll tile the roof of our house so it won't let in the rain.'

'Then?'

'You'll be just like your father.'

'And if my father hadn't died?'

'You'd have gone to school and studied and become a great man. . . .'

'But now?'

'If your father had been alive. . . .'

'Look,' said Mustafa, 'I'll have a gold watch when I'm big, won't I?'

The next morning he was up and away before sunrise. The dust on the road felt cool and soft under his bare feet. A flood of light was surging up behind the hill. When he came to the kiln, the sun was sitting on the crest like a great round ember. He bent over to the mouth of the kiln. It was dark inside. Around it brushwood had been heaped in little hillocks.

It was almost noon when Jumali arrived. He was a big man who walked ponderously, picking his way. Ignoring Mustafa, he stopped before the kiln and thrust his head inside. Then he turned back.

'What're you doing around here, hey?' he barked.

The boy was struck with fear. He felt like taking to his heels.

'What're you standing there stuck for, hey?' shouted Jumali.

'Hassan Bey sent me,' stammered Mustafa. 'To help you. . . .'

With surprising agility Jumali swung his heavy frame impatiently back to the kiln.

'Now that's fine!' he growled. 'What does Hassan Bey think he's doing, sending along a child not bigger than the palm of your hand?' He flung his hand out. 'Not bigger than this hand! You go right back and tell him to find someone else.'

Mustafa was dumb with dismay. He took a few wavering steps toward the town. Then he stopped. The white trousers danced before his eyes. He wanted to cry.

'Uncle Jumali,' he begged weakly, 'I'll work harder than a grown man. . . .'

'Listen to the pup! Do you know what it means to fire a kiln?'

'Oh, yes. . . .'

'Why, you little bastard, three days, three nights of feeding wood into this hole you see here, taking it in turns, you and I. . . .'

'I know, I know!'

'Listen to the little bastard! Did you learn all this in

your mother's womb? Now bugger off and stop pestering me.'

Mustafa had a flash of inspiration.

'I can't go back,' he said. 'Hassan Bey paid me in advance and I've already spent the money.'

'Go away!' shouted Jumali. 'You'll get me into trouble.'

Mustafa rebelled.

'But why? Why d'you want to take the bread out of my mouth? Just because I'm a child. . . . I can work as hard as anyone.' Suddenly he ran up to Jumali and grasped his hand. 'I swear it, Uncle Jumali! You'll see how I'll feed that kiln. Anyway, I've spent the pay. . . .'

'Well, all right,' Jumali said at last. 'We'll see. . . .'

He lit a stick of pinewood and thrust it in. The wood crackled and a long tongue of flame spurted out.

'Damn!' he cursed. 'Filled it up to bursting, they have, the bastards! Everything they do is wrong.'

Still cursing, he gave Mustafa a few instructions. Then he lit a cigarette and moved off into the shade of a fig-tree.

When the flames that were lapping the mouth of the kiln had receded, Mustafa picked up an armful of brushwood and threw it in. Then another. . . . And another. . . .

The dusty road, the thick-spreading fig-trees, the stream that flowed like molten tin, the ashen sky, the lone bird flapping by, the scorched grass, the small wilting yellow flowers, the whole world drooped wearily under the impact of the noonday heat. Mustafa's face was as red as the flames, his shirt dripping, as he ran carrying the brushwood from the heat of the sun to the heat of the kiln.

At the close of the sizzling afternoon, little white clouds rise up in clusters far off in the south over the Mediterranean, heralding the cool moist breeze that will soon enwrap the heat-baked creatures as in a wet soothing towel. As the first fresh puff of wind stirred up the dust on the road, Jumali called to Mustafa from where he lay supine in the heavy shade of the fig-tree.

'Hey, boy, come along and let's eat!'

Mustafa was quivering with exhaustion and hunger.

Hassan Bey had provided Jumali with a bundle of food. There was white cheese, green onions, and wafer-bread. They fell to without a word. The sun sank down behind the poplar trees that stood out like a dark curtain against the glow. Mustafa picked up the jug and went to the stream. The water tasted like warm blood. They drank it thirstily. Jumali wiped his long moustache with the back of his hand.

'I'm going to sleep a while, Mustafa,' he said. 'Wake me up when you're tired, eh?'

It was long past midnight. The moon had dropped behind the wall of poplars. Mustafa's thin sweating face shone red in the blaze. He threw in an armful of wood and watched the wild onrush of flames swallow it up. There was a loud crackling at first, then a long, long moaning sound that was almost human.

Like a baby crying its heart out, he thought.

'Are you tired? D'you want me?' came Jumali's sleepy voice.

A tremor shook his body. He felt a cold sweat breaking out all over him.

'Oh no, Uncle Jumali!' he cried. 'I never get tired. You go on sleeping.'

He could not bear to go near the kiln any more. Now he heaped as much wood as possible close to the opening and shoved it in with the long wooden fork. Then, backing before the sudden surge of heat, he scrambled onto a mound nearby and stood awhile against the night breeze. But the air bore down, heavy and stifling, drowning him.

There is a bird that sings just before the break of dawn. A very tiny bird. Its call is long-drawn and piercing. He heard the bird's call and saw a widening ribbon of light brighten up the sky behind the hill.

Just then Jumali woke up.

'Are you tired?' he asked.

'No . . . No . . . I'm not tired.' But his voice broke, strangling with tears.

Jumali rose and stretched himself.

'Go and sleep a little now,' he said.

He was asleep when Hassan Bey arrived.

'How's the boy doing?' he asked. 'Working all right?'

Jumali's lips curled.

'A chit of a child. . . .' he said.

'Well, you'll have to shift along as best you can. I'll make it worth your while,' said Hassan Bey as he left.

When Mustafa awoke the sun was heaving down upon him and the earth was like red-hot iron. His bones ached as though they had been pounded in a mortar. Setting his teeth, he struggled up and ran to the kiln.

'Uncle Jumali,' he faltered, 'I'm sorry I slept so long. . . .'

'I told you you'd never make it,' said Jumali sourly.

Mustafa did not answer. He scraped up some brushwood and began feeding the kiln. After a while he felt a little better.

Hurray! he thought. We've weathered the first day.

But the two huge searing days loomed before him and the stifling clamminess of the infernal nights. He chased the thought away and conjured up the image of the white trousers. . . .

The last night. . . . The moon bright over the poplar trees. . . .

'Wake me up if you get tired,' says Jumali. . . .

The fire has to be kept up at the same level or the bricks will not bake and a whole two days' work will have been in vain. The flames must flare out greedily licking at the night. The hated flames. . . . He has not the strength to reach the refreshing mound any longer. He can only throw himself on the ground and let the moist coolness of the earth seep into his body. But always the fear in his heart that sleep will overcome him. . . .

His eyes were clinging to the east, groping for the ribbon of light. But it was pitch dark and Jumali snored on loudly.

Damn you, Uncle Jumali! Damn you. . . .

Suddenly, the whole world started trembling. The dark curtain of poplars, the hills, the flames, the kiln were turning round and round. He was going to vomit.

'Jumali! Uncle Jumali. . . .'

He had fainted.

It was a good while before Jumali called again in his drowsy voice.

'Are you tired, Mustafa?'

There was no answer. Then he caught sight of the darkened kiln. He rushed up and fetched the child a furious kick.

'You've done for me, you little bastard! They'll make me pay for the bricks now. . . .'

He peered into the opening and took hope. A few small flames were still wavering against the inner wall.

Mustafa came to as the dawn was breaking. His heart quaked at the sight of Jumali, his hairy chest bared, stoking the kiln.

'Uncle Jumali,' he faltered, 'really, I never meant to. . . .'

Jumali cast an angry glance over his shoulder.

'Shut up, damn you! Go to hell!'

Mustafa hung his head and sat there motionless until the sun rose over the hill. Then he fell asleep in the same position.

A brick kiln is large and spacious, rather like a well that has been capped with a dome. When it is first set alight the bricks take on a leaden hue. The second day, they turn a dull black. But on the morning of the third day, they are a fiery red. . . .

Mustafa awoke with fear in his heart. The sun was quarter high and Hassan Bey was standing near the kiln. The bricks were sparkling like red crystal.

'Well, my boy?' Hassan Bey laughed. 'So we came here to sleep, did we?'

'Uncle, I swear that every night. . . .'

Jumali threw him a dour look. He dared not go on. They sealed up the mouth of the kiln.

The cobbler had shaggy eyebrows and a beard. His back was slightly hunched. The shop, dusty and cobwebby, smelled of leather and rawhide.

A week had gone by and still no sign of Hassan Bey. Mustafa was eating his heart out with anxiety, but he said nothing. Then one day Hassan Bey happened to pass before the shop.

'Hey, Hassan!' the cobbler called. 'When are you going to pay the lad here?'

Hassan Bey hesitated. Then he took a one lira note and two twenty-five kurush coins and placed them on the bench.

'Here you are,' he said.

The cobbler stared at the money.

'But that's only a lira and a half. The child worked three days. . . .'

'Well, he slept all the time, so I paid his share to Jumali. This, I am giving him simply out of consideration for you,' said Hassan Bey, turning to leave.

'Uncle, I swear that every night . . .' began Mustafa, but his voice stuck in his throat. He lowered his head.

There was a long, painful silence.

'Look, Mustafa,' said the cobbler at last, 'you're more than an apprentice now. You patch soles really well. From now on you'll get a lira a week for your work.'

Mustafa raised his head slowly. His eyes were shining through the tears.

'Take these five liras,' said the cobbler,' and give them to the tailor Vayis with my compliments. Tell him to cut your white trousers out of the best material he's got. With the rest of the money you can buy your shoes. I'm taking this fellow's money, so you owe me only three and a half weeks' pay. . . .'

Mustafa laughed with glee.

In those days the blue five-lira note carried the picture of a wolf, its tongue hanging out as it galloped swift as the wind.

Inside the story

In pairs

1 Discuss why it is so important to Mustafa to have a pair of white trousers and white shoes.

2 What persuades Mustafa's mother to allow him to fire the kiln?

3 Discuss what Mustafa's dreams for the future are and why they seem so close to his mother's.

4 Mustafa wants to prove himself. Do you think he does in the end?

5 Perhaps you want something or remember wanting something almost as badly as Mustafa wants the white trousers – a toy or a pet maybe, or a pony or a bike or a particular outfit. If so, you may feel able to talk about it.

On your own

Write your own story about somebody who wants something very much and the way in which they set about achieving it. The object could be obtained through hard work but it might equally be managed through cajoling and persuading and wheedling. You may want to base what you write on the discussion you have already had but you could write a story about an entirely imaginary situation: the 'somebody' doesn't have to be you. Try to capture the sense of what it feels like to want something so intensely and try to capture the sense of what it feels like to have achieved it.

Thank You, M'am

Langston Hughes

She was a large woman with a large purse that had everything in it but a hammer and nails. It had a long strap, and she carried it slung across her shoulder. It was about eleven o'clock at night, dark, and she was walking alone, when a boy ran up behind her and tried to snatch her purse. The strap broke with the sudden single tug the boy gave it from behind. But the boy's weight and the weight of the purse combined caused him to lose his balance. Instead of taking off full blast as he had hoped, the boy fell on his back on the sidewalk and his legs flew up. The large woman simply turned around and kicked him right square in his blue-jeaned sitter. Then she reached down, picked the boy up by his shirt front, and shook him until his teeth rattled.

After that the woman said, 'Pick up my pocket-book, boy, and give it here.'

She still held him tightly. But she bent down enough to permit him to stoop and pick up her purse. Then she said, 'Now ain't you ashamed of yourself?'

Firmly gripped by his shirt front, the boy said, 'Yes'm.'

The woman said, 'What did you want to do it for?'

The boy said, 'I didn't aim to.'

She said, 'You a lie!'

By that time two or three people passed, stopped, turned to look, and some stood watching.

'If I turn you loose, will you run?' asked the woman.

'Yes'm,' said the boy.

'Then I won't turn you loose,' said the woman. She did not release him.

'Lady, I'm sorry,' whispered the boy.

'Um-hum! Your face is dirty. I got a great mind to wash your face for you. Ain't you got nobody home to tell you to wash your face?'

'No'm,' said the boy.

'Then it will get washed this evening,' said the large woman, starting up the street, dragging the frightened boy behind her.

He looked as if he were fourteen or fifteen, frail and willow-wild, in tennis shoes and blue jeans.

The woman said, 'You ought to be my son. I would teach you right from wrong. Least I can do right now is to wash your face. Are you hungry?'

'No'm,' said the being-dragged boy. 'I just want you to turn me loose.'

'Was I bothering *you* when I turned that corner?' asked the woman.

'No'm.'

'But you put yourself in contact with *me*,' said the woman. 'If you think that that contact is not going to last awhile, you got another thought coming. When I get through with you, sir, you are going to remember Mrs Luella Bates Washington Jones.'

Sweat popped out on the boy's face and he began to struggle. Mrs Jones stopped, jerked him around in front of her, put a half nelson about his neck, and continued to drag him up the street. When she got to her door, she dragged the boy inside, down a hall, and into a large kitchenette-furnished room at the rear of the house. She switched on the light and left the door open. The boy could hear other roomers laughing and talking in the large house. Some of their doors were open, too, so he knew he and the woman were not alone. The woman still had him by the neck in the middle of her room.

She said, 'What is your name?'

'Roger,' answered the boy.

'Then, Roger, you go to that sink and wash your face,' said the woman, whereupon she turned him loose – at last. Roger looked at the door – looked at the woman – looked at the door – *and went to the sink.*

'Let the water run until it gets warm,' she said. 'Here's a clean towel.'

'You gonna take me to jail?' asked the boy, bending over the sink.

'Not with that face, I would not take you nowhere,' said the woman. 'Here I am trying to get home to cook me a bite to eat, and you snatch my pocketbook! Maybe you ain't been to your supper either, late as it be. Have you?'

'There's nobody home at my house,' said the boy.

'Then we'll eat,' said the woman. 'I believe you're hungry – or been hungry – to try to snatch my pocketbook!'

'I want a pair of blue suede shoes,' said the boy.

'Well, you didn't have to snatch *my* pocketbook to get some suede shoes,' said Mrs Luella Bates Washington Jones. 'You could of asked me.'

'M'am?'

The water dripping from his face, the boy looked at her. There was a long pause. A very long pause. After he had dried his face, and not knowing what else to do, dried it again, the boy turned around, wondering what next. The door was open. He could make a dash for it down the hall. He could run, run, run, *run!*

The woman was sitting on the daybed. After a while she said, 'I were young once and I wanted things I could not get.'

There was another long pause. The boy's mouth opened. Then he frowned, not knowing he frowned.

The woman said, 'Um-hum! You thought I was going to say *but,* didn't you? You thought I was going to say, *but I didn't snatch people's pocketbooks.* Well, I wasn't going to say that.' Pause. Silence. 'I have done things, too, which I would not tell you, son – neither tell God, if He didn't already know. Everybody's got something in common. So you set down while I fix us something to eat. You might run that comb through your hair so you will look presentable.'

In another corner of the room behind a screen was a gas plate and an icebox. Mrs Jones got up and went behind the screen. The woman did not watch the boy to see if he was going to run now, nor did she watch her purse, which she left behind her on the daybed. But the boy took care to sit on the far side of the room, away from the purse, where he thought she could easily see him out of the corner of her eye if she wanted to. He did not trust the woman *not* to trust him. And he did not want to be mistrusted now.

'Do you need somebody to go to the store,' asked the boy, 'maybe to get some milk or something?'

'Don't believe I do,' said the woman, 'unless you just want sweet milk yourself. I was going to make cocoa out of this canned milk I got here.'

'That will be fine,' said the boy.

She heated some lima beans and ham she had in the icebox, made the cocoa, and set the table. The woman did not ask the boy anything about where he lived, or his folks, or anything else that would embarrass him. Instead, as they ate, she told him about her job in a hotel beauty shop that stayed open late, what the work was like, and how all kinds of women came in and out, blondes, redheads, and Spanish. Then she cut him a half of her ten-cent cake. 'Eat some more, son,' she said.

When they were finished eating, she got up and said, 'Now here, take this ten dollars and buy yourself some blue suede shoes. and next time, do not make the mistake of latching onto *my* pocketbook *nor nobody else's* – because shoes got by devilish ways will burn your feet. I got to get my rest now. But from here on in, son, I hope you will behave yourself.'

She led him down the hall to the front door and opened it. 'Good night! Behave yourself, boy!' she said, looking out into the street as he went down the steps.

The boy wanted to say something other than, 'Thank you, M'am,' to Mrs Luella Bates Washington Jones, but although his lips moved, he couldn't even say that as he turned at the foot of the barren stoop and looked up at the large woman in the door. Then she shut the door.

Inside the story

On your own

How do *you* imagine Mrs Luella Bates Washington Jones? Jot down a few thoughts about her appearance, her character and her position in society. Jot down similar points about the boy. Spend no more than about four or five minutes on this activity.

In pairs or small groups

1 Now share your ideas with others and see if your mental pictures of the two characters are similar. Discuss why you imagine the woman and the boy the way you do.

2 Why does the woman behave as she does to the boy rather than calling the police?

3 Discuss the effect the woman's treatment of the boy has on his behaviour.

On your own

The boy, Roger, returns to the streets dumbfounded at his treatment. But sometime he will want to tell somebody else, another street urchin maybe, what happened. Write down what you imagine he might say about his experience. Think carefully about how he sees Mrs Luella Bates Washington Jones.

In groups

Roger in this story wants a pair of blue suede shoes perhaps as intensely as Mustafa in the story on p.130 wants a pair of white trousers. When you have read both stories, discuss any points of similarity and difference between their two situations.

THE BELLOWS OF THE FIRE

Rose Tremain

The two things I cared about most in the world until this morning were my dog, Whisper, and the bungalow under the viaduct.

Whisper is black and white with black blobs round her eyes and my aunt Nellie Miller says she reminds her of a panda.

Whisper is a one-person panda. The one person she loves is me. She waits for me to get home from school with her nose in the letter-box flap.

The viaduct is about a mile from our house. In winter, I can't get to it before dark, but in summer I take Whisper there every day. Trains used to go over it, but the railway line was torn up before I was born, so I've always known it like it is now, which is like a roof garden of weeds.

On rainy days, I hardly stop on the viaduct to look at the bungalow, because down there in the mist and drizzle it looks a bit sorry for itself. But in the sunshine, you see that it isn't sorry for itself at all and that the people who live there give it so much love and attention, you can't imagine they've got time for normal life.

Despite what's happened and what may happen in the future, I still feel that if that bungalow was mine, I'd be one of the happiest people in Devon. The only thing I'd add to the garden would be a wall all round it to keep Whisper in, so that she couldn't roam off to the sea when I wasn't there and drown.

The sea's second on my list of places I like, except that the sea does something to me: it makes me long for things. I sit down on the beach and stare out at invisible France, and this feeling of longing makes me dreamy as a fish. One of the things I long for is for time to pass.

It was my fourteenth birthday last week. We don't seem to celebrate my birthday in our family any more and I think this is because my mother says it only reminds her how fast her life is slipping away.

The only birthday I remember well is when I was six. My mother still considered herself young then and we had a new car and we drove to Dartmoor. The plan was, we were going to make a fire and cook sausages in it. I thought this was the best idea my parents had ever had.

But in the car, on the way to Dartmoor, my brothers bagged all the good jobs in advance. 'Bags collect the wood.' 'Bags light the fire.' 'Bags be in charge of cooking.' Only after a long time did my mother remember me and say, 'What about you, Susan? What job are you going to do, dear?' I didn't know what other jobs there were. 'She can't do anything, she's too little,' said my brothers.

We drove for ages in silence, but then my father had an idea. 'You can be the bellows of the fire, Susie. That means you have to blow on it and your breath keeps it going.' This didn't seem like a nice job to me. Blowing out cake candles was horrible enough. So I thought, I'm not going to breathe on their fire. I'm going to be absolutely quiet and hardly breathe at all.

I'm going to be as silent as a stone.

Since then – or perhaps always, I don't know – I've been very quiet in my family. I notice things about them, like how they all love noise and seem to believe that happiness is *in* noise somewhere and that misery is in silence. They think that I'm a miserable person. What I think is that there are millions of things they'll never understand.

Our house is a modern house in a terrace of identical ones. Noise and mess from these houses spills out all over the puny little gardens and all over the street. If you were a visitor from France or somewhere and you thought all of Britain was like our terrace, you'd say it was the most hideous country in the world. Getting away from our house is something I think about every day of my life. My brothers are trying to get work in this town. They're trying to get jobs, so they can stay on and live in houses like these ones, or worse. And girls I know at school, that's what they want too. They want to be beauticians or hairdressers in the crappy shopping arcade. If I thought that was going to happen to me, I'd drown myself.

I took Whisper to the sea this evening. I throw things into the waves and she gets them out. She's terrific at this, much better than other dogs we see. Then we lay in the sun while her coat dried and I told her the news that came this morning.

I like secrets. I'm going to keep this one as long as I can. It'll come out eventually, though, and then my mother will say, '*Film*, Susan? What film?' And I will have to tell her the story.

It's a story about a community. It's set in a town like ours, not far from the coast. It's based on something which actually happened, on a person who actually lived, a girl called Julie who was fourteen and a fire raiser. She was a Girl Guide and her Dad worked for the town council. These things were important in the story, because the places where she started the fires were the places where new things were getting done, like a new Leisure Centre was being built and a new Bingo Palace.

Being a Girl Guide, she knew how to start fires without matches or paraffin or anything, so there was never any evidence left lying about, and this is why it took the police ages and ages to track Julie down. And also, they decided all the wrong things to start with. They decided the fires were started by a person from an ethnic minority, who resented the clubs and places where he wasn't welcome, so all they were really looking for were young Indians or West Indian youths. It took them a year before they suspected the daughter of a town councillor, and by that time, seven fires had been raised and the Bingo Palace had burned to the ground. She was caught in the end only because she set fire to the Girl Guide hut.

So, anyway, the thing is, they're making a film about her. The TV company came down here months ago. They arranged auditions in all the schools. All they said was, you had to be about fourteen and interested in acting. I haven't been in many school plays. When we did *The Insect Play*, I was only a moth with nothing to say. But I am very interested in acting, because in the last year I've realised that what I do all the time at home is *act*. I act the sort of person my family think I am, with nothing to say for herself and no opinions on anything, when inside me I'm not like that at all, I just don't let my opinions out. I'd rather save my breath. I plan, though. At school with one or two of the teachers and then on my walks with Whisper to the viaduct and the sea, I plan a proper life.

Not that many people from our school went to the

auditions. They thought it was going to be too hard, and anything that seems hard to them, they let it go. But it wasn't difficult. You had five minutes to look at the script and then you had to read out a speech from near the end of the film, where they ask Julie why she started the fires, and she tells them. She tells them what she feels about communities like this one. She despises them. She thinks they've been hypnotised and corrupted. She thinks greed is all they understand.

It was quite a long, angry speech. When it came to my turn to read it, I pretended I was saying it all to my brothers and that they didn't understand a word of it and the more confused they looked, the more angrily the words came out. When I ended it, I knew I'd made an impression on the person who had asked me to read it. He was staring at me in amazement and then he said would I be able to come down to London in July for a second audition, which would be in front of a camera.

In the letter that came this morning, they told me that over two hundred girls had been seen for the part of Julie and that now there are just six of us. And us six will go to London – not all together, but each of us on a different day – and we will all pretend to be Julie, the arsonist, and other real actors will pretend to be her Mum and Dad and everyone and they'll decide at the end of all that who they're going to cast.

When I think about this now, I realise that although I've longed to get away from this town and longed to be the owner of the bungalow under the viaduct, I've never before longed for anything I could actually have, *now*. Getting away and living in that little house were all way-into-the-future kinds of things, but this, this part in the film is waiting for someone now, this year, now, and I've got a one-in-six chance of getting it and I want to get it so badly that it's been impossible, since this morning, to concentrate on lessons or eat a shitty school dinner because what I could feel all the time was my heart beating.

The only time I could feel calmer about it was on my walk with Whisper. What I told myself then was that I have had years of 'acting experience' at home and probably those other five girls have had none and what you see and hear of them is all there is. But me, I've been saving my breath. Saving it up for now.

When we walked back, by the time we got to the viaduct, I'd made myself believe – and I'm going to stick to this – that I am definitely the right person for this part and that the TV people are intelligent enough to recognise this and to offer it to me. And when I get it, that's going to be something.

But I still, to be on the safe side, looked for a long time at the bungalow under the viaduct and told myself that if you know how and where to look for them, there are loads of different ways you can be happy. Being an actress is one. Having a nice home in a place where there's silence is another. You just have to work at it all, slowly and carefully, like Dad made that fire catch on Dartmoor in the rain, one stick at a time.

Inside the story

On your own

Which four of these words (if any) do you think best describe the character of Susan: *ambitious, solitary, lonely, intelligent, selfish, caring, hard, kind, thoughtful, calculating, miserable, discontented, unhappy, sentimental, snobbish, angry*? Jot down a phrase or two from the story to show why you think so. If you prefer, choose other words that you think describe her.

In pairs or small groups

1 Compare your own ideas with a partner or in a group and see how far you are agreed on your reading of Susan's character. Discuss what experiences have influenced her way of seeing the world and her behaviour.

2 What would you say Susan needs and wants most in her life? Discuss why these things matter to her.

3 Do you feel any sympathy with her feelings about her life and the world she lives in?

4 Why do you think Rose Tremain chose 'The Bellows of the Fire' as the title of her story?

In small groups

Imagine Susan gets the part in the film. It is made and televised and is a great success, catapulting Susan to fame overnight. Next day, newspapers and magazines scramble for interviews with the new teenage star. Decide what questions they would want to ask her about her performance, her background and her beliefs. Decide how she would answer these questions. Write the script of the interview basing Susan's answers on what we learn of her from the story. You may choose to work individually on providing answers to particular questions and then put the interview together as a whole. You could tape record it when you are satisfied.

On your own

Write your own story about a person who desperately longs to achieve an ambition and has the opportunity to do so: perhaps to be a champion athlete, a singer, a player for a county or national team, a published writer, or whatever . . . Think about what drives them on and about their feelings when the opportunity presents itself.

Surprised

Catherine Storr

Have you ever thought how when you think you know what something's going to be like, it turns out to be quite different? Or if it is anything like you imagined, it's somehow flat, as if you'd had it before. There may be a minute when you say, 'It's perfect, it's exactly like I imagined.' Then, another minute later, it's disappointing, just because it is how you'd imagined it. Like staying too long at a party, or thinking too much about Christmas before it comes.

My sister Tossie was always disappointed long before the end of Christmas day. She was the one of us who got most excited about Christmas; she was always awake long before we were supposed to get up on Christmas morning, waking the rest of us up too, poking at our stockings and guessing what was inside them. I remember one Christmas, she can't have been more than ten, because I know I was nearly six – it was the year we'd all had chicken-pox. She poked round a sort of long, thin thing in her stocking and said, 'It's a watch.'

'It couldn't be a *watch*. It's much too expensive,' we said.

'It could. It could be a watch. What else would be that shape?'

'A pencil.'

'Too flat.'

'A bracelet.'

'Not in that shaped box.'

'A paperknife.'

'Mum wouldn't.'

We guessed all sorts of things, but Tossie wouldn't listen to any of them. She went off on a sort of dream which she told out loud, about how she'd wear the watch and how surprised her friends were going to be, and how no one except her in the upper thirds had a watch. How she'd lend it to me for parties – as long as she wasn't going to them herself, of course – and how when she was an old, old lady and died, she'd leave it to her grandchildren, with a message telling them it was the first watch she'd ever had, and she'd been given it the Christmas she was ten.

It turned out to be a pair of compasses, something she'd always wanted before, but of course not like having a proper watch. That was another sad Christmas. Somehow, when Tossie was sad it made us all feel as if we'd been disappointed about our presents too. Our Mum used to say she built up such a rigmarole in her head about how marvellous everything was going to be that nothing, not watches or bicycles or diamond rings or the Queen's crown could have come up to what she'd imagined. And it was always like that. She'd come back sad from parties, because each one was going to be the most marvellous party she'd ever been to; then, when it turned out to be just being with the same lot of people she'd seen every day at school all term, but wearing different clothes and not having anything special to do, she felt let down and awful. I used to dread Tossie's parties because of her and me sharing the room. I'd be asleep when she came in, but when it had been a bad evening she wouldn't bother about being quiet. She'd drop her shoes, shut the wardrobe door so it slammed as well as squeaked – which you couldn't help – and then lie in bed sighing. Tossie had the biggest sighs I've ever heard; it was like hearing a hippopotamus feeling sad. Sometimes I'd say, 'Tossie?'

'What?' she'd say, sounding cross, though she wasn't.

'Was the party fun?'

'No.'

'Tell.'

'Nothing to tell.'

'What happened?'

'Nothing happened.'

'Didn't they like your dress?'

'No one said.'

'What did you do?'

'Nothing.'

'Did you meet any boys?' I knew it was risky asking this, but I generally couldn't stop myself.

'I suppose so.'

If I was feeling brave I'd go one step further.

'Did any of them try to kiss you?'

'Go to sleep. It's long past your bedtime.'

But I couldn't get to sleep until Tossie had stopped those awful deep sighs, and the restless turning in bed. Even that wasn't the worst, though. The worst was when I heard her sniffing into the pillow. I didn't feel better about this until one morning when I heard Tossie tell Mum that she'd cried till her pillow was wet with tears. So at least one of Tossie's imaginings had been made to come true.

When Tossie started going with boys, I mean really, not just seeing them gooping at the parties, but having them call for her and taking her out to coffee bars, I knew we had a bad time coming. When I said

this to Mum she said not to be a something or other.

'What's that?'

'Jeremiah. Sad sort of chap, always saw bad things coming.'

'Am I? I mean, do I?'

'Not more than most, I daresay. Still, you and Tossie, you are a pair.'

'I see things the way they are. Tossie sees them how she wants them to be.'

Mum said, 'Well, I don't know.' She often said that, but I thought she knew quite a lot, really.

As it turned out, Tossie's love affairs weren't so much awful as wearing. That isn't quite true, because the first few were awful. Then I got used to the way they happened. In fact I got so used, I could almost tell when the next stage was due. They went like this. First of all Tossie would go very quiet and mysterious. If you said anything to her, she'd sort of come back to earth with a start, as if she'd been miles away. If you asked, she'd say no, she wasn't thinking about anything in particular, smiling all the time a secret smile that meant just the opposite of what she said. This was while she and the boy were sort of eyeing each other, they hadn't said anything yet. Then when he'd come out with saying he was crazy about her, or whatever it was, and they'd kissed a bit, Tossie couldn't talk about anything else. As far as I can remember, with the first one or two, or perhaps three, I really did think, 'This is it. Tossie's going to marry John' (or perhaps it was Martin or David or Joe). 'She'll be a bride at sixteen, I'll be an aunt before I take my "O" levels.' It would be a marvellous time – it got boring later – with Tossie on top of the world, telling us how tremendous John (or Martin or David) was, and how she'd never felt like this before, how it was all that love was written up to be, and better. She'd keep me awake late into the night, talking about whichever it was, how she loved him, how he loved her, how clever he was, how they must have been meant for each other, the lot. Of course when she got on to the later ones there'd be a lot of comparing: how John had really been too changeable, she could see that now, and how she'd wondered at the time if Martin was a strong enough character for her, and how David had been slow in the uptake, but how now Joe . . .

Then there'd come the time that was like opening the stocking and finding it wasn't a watch after all. First of all she'd be home evenings when we'd thought she'd be out, sometimes explaining, sometimes not. Then she'd be very touchy; you couldn't say anything without having your head bitten off. After a bit of this, there'd be a night when she'd keep me awake gulping and sighing, even groaning sometimes, saying things in between like, 'Don't ever fall in love, Barb, it's bloody hell,' (her language always got a bit lurid at these times), or 'I know now, everything they say about not trusting men is true.' After a week or so of this, with Tossie going around looking like Ophelia and The Lady of the Camellias rolled into one (a lot of eyeshadow, and I swear that even Mum got worried once or twice about the cough she used to get at these times) she'd begin to recover. First of all she'd be a brave little woman who was going to bury herself in her work (it was a tremendous piece of luck that she had a month just before her 'A' levels in between Sammy and Dan) and then, sometimes gradually, sometimes suddenly, it would begin all over again. She'd forget her career and it would be all romance. She had a bottom drawer she put things into when she got something new and pretty. The trouble was it went through off-seasons like Tossie's love life, and when she was going to be a career woman she'd take out the new nylon nightie

she'd put there for her wedding to John/Martin/David/Joe, etc. and she'd wear it, enjoying herself, in a way, doing it and suffering. She talked a lot about suffering during this time. She'd get me worried sometimes, thinking that whatever happened to Tossie was, of course, going to happen to me as soon as I was old enough. For me, you see, it was almost like having a crystal ball showing me what my life would be like in a year or so, and though I wanted this business of being in love and going out with boys and everything, I didn't want to suffer. Or at least, not like Tossie did.

I think I'm sounding rather bitchy about Tossie and her sufferings, but this really isn't fair. She certainly did suffer. The trouble is that when you share a room with someone who suffers such a lot you sort of get used to it. You even get a bit bored.

I can't remember now how long Tossie went on like that. It was probably quite a time, because I know that I'd got to that sort of stage myself, where I was wondering all the time when some boy would want to take me out, and feeling sure none of them ever would. So perhaps I didn't notice so much about Tossie; or it may have been that if something goes on long enough, you don't notice all at once if it stops. Like a headache. You suddenly realize you haven't been noticing it for the last quarter of an hour, which means that it's gone. I suddenly noticed about Tossie that way. Not that she'd gone, but that she was different.

I said before how at the beginning of a new boy she'd go quiet; but it never lasted. What I realized this time was that she'd been quiet for ever so long.

I would have said it wasn't natural, only that she didn't feel unnatural. She was kind of peaceful, and yet it wasn't peaceful like being asleep. It was more like waiting. Even that's not quite right because it wasn't like waiting for something you're worried about; nor like that feeling that you *can't* wait it's so exciting, like a birthday or a party or a match. More like waiting for something to grow, like mustard and cress on a flannel in a saucer, where you notice each leaf as it comes out, and it almost doesn't matter when you eat it, because growing it's been exciting too.

But it wasn't like Tossie. It wasn't like her to wait that way. It wasn't like her not to have to talk about it. I could see she wasn't unhappy, either. Every night she was out, and every night she'd come in so quietly I never woke up. There wasn't any sighing and groaning. I couldn't understand it. It was funny. Different.

At last I said to her, 'Tossie. What's going on?'

'What's going on?' she said back.

'It isn't Jamie, is it?' I knew it wasn't really. Jamie had been weeks back.

'Jamie and I broke up seven weeks and two days ago.'

I saw then what a long time I'd taken to catch on. And I was interested she'd got it so exact too, Tossie being apt to exaggerate a lot.

'What's up, then, Toss?'

She said, 'I don't really know.'

Now that was the first time I'd heard my sister Tossie admit she didn't know what was up.

'Is it Barry, Tossie?' Barry was the fellow she'd been going out with lately.

''Course it's Barry.'

'Is he crazy about you?'

'I don't know,' she said again.

'Are you in love with him?'

This time, when she said, 'I don't know,' again, she really shook me. I'd been a bit drowsy before, but that really woke me up with a jolt.

'But Tossie, you must know. You've been in love before.'

'I'm not sure I have,' she said.

I thought about this.

'What does it feel like, then?' I asked.

She said, 'Barb, it's different.'

'Well, do you love him?' I asked.

'He's not the sort of boy I generally go for,' she said.

'Go on.'

'I sort of can't help liking him. You know. I like him being around. I feel sort of . . .'

'Sort of what?'

'Comfortable. When he's there.'

'Not in love, then?' I said, disappointed.

'I don't know.'

Tossie seemed to me, by this time, so experienced I couldn't understand how it was she didn't know if she was in love or not. I said, 'Well, what then?'

She said, slowly, 'Perhaps I am. P'raps this is what it's really like. Not like anything you thought it would be.'

'What then?' I asked again wanting to know, so I'd be able to tell when it happened to me.

Tossie said, 'Surprised. All the time I don't feel like what I thought I would. I'm always being surprised.'

Inside the story

In pairs or small groups

1 Read the first paragraph of the story again and talk about whether the feelings of disappointment that are described are ones you recognise. Share any memories of things that were a bit of a let down when you were smaller and of how you felt at the time. It may perhaps have been a party or a treat or a present or a holiday or a visit that didn't quite live up to all your expectations.

2 Discuss the similarities between the way Tossie used to build up expectations over presents when she was younger and the way she thinks about her boy-friends. Does her behaviour seem convincing to you?

3 Discuss how the character of the younger sister telling the story is different from that of the elder sister.

4 'Surprised' – Does Tossie's behaviour when she falls in love seem convincing to you? Why do you think Catherine Storr chose this title for the story?

On your own

1 Recalling the discussion you had earlier about disappointments when you were younger, write your own story about an event that did not come up to expectations. Try to capture the main character's excitement as the event approaches and then the sense of things going flat. You may choose to write an autobiographical piece based on something you remember from your own past but you could equally well write about a brother's or a sister's disappointment, or even invent a situation.

2 Tossie changes as a result of being in love. Write an entry from her diary describing her feelings about Barry, her new boy-friend, and reflecting on how this time they are somehow different.

5
GENERATIONS

Olive Senior is one of the most exciting and refreshing writers to come from the Caribbean in recent years. Her collection of stories, *Summer Lightning*, from which the first story in this section is taken, won the Commonwealth Writers Prize for 1987. Beccka, the little girl in 'Do Angels Wear Brassieres?', enjoys wrongfooting not only the rather proper adults in whose house she lives but also a visiting church dignitary. Beccka's testing of the wisdom of her elders and her general irreverence is pursued with great zest on her part but there is no sense of her being some sickening know-it-all. The language of the story is a joy and it really needs to be heard read aloud. The distinct voices of the poor harrassed Cherry (Beccka's mother), righteous Auntie Mary, fat, sly-eyed Katie, bright, bubbling Beccka and the booming Archdeacon weave in and out of the narrative. Notice how it is all told in the continuous present tense and thus seems to unfold breathlessly, immediately, before us.

Jane Gardam's story, 'The Best Day of My Easter Holidays', is also set in Jamaica and it is interesting to contrast the tourist picture of the country presented in this story with the one we take from Olive Senior's tale of Beccka and the Archdeacon. Again, a central feature of the story is the gap between the generations, between the parents and their schoolboy son whose story this is. It is hardly surprising that Ned finds he responds more to Jolly Jackson, the amazing, larger than life Jamaican who acts as the family's tour guide, than to his very proper and repressed parents. Jolly Jackson carries all before him. His innocent, child-like belief in his powers and his enormous pride in his country, coupled with vast stores of good humour and energy, propel us through the story in much the same way that the Egerton family are propelled around the sights.

Larry, the little boy who is the focus of Frank O'Connor's story, 'The Genius', feels himself frustrated at the way the adult world can never take him as seriously as he would wish; a situation which children of all ages may experience. Larry's relationships with those older than himself – his parents, Miss Cooney, Una and Mrs Dwyer – are the mainspring of the story. His own earnest musings on life and love are interwoven with the poignant story of Una's brother, mingling humour and sadness in true Irish fashion so that we don't quite know whether to laugh or cry.

DO ANGELS WEAR BRASSIERES?

Olive Senior

Beccka down on her knees ending her goodnight prayers and Cherry telling her softly, 'And Ask God to bless Auntie Mary.' Beccka vex that anybody could interrupt her private conversation with God so, say loud loud, 'No. Not praying for nobody that tek weh mi best glassy eye marble.'

'Beccka!' Cherry almost crying in shame, 'Shhhhh! She wi hear you. Anyway she did tell you not to roll them on the floor when she have her headache.'

'A hear her already' – this is the righteous voice of Auntie Mary in the next room – 'But I am sure that God is not listening to the like of she. Blasphemous little wretch.'

She add the last part under her breath and with much lifting of her eyes to heaven she turn back to her nightly reading of the Imitations of Christ.

'Oooh Beccka, Rebecca, see what you do,' Cherry whispering, crying in her voice.

Beccka just stick out her tongue at the world, wink at God who she know right now in the shape of a big fat anansi in a corner of the roof, kiss her mother and get into bed.

As soon as her mother gone into Auntie Mary room to try make it up and the whole night come down with whispering, Beccka whip the flash light from off the dressing table and settle down under the blanket to read. Beccka reading the Bible in secret from cover to cover not from any conviction the little wretch but because everybody round her always quoting that book and Beccka want to try and find flaw and

question she can best them with.

Next morning Auntie Mary still vex. Auntie Mary out by the tank washing clothes and slapping them hard on the big rock. Fat sly-eye Katie from the next yard visiting and consoling her. Everybody visiting Auntie Mary these days and consoling her for the crosses she have to bear (that is Beccka they talking about). Fat Katie have a lot of time to walk bout consoling because ever since hard time catch her son and him wife a town they come country to cotch with Katie. And from the girl walk through the doors so braps! Katie claim she too sickly to do any washing or housework. So while the daughter-in-law beating suds at her yard she over by Auntie Mary washpan say she keeping her company. Right now she consoling about Beccka who (as she telling Auntie Mary) every decent-living upright Christian soul who is everybody round here except that Dorcas Waite about whom one should not dirty one's mouth to talk yes every clean living person heart go out to Auntie Mary for with all due respect to a sweet mannersable child like Cherry her daughter is the devil own pickney. Not that anybody saying a word about Cherry God know she have enough trouble on her head from she meet up that big hard back man though young little gal like that never shoulda have business with no married man. Katie take a breath long enough to ask question:

'But see here Miss Mary you no think Cherry buck

up the devil own self when she carrying her? Plenty time that happen you know. Remember that woman over Allside that born the pickney with two head praise Jesus it did born dead. But see here you did know one day she was going down river to wash clothes and is the devil own self she meet. Yes'm. Standing right there in her way. She pop one big bawling before she faint weh and when everybody run come not a soul see him. Is gone he gone. But you no know where he did gone? No right inside that gal. Right inna her belly. And Miss Mary I telling you the living truth, just as the baby borning the midwife no see a shadow fly out of the mother and go right cross the room. She frighten so till she close her two eye tight and is so the devil escape.'

'Well I dont know about that. Beccka certainly dont born with no two head or nothing wrong with her. Is just hard ears she hard ears.'

'Den no so me saying?'

'The trouble is, Cherry is too soft to manage her. As you look hard at Cherry herself she start cry. She was never a strong child and she not a strong woman, her heart just too soft.'

'All the same right is right and there is only one right way to bring up a child and that is by bus' ass pardon my french Miss Mary but hard things call for hard words. That child should be getting blows from the day she born. Then she wouldn't be so force-ripe now. Who cant hear must feel for the rod and reproof bring wisdom but a child left to himself bringeth his mother to shame. Shame, Miss Mary.'

'Is true. And you know I wouldn't mind if she did only get into mischief Miss Katie but what really hurt me is how the child know so much and show off. Little children have no right to have so many things in their brain. Guess what she ask me the other day nuh? – if me know how worms reproduce.'

'Say what, maam?'

'As Jesus is me judge. Me big woman she come and ask that. Reproduce I say. Yes Auntie Mary she say as if I stupid. When the man worm and the lady worm come together and they have baby. You know how it happen? – Is so she ask me.'

'What you saying maam? Jesus of Nazareth!'

'Yes, please. That is what the child ask me. Lightning come strike me dead if is lie I lie. In my own house. My own sister pickney. So help me I was so frighten that pickney could so impertinent that right away a headache strike me like autoclaps. But before I go lie down you see Miss Katie, I give her some licks so hot there she forget bout worm and reproduction.'

'In Jesus name!'

'Yes. Is all those books her father pack her up with. Book is all him ever good for. Rather than buy food put in the pickney mouth or help Cherry find shelter his only contribution is book. Nuh his character stamp on her. No responsibility that man ever have. Look how him just take off for foreign without a word even to his lawful wife and children much less Cherry and hers. God knows where it going to end.'

'Den Miss M. They really come to live with you for all time?'

'I dont know my dear. What are they to do? You know Cherry cant keep a job from one day to the next. From she was a little girl she so nervous she could never settle down long enough to anything. And you know since Papa and Mama pass away is me one she have to turn to. I tell you even if they eat me out of house and home and the child drive me to Bellevue I accept that this is the crosses that I put on this earth to bear ya Miss Katie.'

'Amen. Anyway dont forget what I was saying to you about the devil. The child could have a devil inside her. No pickney suppose to come facety and force-ripe so. You better ask the Archdeacon to check it out next time he come here.'

'Well. All the same Miss Katie she not all bad you know. Sometime at night when she ready to sing and dance and make up play and perform for us we laugh so till! And those times when I watch her I say to myself, this is really a gifted child.'

'Well my dear is your crosses. If is so you see it then is your sister child.'

'Aie. I have one hope in God and that is the child take scholarship exam and God know she so bright she bound to pass. And you know what, Miss Katie, I put her name down for the three boarding school them that furthest from here. Make them teacher deal with her. That is what they get paid for.'

Beccka hiding behind the tank listening to the conversation as usual. She think about stringing a wire across the track to trip fat Katie but she feeling too lazy today. Fat Katie will get her comeuppance on Judgement Day for she wont able to run quick enough to join the heavenly hosts. Beccka there thinking of fat Katie huffing and puffing arriving at the pasture just as the company of the faithful in their white robes are rising as one body on a shaft of light. She see Katie a-clutch at the hem of the gown of one of the faithful and miraculously, slowly, slowly, Katie start to rise. But her weight really too much and with a tearing sound that spoil the solemn moment the hem tear way from the garment and Katie fall back to earth with a big buff, shouting and wailing for them to wait on her. Beccka snickering so hard at the sight she have to scoot way quick before Auntie Mary and Katie hear her. They think the crashing about in the cocoa walk is mongoose.

Beccka in Auntie Mary room – which is forbidden – dress up in Auntie Mary bead, Auntie Mary high heel shoes, Auntie Mary shawl, and Auntie Mary big floppy hat which she only wear to wedding – all forbidden. Beccka mincing and prancing and mincing in front of the three-way adjustable mirror in Auntie Mary vanity she brought all the way from Cuba with her hard earned money. Beccka seeing herself as a beautiful lady on the arms of a handsome gentleman who look just like her father. They about to enter a night club neon sign flashing for Beccka know this is the second wickedest thing a woman can do. At a corner table lit by Chinese lantern soft music playing Beccka do the wickedest thing a woman can do – she take a drink. Not rum. One day Beccka went to wedding with Auntie Mary and sneak a drink of rum and stay sick for two days. Beccka thinking of all the bright-colour drink she see advertise in the magazine Cherry get from a lady she use to work for in town a nice yellow drink in a tall frosted glass . . .

'Beccka, Rebecca O My god!' That is Cherry rushing into the room and wailing. 'You know she wi mad like hell if she see you with her things you know you not to touch her things.'

Cherry grab Auntie Mary things from off Beccka and fling them back into where she hope is the right place, adjust the mirror to what she hope is the right angle, and pray just pray that Auntie Mary wont find out that Beccka was messing with her things. Again. Though Auntie Mary so absolutely neat she always know if a pin out of place. 'O God Beccka,' Cherry moaning.

Beccka stripped of her fancy clothes dont pay no mind to her mother fluttering about her. She take the story in her head to the room next door though here the mirror much too high for Beccka to see the sweep of her gown as she does the third wickedest thing a woman can do which is dance all night.

*

Auntie Mary is a nervous wreck and Cherry weeping daily in excitement. The Archdeacon is coming. Auntie Mary so excited she cant sit cant stand cant do her embroidery cant eat she forgetting things the house going to the dog she dont even notice that Beccka been using her lipstick. Again. The Archdeacon coming Wednesday to the churches in the area and afterwards – as usual – Archdeacon sure to stop outside Auntie Mary gate even for one second – as usual – to get two dozen of Auntie Mary best roses and a bottle of pimento dram save from Christmas. And maybe just this one time Archdeacon will give in to Auntie Mary pleading and step inside her humble abode for tea. Just this one time.

Auntie Mary is due this honour at least once because she is head of Mothers Union and though a lot of them jealous and back-biting her because Archdeacon never stop outside their gate even once let them say anything to her face.

For Archdeacon's certain stop outside her gate Auntie Mary scrub the house from top to bottom put up back the freshly laundered Christmas Curtains and the lace tablecloth and the newly starch doilies and the antimacassars clean all the windows in the house get the thick hibiscus hedge trim so you can skate across the top wash the dog whitewash every rock in the garden and the trunk of every tree paint the gate polish the silver and bring out the crystal cake-plate and glasses she bring from Cuba twenty-five years ago and is saving for her old age. Just in case Archdeacon can stop for tea Auntie Mary bake a fruitcake a upside-down cake a three-layer cake a chocolate cake for she dont know which he prefer also some coconut cookies for although the Archdeacon is an Englishman dont say he dont like his little Jamaican dainties. Everything will be pretty and nice for the Archdeacon just like the American

lady she did work for in Cuba taught her to make them.

The only thing that now bothering Auntie Mary as she give a last look over her clean and well ordered household is Beccka, dirty Beccka right now sitting on the kitchen steps licking out the mixing bowls. The thought of Beccka in the same house with Archdeacon bring on one of Auntie Mary headache. She think of asking Cherry to take Beccka somewhere else for the afternoon when Archdeacon coming but poor Cherry work so hard and is just excited about Archdeacon coming. Auntie Mary dont have the courage to send Beccka to stay with anyone for nobody know what that child is going to come out with next and a lot of people not so broadmind as Auntie Mary. She pray that Beccka will get sick enough to have to stay in bed she – O God forgive her but is for a worthy cause – she even consider drugging the child for the afternoon. But she dont have the heart. And anyway she dont know how. So Auntie Mary take two asprin and a small glass of tonic wine and pray hard that Beccka will vanish like magic on the afternoon that Archdeacon visit.

Now Archdeacon here and Beccka and everybody in their very best clothes. Beccka thank God also on her best behaviour which can be very good so far in fact she really look like a little angel she so clean and behaving.

In fact Archdeacon is quite taken with Beccka and more and more please that this is the afternoon he decide to consent to come inside Auntie Mary parlour for one little cup of tea. Beccka behaving so well and talking so nice to the Archdeacon Auntie Mary feel her heart swell with pride and joy over everything. Beccka behaving so beautiful in fact that Auntie Mary and Cherry dont even think twice about leaving her to talk to Archdeacon in the parlour while they out in the kitchen preparing tea.

By now Beccka and the Archdeacon exchanging Bible knowledge. Beccka asking him question and he trying his best to answer but they never really tell him any of these things in theological college. First he go ask Beccka if she is a good little girl. Beccka say yes she read her Bible every day. Do you now say the Archdeacon, splendid. Beccka smile and look shy.

'Tell me my little girl, is there anything in the Bible you would like to ask me about?'

'Yes sir. Who in the Bible wrote big?'

'Who in the Bible wrote big. My dear child!'

This wasnt the kind of question Archdeacon expecting but him always telling himself how he have rapport with children so he decide to confess his ignorance.

'Tell me, who?'

'Paul!' Beccka shout.

'Paul?'

'Galations six eleven "See with how large letters I write onto you with mine own hands".'

'Ho Ho Ho Ho' Archdeacon laugh. – 'Well done. Try me with another one.'

Beccka decide to ease him up this time.

'What animal saw an angel?'

'What animal saw an angel? My word. What animal . . . of course. Balaam's ass.'

'Yes you got it.'

Beccka jumping up and down she so excited. She decide to ask the Archdeacon a trick questions her father did teach her.

'What did Adam and Eve do when they were driven out of the garden?'

'Hm,' the Archdeacon sputtered but could not think of a suitable answer.

'Raise Cain ha ha ha ha ha.'

'They raised Cain Ho Ho Ho Ho Ho.'

The Archdeacon promise himself to remember that one to tell the Deacon. All the same he not feeling strictly comfortable. It really dont seem dignified for an Archdeacon to be having this type of conversation with an eleven-year-old girl. But Beccka already in high gear with the next question and Archdeacon tense himself.

'Who is the shortest man in the Bible?'

Archdeacon groan.

'Peter. Because him sleep on his watch. Ha Ha Ha.'

'Ho Ho Ho Ho Ho.'

'What is the smallest insect in the Bible?'

'The widow's mite,' Archdeacon shout.

'The wicked flee,' Beccka cry.

'Ho Ho Ho Ho Ho Ho.'

Archdeacon laughing so hard now he starting to cough. He cough and cough till the coughing bring him to his senses. He there looking down the passage where Auntie Mary gone and wish she would hurry come back. He sputter a few time into his handkerchief, wipe his eye, sit up straight and assume his most religious expression. Even Beccka impress.

'Now Rebecca. Hm. You are a very clever very entertaining little girl. Very. But what I had in mind were questions that are a bit more serious. Your aunt tells me you are being prepared for confirmation. Surely you must have some questions about doctrine hm, religion, that puzzle you. No serious questions?'

Beccka look at Archdeacon long and hard. 'Yes,' she say at long last in a small voice. Right away Archdeacon sit up straighter.

'What is it my little one?'

Beccka screwing up her face in concentration.

'Sir, what I want to know is this for I cant find it in the Bible. Please sir, do angels wear brassieres?'

Auntie Mary just that minute coming through the

doorway with a full tea tray with Cherry carrying another big tray right behind her. Enough food and drink for ten Archdeacon. Auntie Mary stops braps in the doorway with fright when she hear Beccka question. She stop so sudden that Cherry bounce into her and spill a whole pitcher of cold drink all down Auntie Mary back. As the coldness hit her Auntie Mary jump and half her tray throw way on the floor milk and sugar and sandwiches a rain down on Archdeacon. Archdeacon jump up with his handkerchief and start mop himself and Auntie Mary at the same time he trying to take the tray from her. Auntie Mary at the same time trying to mop up the Archdeacon with a napkin in her mortification not even noticing how Archdeacon relieve that so much confusion come at this time. Poor soft-hearted Cherry only see that her sister whole life ruin now she dont yet know the cause run and sit on the kitchen stool and throw kitchen cloth over her head and sit there bawling and bawling in sympathy.

Beccka win the scholarship to high school. She pass so high she getting to go to the school of Auntie Mary choice which is the one that is furthest away. Beccka vex because she dont want go no boarding school with no heap of girl. Beccka dont want to go to no school at all.

Everyone so please with Beccka. Auntie Mary even more please when she get letter from the headmistress setting out Rules and Regulation. She only sorry that the list not longer for she could think of many things she could add. She get another letter setting out uniform and right away Auntie Mary start sewing. Cherry take the bus to town one day with money coming from God know where for the poor child dont have no father to speak of and she buy shoes and socks and underwear and hair ribbon and towels and toothbrush and a suitcase for Beccka. Beccka normally please like puss with every new thing vain like peacock in ribbons and clothes. Now she hardly look at them. Beccka thinking. She dont want to go to no school. But how to get out of it. When Beccka think done she decide to run away and find her father who like a miracle have job now in a circus. And as Beccka find him so she get job in the circus as a tight-rope walker and in spangles and tights lipstick and powder (her own) Beccka perform every night before a cheering crowd in a blaze of light. Beccka and the circus go right round the world. Every now and then, dress up in furs and hats like Auntie Mary wedding hat Beccka come home to visit Cherry and Auntie Mary. She arrive in a chauffeur-driven limousine pile high with luggage. Beccka shower them with presents. The whole village. For fat Katie Beccka bring a years supply of diet pill and a exercise machine just like the one she see advertise in the magazine the lady did give to Cherry.

Now Beccka ready to run away. In the books, the picture always show children running away with their things tied in a bundle on a stick. The stick easy. Beccka take one of the walking stick that did belong to Auntie Mary's dear departed. Out of spite she take Auntie Mary silk scarf to wrap her things in for Auntie Mary is to blame for her going to school at all. She pack in the bundle Auntie Mary lipstick Auntie Mary face powder and a pair of Auntie Mary stockings for she need these for her first appearance as a tight rope walker. She take a slice of cake, her shiny eye marble and a yellow nicol which is her best taa in case she get a chance to play in the marble championship of the world. She also take the Bible. She want to find some real hard question for the Archdeacon next time he come to Auntie Mary house for tea.

When Auntie Mary and Cherry busy sewing her school clothes Beccka take off with her bundle and cut across the road into the field. Mr O'Connor is her best friend and she know he wont mind if she walk across his pasture. Mr O'Connor is her best friend because he is the only person Beccka can hold a real conversation with. Beccka start to walk toward the mountain that hazy in the distance. She plan to climb the mountain and when she is high enough she will look for a sign that will lead her to her father. Beccka walk and walk through the pasture divided by stone wall and wooden gates which she climb. Sometime a few trees tell her where a pond is. But it is very lonely. All Beccka see is john crow and cow and cattle egret blackbird and parrotlets that scream at her from the trees. But Beccka dont notice them. Her mind busy on how Auntie Mary and Cherry going to be sad now she gone and she composing letter she will write to tell them she safe and she forgive them everything. But the sun getting too high in the sky and Beccka thirsty. She eat the cake but she dont have water. Far in the distance she see a bamboo clump and hope is round a spring with water. But when she get to the bamboo all it offer is shade. In fact the dry bamboo leaves on the ground so soft and inviting that Beccka decide to sit and rest for a while. Is sleep Beccka sleep. When she wake she see a stand above her four horse leg and when she raise up and look, stirrups, boots, and sitting atop the horse her best friend, Mr O'Connor.

'Well Beccka, taking a long walk?'

'Yes sir.'

'Far from home eh?'

'Yes sir.'

'Running away?'

'Yes sir.'

'Hm. What are you taking with you?'

Beccka tell him what she have in the bundle. Mr O'Connor shock.

'What, no money?'

'Oooh!'

Beccka shame like anything for she never remember anything about money.

'Well you need money for running away you know. How else you going to pay for trains and planes and taxis and buy ice cream and pindar cake?'

Beccka didn't think about any of these things before she run away. But now she see that is sense Mr O'Connor talking but she dont know what to do. So the two of them just stand up there for a while. They thinking hard.

'You know Beccka if I was you I wouldn't bother with the running away today. Maybe they dont find out you gone yet. So I would go back home and wait until I save enough money to finance my journey.'

Beccka love how that sound. To finance my journey. She think about that a long time. Mr O'Connor say, 'Tell you what. Why dont you let me give you a ride back and you can pretend this was just a practice and you can start saving your money to run away properly next time.'

Beccka look at Mr O'Connor. He looking off into the distance and she follow where he gazing and when she see the mountain she decide to leave it for another day. All the way back riding with Mr O'Connor Beccka thinking and thinking and her smile getting bigger and bigger. Beccka cant wait to get home to dream up all the tricky question she could put to a whole school full of girl. Not to mention the teachers. Beccka laughing for half the way home. Suddenly she say –

'Mr Connor, you know the Bible?'

'Well Beccka I read my Bible every day so I should think so.'

'Promise you will answer a question.'
'Promise.'
'Mr Connor, do angels wear brassieres?'
'Well Beccka, as far as I know only the lady angels

need to.'

Beccka laugh cant done. Wasnt that the answer she was waiting for?

Inside the story

Olive Senior was born and brought up in Jamaica, largely by her grandparents who were better off than her own parents struggling to make ends meet with ten children. The story, then, perhaps reflects something of her own experience but stands in its own right as a delightful tale. It reflects too the strong part played by the Christian church in the everyday life of many Jamaicans. In a society such as our own, which is both less religious and also has people of many faiths, the Biblical references may present a problem. After all, if Beccka's puzzles are enough to floor a high-ranking Christian clergyman such as the Archdeacon, it is no surprise if we don't find them easy! To help you, here are keys to the Biblical quotations that Beccka was using:

'Who in the Bible wrote big?' refers to Chapter 6, v11 of St Paul's epistle (or letter) to the Galatians where he writes 'You see how large a letter I have written unto you with mine own hand.'

'What animal saw an angel?' refers to the story of Balaam as recorded in the book of Numbers, Chapter 22, vv22–23: 'Now he (Balaam) was riding upon his ass, and his servants were with him. And the ass saw the angel of the Lord standing in the way, and his sword drawn in his hand and the ass turned aside out of the way and went into the field.'

'Raising Cain' is a pun on the name. Cain was the name of the first son of Adam and Eve. In modern times, the phrase 'to raise Cain' has come to mean 'to have tremendous row'.

Peter sleeping on his watch refers to the story in St Mark's

Gospel, Chapter 14, v37 about the disciple Simon Peter and his fellows being charged to stay on watch and then falling asleep: 'And he (Jesus) cometh and findeth them sleeping and said unto Peter, Simon sleepest thou? Couldst thou not watch one hour?'

'The smallest insect in the Bible' is another of Beccka's ghastly puns. In St Mark's Gospel, Chapter 14, v37 there is a story which has the words: 'And there came a certain poor widow, and she threw in two mites (tiny coins) which make a farthing' (less than a quarter of one old penny). A mite is, of course, also a tiny insect.

'The wicked flee' is another play on words. In the Biblical book of Proverbs, Chapter 28, v1, we read: 'The wicked flee when no man pursueth; but the righteous are bold as a lion.'

In pairs

1 It's not just in Beccka's irreverent jokes that we are made aware of the importance of religion in the household and the community. Look back to the beginning of the story and list the points at which religion, or prayer, or God are mentioned in the space of the first few pages. Discuss how religion is used by the adults and what effect this might have on the independent-minded Beccka.

2 We suggested that Beccka was an *independent* spirit. List other words *you* would use to describe her character. In a second column, jot down words and phrases you think best describe her Auntie Mary.

3 Discuss what is suggested about Beccka's family circumstances and why this makes Cherry, her mother, so nervous all the time.

4 Why is the visit of the Archdeacon so important to Auntie Mary?

5 The language in which the story is told is not standard English but the lively, vivid English of Olive Senior's native Jamaica – an English which has its own rules and structures. Pick out a few of the phrases and structures that are not standard and discuss how they work. What do you make of words like 'braps' and 'autoclaps'? Do they have an acceptable alternative in standard English?

On your own

1 Write either Beccka's school report at the end of her first term or a letter from her new Headmistress to Auntie Mary, explaining how Beccka has settled down (or not).

2 Write your own story about a bright, questioning child up against the rules of a very traditional school. What problems does he or she run into and how does he or she get around them?

THE BEST DAY OF MY EASTER HOLIDAYS

Jane Gardam

The best day of my Easter holidays was the day we met Jolly Jackson. This year we went to Jamaica for our holidays because my father was working there and so we spent all his fees although it was still expensive and we didn't get any rake-off. When I told all the American people in our hotel we were there on my father's fees they thought it was very funny and said things to my father like 'I hear you're travelling light, bud,' and slapped him over the back in a way that puzzled him and made him angry.

The people in our hotel were all very, very rich. One was so rich he got paralysed, the beach boy told me. Like Midas one side of him got turned to gold. He dribbled. The only one not rich was a vicar. He had gone there to a conference. My mother met him in the sea and they talked up to their knees. 'How lucky we are,' said the vicar in a HUGE American accent, 'in this so glorious country, enjoying the gifts of God. It is Eden itself.' Then he shouted 'FLAMING HADES' and fell flat on his stomach in the sea because he had been stung by a sea-egg. 'Help, help,' called my mother and everyone came running off the beach and dragged the vicar up the sand – blood everywhere. 'Ammonia!' cried someone. 'Only thing for a sea-egg is to pee on it,' said the beach-raker. 'Git gone,' said the beach-boy and my mother said, 'Come along now, Ned dear, it's time we set off for Duns River Falls.' The other women turned away too, and only the men were left standing around the vicar who had five black spikes sticking out of his foot and was

rolling about in agony. 'They never do no permanent harm, ma'am,' said the beach-boy to my mother, 'just pain and anguish for a day,' and he was laughing like anything – well, like a Jamaican and they laugh a great deal. I don't know if they did try peeing on the vicar or if they did if it was one or all of them. I kept thinking of the whole crowd standing round and peeing on the vicar and I laughed like a Jamaican all the way to Duns River Falls until my parents said, 'Shut up or there'll be trouble.'

Duns River Falls are some waterfalls that drop into the sea. I had expected them about as high as a tower but they were only about as high as my father. Also they had built a road over them and kiosks etc., and ticket offices and I was fed up because I had wanted to stay on the beach.

My mother said, 'Well, now we're here—' and we began to park the car when a huge man came dancing along the road in pink and blue clothes and a straw hat and opened the door and shook hands with my father. 'Hullo Daddy,' he shouted, 'an' how are you today?' (Everyone starts 'An' how are you today.') 'Now then Daddy, outs you get and in the back. I gonna sit with Mummy.'

Now my father is a man who is very important at home and nobody tells him what to do. In Jamaica he doesn't wear his black suit and stiff collar or his gold half-glasses, but even in an orange shirt and a straw hat you can tell he is very important. Oh yes man. But when this great big man told him to get out and sit in the back he got out and sat in the back, and my mother's eyes went large and wide. 'Stop for nobody and dat's advice,' they had said in our hotel, 'Jamaica is a very inflammatory place. Yes sir.' Well this man held out the biggest hand I've ever seen, pink on the front and said, 'My name's Jolly Jackson and what's yours?'

My father said, 'Hum. Hum. Ahem,' but my mother said, 'Mrs Egerton,' and held out her hand and I sprang up and down and said, 'My name's Ned, man,' and my father said, 'That will do.'

'This boy talks Jamaican, yes sir,' said Jolly Jackson, 'and now I gonna take you to see the wonderful Public Gardens followed by a tour of the surrounding countryside where you will find growing, pineapples, coffee beans, tea, avocado, coconuts and every single thing. Every fruit in all the world grow in Jamaica. Jamaica is the best country in the world and the sun is always shining.'

At that moment it began to rain in the most tremendous torrents and as our car was going up a hill which was probably once part of the waterfall and going about the same sort of angle, great waves began to come rushing down on us and the car spluttered and stopped and then turned sideways and began to be washed away.

'This is one of the famous Jamaican rainstorms,' said Jolly Jackson. 'The rain in Jamaica is the best in the world. It is very necessary rain. It rushes over the ground and disappears into the sea. In a minute it will be gone.'

We sat there for about half an hour and the rain hit the road like ten million bullets and went up from it in steam and the trees above dripped it back. Waves washed round our sideways wheels and my mother said, 'What happens if a car comes the other way?'

'Don't worry,' said Jolly Jackson, 'everything stop in a Jamaica rainstorm,' and then a huge great petrol tanker with all its lights on came tearing round the corner and down the hill towards us, screeched its brakes and skidded into the side of the road and fell into a ditch.

'Here comes the sun now,' said Jolly Jackson in a hasty voice, 'away we go,' and he got the car going and turned up the hill again and off before the driver of the petrol tanker had got the door open and got a look at us.

He was right and the sun came out and everything shone and steamed. When we got to the Public Gardens Jolly Jackson put his foot on the accelerator and roared through, past the ticket office. He was out and had all of us out in about a quarter of a second and all of us off down a path before my mother could even mop up her face.

'This here is the famous Jamaica red tree,' he said. 'This here is oleander, that there is the ban-yan tree only fifty year old, big as a mountain. That there is a waterfall. Now this boy and Mummy are gonna stand in the waterfall and have a photo.' He took the camera from round my father's neck, undid it and went click, click. Sometimes he turned the camera towards himself and went click, click and my father said, 'I say, look here—'

'Now,' he said, 'you will take a photograph of me,' and he stood inside a very dark trellis tunnel full of great big pale green lilies like long bells hanging, and stretched up and smelled one, arching his very long back, and a big white smile on his face. He stood there for a very long time even though my mother said, 'It's in the dark.' In the end she said, 'Oh well,' and went click and then Jolly Jackson moved on.

I've never seen my parents go so fast. He simply ran up and down paths, in and out of groves and places, pointing things out, picking things – sometimes great huge branches of things. 'Take it, take it. Plenty more. Jamaica can grow everything.' Once he stopped dead and we all crashed into his back. He gathered us all together and said, 'Look now, just there. That is the true Jamaica humming bird,' and there of course was a humming bird with its lovely curly tail. It was sipping from a rosy flower. There are thousands of them at our hotel all round our table at lunch every single day. We didn't even notice them much after the first week, but now we all said 'Oooooooooooh.' Jolly Jackson somehow made you say 'Oooooooooooooh.' Yes man.

Well, before my mother had seen half she wanted to he shovelled us into the car again and we stormed the barricades like James Bond or something and were off up a terribly narrow stony road with little Jamaican chicken-hut houses on each side in the trees and ladies doing their washing with lovely pink and yellow handkerchiefs on their heads, but we went so fast we couldn't get more than glimpses. My father said, leaning forward and tapping Jolly Jackson's shoulder, 'I think I should just mention that the car is only insured for myself,' and Jolly Jackson said, 'Now don't you worry Daddy, I been driving ten years. I fully qualified Private Guide and never an accident yet.' Just then a police car came rocketing round the corner and got into a tangle with our front bumper which fell off. 'Never mind,' said Jolly Jackson, 'these are my friends,' and everybody got out. There were three police men and two police women and they all laughed and laughed and shook hands with Jolly Jackson and Jolly Jackson introduced us. 'This is Daddy,' he said. 'A very important man in business from London, England, this is Ned and this is Mummy who is just at home.' This annoyed my mother who does a lot of writing work at home and gives speeches on how women are as important as men.

Well, we picked up the bumper and Jolly Jackson tried to put it in the boot and then threw it away under a banana tree. Then we went to see a lot of his aunts, cousins, great aunts, grandmothers and mother. They were all very nice and gathered round the car and told us about all their daughters who were all matrons in hospitals in London. Jolly Jackson's mother said that his sister was matron of several hospitals in London. 'That right,' said Jolly Jackson, 'my sister called Polly Jackson. I Jolly Jackson. She Polly Jackson. You go back to London and ask for Polly Jackson. She'll be there.'

My mother said to my father, 'I don't believe all this is happening.'

At one chicken-house place a whole lot of children gathered round who all seemed to be relations. One of them put his tongue out at me and said, 'White face', but Jolly Jackson hit him. My father, after we'd waited simply ages, gave some dollars round and we went on. Once we went up a very steep road and stopped to see coffee growing by the road and a woman came out of the trees, very pretty, with a baby with a sore leg. The leg had gone yellow, orange, and purple all round the cut. She had cut it on a bottle last week, the mother said. The baby was hot and crying and my mother said, 'That child has a temperature, he needs penicillin,' (very fierce) and the mother of the baby drew back with a cold look and said, 'No Missis, I put on coconut oil. You think me Jamaican monkey.' A bad look passed between them. The woman said, 'White face' and my father said, 'Oh come now' and handed more dollars.

'Do you think things are going to change in Jamaica?' my father asked Jolly Jackson as we went tearing on after this and he said, still in the same happy voice, 'Oh yes, man. Ninety thousand soldiers.' Actually he might have said, 'Nine thousand soldiers,' or 'Nineteen thousand soldiers' but it sounded like 'Ninety thousand soldiers,' and after that we were all quiet for a bit.

We seemed somehow after a very long time to get back to the same place, I don't know how. But it was terribly hot in the car and we didn't have any idea where we were. Then we saw the petrol tanker in the ditch and crowds and crowds trying to get it out and everybody smiling. Jolly Jackson's police friends were there and lot of his other friends and we all got out again to shake hands, and we bought a pineapple for one dollar thirty which made my mother say, 'Fortnum and Mason!' Jolly Jackson introduced us to hundreds of his friends. Afterwards we went back towards the Falls again and we nearly hit another car and the driver leaned out and shouted a lot of queer language at us ending in Jackson. 'Is he your friend, too?' my mother asked, and Jolly Jackson said, 'No, I know him but he is not my friend.'

'Now, we all go in the Falls,' he said when we got to the parking place. 'All take off your clothes and we walk up the Falls, five hundred feet of pure Jamaican waterfall. Perfectly safe. Nobody never falls in, never.'

'NO,' said my father and gave him six dollars.

'Seven,' said Jolly Jackson, and my father gave him seven dollars, and we went off to look at the Falls by ourselves, my mother saying things like, 'Quite ridiculous. You are an utter fool, James. Daylight robbery,' and my father saying it was worth it just to be still alive.

Somehow going up the Falls was very dull though, without Jolly Jackson and we didn't stay long. Everyone looked very white and ugly and touristy and quiet. My mother even said as we left, and went to the car again, 'I suppose seven dollars was *enough*, James? He really did us rather well I suppose. We did *see* a lot. It took two hours.' But my father said 'Pah! Enough. Look!' and we saw Jolly Jackson by the car park all alone and dancing in the road.

I said I wanted to go and say goodbye to him again but they said, no. I said it wouldn't take long but they said, no dear, come along. 'Come along,' they said. 'let's go back to the beach, let's see what's happened to the poor old vicar.' But that – the silly vicar and the man all paralysed with gold – didn't interest me any more. All that interested me was Jolly Jackson and I watched him and watched him, so beautiful, out of the back window of the car, getting smaller and smaller. And he waved and waved to me as he danced and danced. He danced and danced not moving his feet but with all his body and his lovely smiling face. He was dancing and dancing and dancing and dancing in the very middle of the big main road.

That was the best day of my Easter holidays.

(B—Egerton. Rubbish. See me.)

Inside the story

In pairs

1 Jolly Jackson is a self-appointed tour guide who virtually hi-jacks the family for an express sight-seeing tour. Discuss how the different members of the family – Ned, his father and his mother – react to Jolly Jackson's style. What do their reactions tell you about their characters?

2 Jolly Jackson only has to say one thing for the exact opposite to happen. How many examples of this can you find in the story?

3 Near the end of the story Ned writes, 'All that interested me was Jolly Jackson and I watched him, so beautiful, out of the back window of the car, getting smaller and smaller.' Discuss what it is about Jolly Jackson that causes Ned to call him 'beautiful'. What does Jolly Jackson bring into Ned's life that is probably not there when he is back home in England?

4 The story is written in the style of a schoolboy's essay and the teacher's comment at the end makes it clear that he or she doesn't think much of it. Discuss what comments you would have written at the end of this piece if you had been the teacher who received it. What did you particularly enjoy about it either in terms of the story or the way it is told?

On your own

1 The story we have here is Ned's. We can be sure that he sees what happened very differently from his very stuffy father or rather less stuffy mother. Write an account of the day's events from the point of view of one of Ned's parents. You could write your version as a letter to another adult back home, one of Ned's aunts or uncles perhaps.

2 Jolly Jackson is a larger than life character who seems quite impervious to the chaos that follows him wherever he goes. Part of his attraction to Ned is that he is so lively and unpredictable. He is totally different from any other adult Ned has met, a bringer of light and laughter. You may have met – or even be related to – similar larger than life characters yourself or could, perhaps, imagine them. Write your own story about such a character.

The Genius

Frank O'Connor

Some kids are cissies by nature but I was a cissy by conviction. Mother had told me about geniuses; I wanted to be one, and I could see for myself that fighting, as well as being sinful, was dangerous. The kids round the Barrack where I lived were always fighting. Mother said they were savages, that I needed proper friends, and that once I was old enough to go to school I would meet them.

My way, when someone wanted to fight and I could not get away, was to climb on the nearest wall and argue like hell in a shrill voice about Our Blessed Lord and good manners. This was a way of attracting attention, and it usually worked because the enemy, having stared incredulously at me for several minutes, wondering if he would have time to hammer my head on the pavement before someone came out to him, yelled something like 'blooming cissy' and went away in disgust. I didn't like being called a cissy but I preferred it to fighting. I felt very like one of those poor mongrels who slunk through our neighbourhood and took to their heels when anyone came near them, and I always tried to make friends with them.

I toyed with games, and enjoyed kicking a ball gently before me along the pavement till I discovered that any boy who joined me grew violent and started to shoulder me out of the way. I preferred little girls because they didn't fight so much, but otherwise I found them insipid and lacking in any solid basis of information. The only women I cared for were grown-ups, and my most intimate friend was an old washerwoman called Miss Cooney who had been in the lunatic asylum and was very religious. It was she who had told me all about dogs. She would run a mile after anyone she saw hurting an animal, and even went to the police about them, but the police knew she was mad and paid no attention.

She was a sad-looking woman with grey hair, high cheekbones and toothless gums. While she ironed, I would sit for hours in the hot, steaming, damp kitchen, turning over the pages of her religious books. She was fond of me too, and told me she was sure I would be a priest. I agreed that I might be a bishop, but she didn't seem to think so highly of bishops. I told her there were so many other things I might be that I couldn't make up my mind, but she only smiled at this. Miss Cooney thought there was only one thing a genius could be and that was a priest.

On the whole I thought an explorer was what I would be. Our house was in a square between two roads, one terraced above the other, and I could leave home, follow the upper road for a mile past the Barrack, turn left on any of the intervening roads and lanes, and return almost without leaving the pavement. It was astonishing what valuable information you could pick up on a trip like that. When I came home I wrote down my adventures in a book called *The Voyages of Johnson Martin*, 'with many Maps and Illustrations, Irishtown University Press, 3s. 6d. nett'. I was also compiling *The Irishtown*

University Song Book for Use in Schools and Institutions by Johnson Martin, which had the words and music of my favourite songs. I could not read music yet but I copied it from anything that came handy, preferring staff to solfa because it looked better on the page. But I still wasn't sure what I would be. All I knew was that I intended to be famous and have a statue put up to me near that of Father Matthew, in Patrick Street. Father Matthew was called the Apostle of Temperance, but I didn't think much of temperance. So far our town hadn't a proper genius and I intended to supply the deficiency.

But my work continued to bring home to me the great gaps in my knowledge. Mother understood my difficulty and worried herself endlessly finding answers to my questions, but neither she nor Miss Cooney had a great store of the sort of information I needed, and Father was more a hindrance than a help. He was talkative enough about subjects that interested himself but they did not greatly interest me. 'Ballybeg,' he would say brightly. 'Market town. Population 648. Nearest station, Rathkeale.' He was also forthcoming enough about other things, but later, Mother would take me aside and explain that he was only joking again. This made me mad, because I never knew when he was joking and when he wasn't.

I can see now, of course, that he didn't really like me. It was not the poor man's fault. He had never expected to be the father of a genius and it filled him with forebodings. He looked round him at all his contemporaries who had normal, blood-thirsty, illiterate children, and shuddered at the thought that I would never be good for anything but being a genius. To give him his due, it wasn't himself he worried about, but there had never been anything like it in the family before and he dreaded the shame of it. He would come in from the front door with his

cap over his eyes and his hands in his trouser pockets and stare moodily at me while I sat at the kitchen table, surrounded by papers, producing fresh maps and illustrations for my book of voyages, or copying the music of 'The Minstrel Boy'.

'Why can't you go out and play with the Horgans?' he would ask wheedlingly, trying to make it sound attractive.

'I don't like the Horgans, Daddy,' I would reply politely.

'But what's wrong with them?' he would ask testily. 'They're fine manly young fellows.'

'They're always fighting, Daddy.'

'And what harm is fighting? Can't you fight them back?'

'I don't like fighting, Daddy, thank you,' I would say, still with perfect politeness.

'The dear knows, the child is right,' Mother would say coming to my defence. 'I don't know what sort those children are.'

'Ah, you have him as bad as yourself,' Father would snort, and stalk to the front door again, to scald his heart with thoughts of the nice natural son he might have had if only he hadn't married the wrong woman. Granny had always said Mother was the wrong woman for him and now she was being proved right.

She was being proved so right that the poor man couldn't keep his eyes off me, waiting for the insanity to break out in me. One of the things he didn't like was my Opera House. The Opera House was a cardboard box I had mounted on two chairs in the dark hallway. It had a proscenium cut in it, and I had painted some back-drops of mountain and sea with wings that represented trees and rocks. The characters were pictures cut out, mounted and coloured, and moved on bits of stick. It was lit with candles, for which I had made coloured screens, greased so that they were transparent, and I made up operas from story-books and bits of songs. I was singing a passionate duet for two of the characters while twiddling the screens to produce the effect of moonlight when one of the screens caught fire and everything went up in a mass of flames. I screamed and Father came out to stamp out the blaze, and he cursed me till even Mother lost her temper with him and told him he was worse than six children, after which he wouldn't speak to her for a week.

Another time I was so impressed with a lame teacher I knew that I decided to have a lame leg myself, and there was hell in the home for days because Mother had no difficulty at all in seeing that my foot was already out of shape while Father only looked at it and sniffed contemptuously. I was furious with him, and Mother decided he wasn't much better than a monster. They quarrelled for days over that until it became quite an embarrassment to me because, though I was bored stiff with limping, I felt I should be letting her down by getting better. When I went down the Square, lurching from side to side, Father stood at the gate, looking after me with a malicious knowing smile, and when I had discarded my limp, the way he mocked Mother was positively disgusting.

2

As I say, they squabbled endlessly about what I should be told. Father was for telling me nothing.

'But, Mick,' Mother would say earnestly, 'the child must learn.'

'He'll learn soon enough when he goes to school,' he snarled. 'Why do you be always at him, putting ideas into his head? Isn't he bad enough? I'd sooner the boy would grow up a bit natural.'

But either Mother didn't like children to be natural

or she thought I was natural enough, as I was. Women, of course, don't object to geniuses half as much as men do. I suppose they find them a relief.

Now one of the things I wanted badly to know was where babies came from, but this was something that no one seemed to be able to explain to me. When I asked Mother she got upset and talked about birds and flowers, and I decided that if she had ever known she must have forgotten it and was ashamed to say so. Miss Cooney only smiled wistfully when I asked her and said, 'You'll know all about that soon enough, child.'

'But, Miss Cooney,' I said with great dignity, 'I have to know now. It's for my work, you see.'

'Keep your innocence while you can, child,' she said in the same tone. 'Soon enough the world will rob you of it, and once 'tis gone 'tis gone for ever.'

But whatever the world wanted to rob me of, it was welcome to it from my point of view, if only I could get a few facts to work on. I appealed to Father and he told me that babies were dropped out of aeroplanes and if you caught one you could keep it. 'By parachute?' I asked, but he only looked pained and said, 'Oh, no, you don't want to begin by spoiling them.' Afterwards, Mother took me aside again and explained that he was only joking. I went quite dotty with rage and told her that one of these days he would go too far with his jokes.

All the same, it was a great worry to Mother. It wasn't every mother who had a genius for a son, and she dreaded that she might be wronging me. She suggested timidly to Father that he should tell me something about it and he danced with rage. I heard them because I was supposed to be playing with the Opera House upstairs at the time. He said she was going out of her mind, and that she was driving me out of my mind at the same time. She was very upset because she had considerable respect for his judgement.

At the same time when it was a matter of duty she could be very, very obstinate. It was a heavy responsibility, and she disliked it intensely – a deeply pious woman who never mentioned the subject at all to anybody if she could avoid it – but it had to be done. She took an awful long time over it – it was a summer day, and we were sitting on the bank of a stream in the Glen – but at last I managed to detach the fact that mummies had an engine in their tummies and daddies had a starting-handle that made it work, and once it started it went on until it made a baby. That certainly explained an awful lot of things I had not understood up to this – for instance, why fathers were necessary and why Mother had buffers on her chest while Father had none. It made her almost as interesting as a locomotive, and for days I went round deploring my own rotten luck that I wasn't a girl and couldn't have an engine and buffers of my own instead of a measly old starting-handle like Father.

Soon afterwards I went to school and disliked it intensely. I was too small to be moved up to the big boys and the other 'infants' were still at the stage of spelling 'cat' and 'dog'. I tried to tell the old teacher about my work, but she only smiled and said, 'Hush, Larry!' I hated being told to hush. Father was always saying it to me.

One day I was standing at the playground gate, feeling very lonely and dissatisfied, when a tall girl from the senior girls' school spoke to me. She was a girl with a plump, dark face and black pigtails.

'What's your name, little boy?' she asked.

I told her.

'Is this your first time at school?' she asked.

'Yes.'

'And do you like it?'

'No, I hate it,' I replied gravely. 'The children can't spell and the old woman talks too much.'

Then I talked myself for a change and she listened attentively while I told her about myself, my voyages, my books and the time of the trains from all the city stations. As she seemed so interested I told her I would meet her after school and tell her some more.

I was as good as my word. When I had eaten my lunch, instead of going on further voyages I went back to the girls' school and waited for her to come out. She seemed pleased to see me because she took my hand and brought me home with her. She lived up Gardiner's Hill, a steep, demure suburban road with trees that overhung the walls at either side. She lived in a small house on top of the hill and was one of a family of three girls. Her little brother John Joe, had been killed the previous year by a car. 'Look at what I brought home with me!' she said when we went into the kitchen, and her mother, a tall, thin woman made a great fuss of me and wanted me to have my dinner with Una. That was the girl's name. I didn't take anything, but while she ate I sat by the range and told her mother about myself as well. She seemed to like it as much as Una, and when dinner was over Una took me out in the fields behind the house for a walk.

When I went home at teatime, Mother was delighted.

'Ah,' she said, 'I knew you wouldn't be long making nice friends at school. It's about time for you, the dear knows.'

I felt much the same about it, and every fine day at three I waited for Una outside the school. When it rained and Mother would not let me out I was miserable.

One day while I was waiting for her there were two

senior girls outside the gate.

'Your girl isn't out yet, Larry,' said one with a giggle.

'And do you mean to tell me Larry has a girl?' the other asked with a shocked air.

'Oh, yes,' said the first. 'Una Dwyer is Larry's girl. He goes with Una, don't you, Larry?'

I replied politely that I did, but in fact I was seriously alarmed. I had not realized that Una would be considered my girl. It had never happened to me before, and I had not understood that my waiting for her would be regarded in such a grave light. Now, I think the girls were probably right anyhow, for that is always the way it has happened to me. A woman has only to shut up and let me talk long enough for me to fall head and ears in love with her. But then I did not recognize the symptoms. All I knew was that going with somebody meant you intended to marry them. I had always planned on marrying Mother; now it seemed as if I was expected to marry someone else, and I wasn't sure if I should like it or if, like football, it would prove to be one of those games that two people could not play without pushing.

A couple of weeks later I went to a party at Una's house. By this time it was almost as much mine as theirs. All the girls liked me and Mrs Dwyer talked to me by the hour. I saw nothing peculiar about this except a proper appreciation of geniuses. Una had warned me that I should be expected to sing, so I was ready for the occasion. I sang the Gregorian *Credo*, and some of the little girls laughed. But Mrs Dwyer only looked at me fondly.

'I suppose you'll be a priest when you grow up, Larry?' she asked.

'No, Mrs Dwyer,' I replied firmly. 'As a matter of fact, I intend to be a composer. Priests can't marry, you see, and I want to get married.'

That seemed to surprise her quite a bit. I was quite prepared to continue discussing my plans for the future, but all the children talked together. I was used to planning discussions so that they went on for a long time, but I found that whenever I began one in the Dwyers, it was immediately interrupted so that I found it hard to concentrate. Besides, all the children shouted, and Mrs Dwyer, for all her gentleness, shouted with them and at them. At first, I was somewhat alarmed, but I soon saw that they meant no particular harm, and when the party ended I was jumping up and down on the sofa, shrieking louder than anyone while Una, in hysterics of giggling, encouraged me. She seemed to think I was the funniest thing ever.

It was a moonlit November night, and lights were burning in the little cottages along the road when Una brought me home. On the road outside she stopped uncertainly and said, 'This is where little John Joe was killed.'

There was nothing remarkable about the spot, and I saw no chance of acquiring any useful information.

'Was it a Ford or a Morris?' I asked, more out of politeness than anything else.

'I don't know,' she replied with smouldering anger. 'It was Donegan's old car. They can never look where they're going, the old shows!'

'Our Lord probably wanted him,' I said perfunctorily.

'I dare say He did,' Una replied, though she showed no particular conviction. 'That old fool, Donegan – I could kill him whenever I think of it.'

'You should get your mother to make you another,' I suggested helpfully.

'Make me a what?' Una exclaimed in consternation.

'Make you another brother,' I repeated earnestly. 'It's quite easy, really. She has an engine in her tummy, and all your daddy has to do is to start it with his starting-handle.'

'Cripes!' Una said, and clapped her hand over her mouth in an explosion of giggles. 'Imagine me telling her that!'

'But it's true, Una,' I said obstinately. 'It only takes nine months. She could make you another little brother by next summer.'

'Oh, Jay!' exclaimed Una in another fit of giggles. 'Who told you all that?'

'Mummy did. Didn't your mother tell you?'

'Oh, she says you buy them from Nurse Daly,' said Una, and began to giggle again.

'I wouldn't really believe that,' I said with as much dignity as I could muster.

But the truth was I felt I had made a fool of myself again. I realized now that I had never been convinced by Mother's explanation. It was too simple. If there was anything that woman could get wrong she did so without fail. And it upset me, because for the first time I found myself wanting to make a really good impression. The Dwyers had managed to convince me that whatever else I wanted to be I did not want to be a priest. I didn't even want to be an explorer, a career which would take me away for long periods from my wife and family. I was prepared to be a composer and nothing but a composer.

That night in bed I sounded Mother on the subject of marriage. I tried to be tactful because it had always been agreed between us that I should marry her and I did not wish her to see that my feelings had changed.

'Mummy,' I asked, 'if a gentleman asks a lady to marry him, what does he say?'

'Oh,' she replied shortly, 'some of them say a lot. They say more than they mean.'

She was so irritable that I guessed she had divined my secret and I felt really sorry for her.

'If a gentleman said, "Excuse me, will you marry me?" would that be all right?' I persisted.

'Ah, well, he'd have to tell her first that he was fond of her,' said Mother who, no matter what she felt, could never bring herself to deceive me on any major issue.

But about the other matter I saw that it was hopeless to ask her any more. For days I made the most pertinacious inquiries at school and received some startling information. One boy had actually come floating down on a snowflake, wearing a bright blue dress, but to his chagrin and mine, the dress had been given away to a poor child in the North Main Street. I grieved long and deeply over this wanton destruction of evidence. The balance of opinion favoured Mrs Dwyer's solution, but of the theory of engines and starting-handles no one in the school had ever heard. That theory might have been all right when Mother was a girl but it was now definitely out of fashion.

And because of it I had been exposed to ridicule before the family whose good opinion I valued most. It was hard enough to keep up my dignity with a girl who was doing algebra while I hadn't got beyond long division without falling into childish errors that made her laugh. That is another thing I still cannot stand, being made fun of by women. Once they begin on it they never stop. Once when we were going up Gardiner's Hill together after school she stopped to look at a baby in a pram. The baby grinned at her and she gave him her finger to suck. He waved his fists and sucked like mad, and she went off into giggles again.

'I suppose that was another engine?' she said.

Four times at least she mentioned my silliness, twice in front of other girls and each time, though I pretended to ignore it, I was pierced to the heart. It made me determined not to be exposed again. Once Mother asked Una and her younger sister, Joan, to tea, and all the time I was in an agony of self-consciousness, dreading what she would say next. I felt that a woman who had said such things about babies was capable of anything. Then the talk turned on the death of little John Joe, and it all flowed back into my mind on a wave of mortification. I made two efforts to change the conversation, but Mother returned to it. She was full of pity for the Dwyers, full of sympathy for the little boy and had almost reduced herself to tears. Finally, I got up and ordered Una and Joan to play with me. Then Mother got angry.

'For goodness' sake, Larry, let the children finish their tea!' she snapped.

'It's all right, Mrs Delaney,' Una said good-naturedly. 'I'll go with him.'

'Nonsense, Una!' Mother said sharply. 'Finish your tea and go on with what you were saying. It's a wonder to me your poor mother didn't go out of her mind. How can they let people like that drive cars?'

At this I set up a loud wail. At any moment now I felt she was going to get on to babies and advise Una about what her mother ought to do.

'Will you behave yourself, Larry!' Mother said in a quivering voice. 'Or what's come over you in the past few weeks? You used to have such nice manners, and now look at you! A little corner boy! I'm ashamed of you!'

How could she know what had come over me? How could she realize that I was imagining the family circle in the Dwyers' house and Una, between fits of laughter, describing my old-fashioned mother who still talked about babies coming out of people's stomachs? It must have been real love, for I have never known true love in which I wasn't ashamed of Mother.

And she knew it and was hurt. I still enjoyed going home with Una in the afternoons and while she ate her dinner, I sat at the piano and pretended to play my own compositions, but whenever she called at our house for me I grabbed her by the hand and tried to drag her away so that she and Mother shouldn't start talking.

'Ah, I'm disgusted with you,' Mother said one day. 'One would think you were ashamed of me in front of that little girl. I'll engage she doesn't treat her mother like that.'

Then one day I was waiting for Una at the school gate as usual. Another boy was waiting there as well – one of the seniors. When he heard the screams of the school breaking up he strolled away and stationed himself at the foot of the hill by the crossroads. Then Una herself came rushing out in her wide-brimmed felt hat, swinging her satchel, and approached me with a conspiratorial air.

'Oh, Larry, guess what's happened!' she whispered. 'I can't bring you home with me today. I'll come down and see you during the week though. Will that do?'

'Yes, thank you,' I said in a dead cold voice. Even at the most tragic moment of my life I could be nothing but polite. I watched her scamper down the hill to where the big boy was waiting. He looked over his shoulder with a grin, and then the two of them went off together.

Instead of following them I went back up the hill alone and stood leaning over the quarry wall, looking at the roadway and the valley of the city beneath me. I knew this was the end. I was too young to marry Una. I didn't know where babies came from and I didn't understand algebra. The fellow she had gone home with probably knew everything about both. I was full of gloom and revengeful thoughts. I, who had considered it sinful and dangerous to fight, was now regretting that I hadn't gone after him to batter his teeth in and jump on his face. It wouldn't even have mattered to me that I was too young and weak and that he would have done all the battering. I saw that love was a game that two people couldn't play at without pushing, just like football.

I went home and, without saying a word, took out the work I had been neglecting so long. That too seemed to have lost its appeal. Moodily I ruled five lines and began to trace the difficult sign of the treble clef.

'Didn't you see Una, Larry?' Mother asked in surprise, looking up from her sewing.

'No, Mummy,' I said, too full for speech.

'Wisha, 'twasn't a falling-out ye had?' she asked in dismay, coming towards me. I put my head on my hands and sobbed. 'Wisha, never mind, childeen!' she murmured, running her hand through my hair. 'She was a bit old for you. You reminded her of her little brother that was killed, of course – that was why. You'll soon make new friends, take my word for it.'

But I did not believe her. That evening there was no comfort for me. My great work meant nothing to me and I knew it was all I would ever have. For all the difference it made I might as well become a priest. I felt it was a poor, sad, lonesome thing being nothing but a genius.

Inside the story

In pairs or small groups

1 Discuss how you feel towards Larry, the little boy of the story. Do you find him engaging and amusing or insufferable, for example? Do you feel sympathetic towards him? Did your feelings change as you read the story?

2 From the following list of words that might be used to describe Larry, each pick four that you think suit him best and compare your choices. When you have said why you chose as you did, *as a group* decide on the four you think describe him best: *innocent, knowledgeable, self-centred, outgoing, confident, shy, grave, funny, humourless, imaginative, weak, strong, intelligent, odd, normal*. If you think of other words you believe describe him better, add them to your list.

3 Discuss what Larry's father regards as being natural behaviour for a boy. Do you agree with him?

4 Perhaps the most frustrating thing for Larry was that older people would never take him seriously. Find examples of this and discuss why he found it so maddening.

5 Discuss why Larry is important to Una and her mother.

On your own

1 In an earlier generation, when Frank O'Connor was writing, the facts of life were often cloaked in mystery and unknown to children until they were quite old. As you see, that didn't stop them theorising about the problem and wondering about the strange stories that adults often told them. Traditionally, gooseberry bushes, storks, and even birds and bees have been used by desperately embarrassed parents trying to evade a clear explanation of what was involved. Write your own embarrassed parental 'explanation' which mentions no part of the human anatomy, totally fails to clear up the mystery, and leaves the child more confused than before.

2 Una is obviously very fond of Larry. Write her three diary entries for when she first met him, the day he went to the party at Una's house and the day Una went off with the older boy from the senior school.

6
SOMETHING NASTY

Most of us enjoy being frightened just a bit – particularly if we know in the back of our minds that we are really safe from harm. That is one of the main reasons for the continuing popularity of ghost stories and tales of horror: we do keep coming back for more.

The stories in this section are a mixed bag with only one of them being about a ghost. The others could be said to be concerned broadly with obsessions – the obsessive killer of tramps or hobos, the man who has an obsessive interest in snails and the landlady who . . .

Enough perhaps to say that they all deal with something nasty.

THE GHOST

Catherine Wells

She was a girl of fourteen, and she sat propped up with pillows in an old four-poster bed, coughing a little with the feverish cold that kept her there. She was tired of reading by lamplight, and she lay and listened to the few sounds that she could hear, and looked into the fire. From downstairs, down the wide, rather dark, oak-panelled corridor hung with brown ochre pictures of tremendous naval engagements exploding fierily in their centres, down the broad stone stairs that ended in a heavy, creaking, nail-studded door, there blew in to her remoteness sometimes a gust of dance music. Cousins and cousins and cousins were down there, and Uncle Timothy, as host, leading the fun. Several of them had danced into her room during the day, and said that her illness was a 'perfect shame,' told her that the skating in the park was 'too heavenly,' and danced out again. Uncle Timothy had been as kind as kind could be. But – Downstairs all the full cup of happiness the lonely child had looked forward to so eagerly for a month, was running away like liquid gold.

She watched the flames of the big wood fire in the open grate flicker and fall. She had sometimes to clench her hands to prevent herself from crying. She had discovered – so early was she beginning to collect her little stock of feminine lore – that if you swallowed hard and rapidly as the tears gathered, that you could prevent your eyes brimming over. She wished some one would come. There was a bell within her reach, but she could think of no plausible excuse for ringing it. She wished there was more light in the room. The big fire lit it up cheerfully when the logs flared high; but when they only glowed, the dark shadows crept down from the ceiling and gathered in the corners against the panelling. She turned from the scrutiny of the room to the bright circle of light under the lamp on the table beside her, and the companionable suggestiveness of the currant jelly and spoon, grapes and lemonade and little pile of books and kindly fuss that shone warmly and comfortingly there. Perhaps it would not be long before Mrs Bunting, her uncle's housekeeper, would come in again and sit down and talk to her.

Mrs Bunting, very probably, was more occupied than usual that evening. There were several extra guests, another house-party had motored over for the evening, and they had brought with them a romantic figure, a celebrity, no less a personage than the actor Percival East. The girl had indeed broken down from her fortitude that afternoon when Uncle Timothy had told her of this visitor. Uncle Timothy was surprised; it was only another schoolgirl who would have understood fully what it meant to be denied by a mere cold the chance of meeting face to face that chivalrous hero of drama; another girl who had glowed at his daring, wept at his noble renunciations, been made happy, albeit enviously and vicariously, by his final embrace with the lady of his love.

'There, there, dear child,' Uncle Timothy had said, patting her shoulder and greatly distressed. 'Never mind, never mind. If you can't get up I'll bring him in to see you here. I promise I will. . . . But the *pull* these chaps have over you little women,' he went on, half to himself. . . .

The panelling creaked. Of course, it always did in these old houses. She was of that order of apprehensive, slightly nervous people who do not believe in ghosts, but all the same hope devoutly they may never see one. Surely it was a long time since any one had visited her; it would be hours, she supposed, before the girl who had the room next her own, into which a communicating door comfortingly led, came up to bed. If she rang it took a minute or two before any one reached her from the remote servants' quarters. There ought soon, she thought, to be a housemaid about the corridor outside, tidying up the bedrooms, putting coal on the fires, and making suchlike companionable noises. That would be pleasant. How bored one got in bed anyhow, and how dreadful it was, how unbearably dreadful it was that she should be stuck in bed now, missing everything, missing every bit of the glorious glowing time that was slipping away down there. At that she had to begin swallowing her tears again.

With a sudden burst of sound, a storm of clapping and laughter, the heavy door at the foot of the big stairs swung open and closed. Footsteps came upstairs, and she heard men's voices approaching. Uncle Timothy. He knocked at the door ajar. 'Come in,' she cried gladly. With him was a quiet-faced greyish-haired man of middle age. Then uncle had sent for the doctor after all!

'Here is another of your young worshippers, Mr East,' said Uncle Timothy.

Mr East! She realised in a flash that she had expected him in purple brocade, powdered hair, and ruffles of fine lace. Her uncle smiled at her disconcerted face.

'She doesn't seem to recognise you, Mr East,' said Uncle Timothy.

'Of course I do,' she declared bravely, and sat up, flushed with excitement and her feverishness, bright-eyed and with ruffled hair. Indeed she began to see the stage hero she remembered and the kindly-faced man before her flow together like a composite portrait. There was the little nod of the head, there was the chin, yes! and the eyes, now she came to look at them. 'Why were they all clapping you?' she asked.

'Because I had just promised to frighten them out of their wits,' replied Mr East.

'Oh, how?'

'Mr East,' said Uncle Timothy, 'is going to dress up as our long-lost ghost, and give us a really shuddering time of it downstairs.'

'*Are* you?' cried the girl with all the fierce desire that only a girl can utter in her voice. 'Oh, why am I ill like this, Uncle Timothy? I'm not ill really. Can't you see I'm better? I've been in bed all day. I'm perfectly well. Can't I come down, Uncle *dear* – can't I?'

In her excitement she was half out of bed. 'There, there, child,' soothed Uncle Timothy, hastily smoothing the bedclothes and trying to tuck her in.

'But *can't* I?'

'Of course, if you want to be thoroughly frightened, frightened out of your wits, mind you,' began Percival East.

'I do, I *do*,' she cried, bouncing up and down in her bed.

'I'll come and show myself when I'm dressed up, before I go down.'

'Oh please, please,' she cried back radiantly. A private performance all to herself! 'Will you be perfectly *awful*? she laughed exultantly.

'As ever I can,' smiled Mr East, and turned to

follow Uncle Timothy out of the room. 'You know,' he said, holding the door and looking back at her with mock seriousness, 'I shall look rather horrid, I expect. Are you sure you won't mind?'

'*Mind* – when it's you?' laughed the girl.

He went out of the room, shutting the door.

'Rum-ti-tum, ti-tum, ti-ty,' she hummed gaily, and wriggled down into her bedclothes again, straightened the sheet over her chest, and prepared to wait.

She lay quietly for some time, with a smile on her face, thinking of Percival East and fitting his grave, kindly face back into its various dramatic settings. She was quite satisfied with him. She began to go over in her mind in detail the last play in which she had seen him act. How splendid he had looked when he fought the duel! She couldn't imagine him gruesome, she thought. What would he do with himself?

Whatever he did, she wasn't going to be frightened. He shouldn't be able to boast he had frightened *her*. Uncle Timothy would be there too, she supposed. Would he?

Footsteps went past her door outside, along the corridor, and died away. The big door at the end of the stairs opened and clanged shut.

Uncle Timothy had gone down.

She waited on.

A log, burnt through the middle to a ruddy thread, fell suddenly in two tumbling pieces on the hearth. She started at the sound. How quiet everything was. How much longer would he be, she wondered. The fire wanted making up, the pieces of wood collecting together. Should she ring? But he might come in just when the servant was mending the fire, and that would spoil his entry. The fire could wait. . . .

The room was very still, and, with the fallen fire, darker. She heard no more any sound at all from downstairs. That was because her door was shut. All day it had been open, but now the last slender link that held her to downstairs was broken.

The lamp flame gave a sudden fitful leap. Why? Was it going out? Was it? – no.

She hoped he wouldn't jump out at her, but of course he wouldn't. Anyhow, whatever he did she wouldn't be frightened – really frightened. Forewarned is forearmed.

Was that a sound? She started up, her eyes on the door. Nothing.

But surely, the door had minutely moved, it did not sit back quite so close into its frame! Perhaps it – She was sure it had moved. Yes, it had moved – opened an inch, and slowly, as she watched, she saw a thread of light grow between the edge of the door and its frame, grow almost imperceptibly wider, and stop.

He could never come through that? It must have yawned open of its own accord. Her heart began to beat rather quickly. She could see only the upper part of the door, the foot of her bed hid the lower third. . . .

Her attention tightened. Suddenly, as suddenly as a pistol shot, she saw that there was a little figure like a dwarf near the wall, between the door and the fireplace. It was a little cloaked figure, no higher than the table. How *did* he do it? It was moving slowly, very slowly, towards the fire, as if it was quite unconscious of her; it was wrapped about in a cloak that trailed, with a slouched hat on its head bent down to its shoulders. She gripped the clothes with her hands, it was so queer, so unexpected; she gave a little gasping laugh to break the tension of the silence – to show she appreciated him.

The dwarf stopped dead at the sound, and turned its face round to her.

Oh! but she was frightened! it was a dead white

face, a long pointed face hunched between its shoulders, there was no colour in the eyes that stared at her! How did he do it, how *did* he do it? It was too good. She laughed again nervously, and with a clutch of terror that she could not control she saw the creature move out of the shadow and come towards her. She braced herself with all her might, she mustn't be frightened by a bit of acting – he was coming nearer, it was horrible, horrible – right up to her bed. . . .

She flung her head beneath her bedclothes. Whether she screamed or not she never knew. . . .

Some one was rapping at her door, speaking cheerily. She took her head out of the clothes with a revulsion of shame at her fright. The horrible little creature was gone! Mr East was speaking at her door. What was it he was saying? *What?*

'I'm ready now,' he said. *'Shall I come in, and begin?'*

Inside the story

In pairs or small groups

1 What aspects of the description suggest the girl's room is a warm, secure and comforting place and what things hold a suggestion of menace? Can some things be seen as either secure or menacing according to the way you look at them?

2 There is quite a long build up to the point where the ghost appears. Discuss why you think Catherine Wells might have spent so long in setting the scene and establishing Mr East's skill as an actor before getting to the unpleasant part.

3 Look at the opening paragraphs of the story and get a sense of how they appear on the page – solid chunks of writing, long sentences, plenty of detail. Now look at the part of the story when the girl is left alone to await Mr East's entrance: 'He shouldn't be able to boast he had frightened *her*. Uncle Timothy would be there too, she supposed. Would he?' and read on to 'What was that sound? She started up, her eyes on the door.

Nothing.' Discuss why the writing is different here from the writing in the opening paragraphs and its effect on the reader.

4 At what point do you think the girl is *convinced* that the figure she sees is not Mr East? And you, when were you sure?

On your own

1 What happens next? Continue the story.

2 Think of things that may have frightened you when you were younger, that may even now make you feel a little uneasy. Maybe it was the shape of coats hanging bat-like on the backs of doors; the movement of curtains in a slight draught; maybe it was the pale ghost-light of mirrors reflecting in a darkened room or maybe the uncertainty of whether that now open wardrobe door was closed when you slipped into bed. Write about a ghostly appearance which, like this one, is located entirely in one room. Your own room perhaps?

Hobo

Robert Bloch

Hannigan hopped the freight in the yards, just as it started to roll. It had already picked up speed before he spotted an empty in the deepening twilight, and in Hannigan's condition it wasn't easy to swing aboard. He scraped all of the cloth and most of the skin from his left knee before he landed, cursing, in the musty darkness of the boxcar.

He sat there for a moment, trying to catch his wind, feeling the perspiration trickle down under the folds of the dirty jacket. That's what Sneaky Pete did to a man.

Staring out of the doorway, Hannigan watched the lights of the city move past in a blinding blur as the train gained momentum. The lights became links in a solid neon chain. That was also what Sneaky Pete could do to a man.

Hannigan shrugged. Hell, he'd been entitled to drink a few toasts to celebrate leaving town!

Unexpectedly the shrug became a twitch and the twitch became a shiver. So all right, he might as well be honest. He hadn't been celebrating anything. He'd drunk up his last dime because he was scared.

That's why he was on the lam again – he had to get out of Knifeville. That wasn't the name of the town, of course, but Hannigan knew he'd always remember it that way. There wasn't enough Sneaky Pete in the world to drown the memory.

He blinked and turned away from the dwindling chain of light, trying to focus his vision in the dimness of the empty boxcar.

Then he froze.

The boxcar wasn't empty.

Sprawling against the opposite side of the wall was the man. He sat there nonchalantly, staring at Hannigan – and he'd been sitting there and staring all the time. The farther reaches of the car were in total darkness, but the man was just close enough to the opposite door so that flashes of light illumined his features in passing. He was short, squat, his bullet-head almost bald. His face was grimy and stubbled, his clothing soiled and wrinkled. This reassured Hannigan. It couldn't be the Knife.

'Brother, you gave me a scare!' Hannigan muttered. The train was passing over a culvert now and the rumbling cut off the man's reply. When the lights flashed by again he was still staring.

'Going South?' Hannigan called.

The man nodded.

'Me, too.' Hannigan wiped the side of his mouth with his sleeve; he could still taste the Sneaky Pete, still feel it warming his churning guts. 'I don't care where I end up, just so's I get the hell out of that burg.'

They were rolling through open country now and he couldn't see his companion. But he knew he hadn't moved, because now, in counterpoint to the steady clickety-clack of the cars, he heard the steady cadence of his hoarse breathing.

Hannigan didn't give a damn whether he saw him or not – the main thing was just to know he was there, hear the reassuring sound of another man's breath. It helped, and talking helped, too.

'I suppose you hit the iron for the same reason I did.' It was really the Sneaky Pete talking, but Hannigan let the words roll. 'You heard about the Knife?'

He caught the man's nod as a farmhouse light flashed by. The guy was probably drunker than he was, but at least he was listening.

'Damnedest thing. Killed four bums in a week – you see what it said in the papers? Some skull doctor figured it out. This loony just has it in for us poor down-and-outers. I was down in Bronson's jungle yesterday. Half the guys had hit the road already and the rest were leaving. Scared they might be next. I gave 'em all the Bronx salute.'

The stranger didn't reply. Listening to his rasping gasps, Hannigan suddenly realized why. He was blind drunk. 'Loaded, huh?' Hannigan grinned. 'Me, too. On account of I was wrong. About giving those guys the Bronx, I mean.' He gulped. 'Because today – I ran into the Knife.'

The man across the way nodded again; Hannigan caught it in a passing beam of light as the cars rolled on. 'I mean it, man,' he said. 'You know Jerry's place – down the alley off Main? I was crawling out of there this afternoon. Nobody in sight. All of a sudden – zing! Something whizzes right past my ear. I look up and there's this shiv, stuck in a post about three inches from my head.

'I didn't see anyone, and I didn't wait to look. I ducked back into Jerry's and stayed there. Drank up my stake and waited until it was time to hop this rattler.' He was twitching again, but he couldn't help it. 'All I wanted was to get out of there.'

Hannigan leaned forward. 'What's the matter, you a dummy or something?' He tried to catch a glimpse of the man's features, but it was too dark. And now he needed the response. He began to edge forward on his hands and knees as the train lurched over the bumpy roadbed.

'How do you figure it?' he asked – knowing that he was really asking himself the question. 'What gets into a guy's skull that makes him kill that way – just creep around in the dark and carve up poor jokers like us?'

There was no answer, only the hoarse breathing.

Hannigan inched forward, just as the train hit the curve. A light flashed by and he saw the man topple forward.

He saw the blood and the gaping hole and the blinding reflection from the blade of the big knife stuck in the man's back.

'Dead!' Hannigan edged away, shivering, then paused. 'But he can't be. *I heard him breathing!*'

Suddenly he realized he could still hear the breathing now. But it was coming from behind him, coming from close behind. In fact, just as the train went into the tunnel, Hannigan could *feel* the breathing – right against the back of his neck . . .

Inside the story

In pairs or small groups

1 Two twists follow rapidly one on the other at the end of this story: first the man is dead, killed by the Knife; second, the Knife is the source of the breathing and he is right behind Hannigan. Discuss how the author manages to keep suggesting earlier in the story that the man is alive and thus to wrong foot us. Look in particular for all the references to him nodding and breathing.

2 Where does the *very first* shock come for Hannigan? What is his immediate thought and how does he behave when he realises he must be wrong? Do you as a reader begin to share his mood?

3 All our senses are brought into play in the course of this story. It is a deliberate ploy to keep us alert and on edge as well as to make the setting seem real. List the things that Hannigan sees in particular and all the things that he hears, smells, feels, tastes.

4 Write the story as a radio script ready for tape recording. Apart from Hannigan's words you will need the sounds of the train, the glug of the whisky bottle and, of course, the sound of hoarse breathing. There are other sounds you might find it helpful to add to convey the atmosphere of the boxcar. How do we know Hannigan has jumped aboard with some difficulty? How do we know he's drunk? that he wipes his mouth on his sleeve? that the man has toppled forward . . . if we have only sounds to suggest these things? Record your version when you are happy with your script.

THE SNAIL-WATCHER

Patricia Highsmith

When Mr Peter Knoppert began to make a hobby of snail-watching, he had no idea that his handful of specimens would become hundreds in no time. Only two months after the original snails were carried up to the Knoppert study, some thirty glass tanks and bowls, all teeming with snails, lined the walls, rested on the desk and windowsills, and were beginning even to cover the floor. Mrs Knoppert disapproved strongly, and would no longer enter the room. It smelled, she said, and besides she had once stepped on a snail by accident, a horrible sensation she would never forget. But the more his wife and friends deplored his unusual and vaguely repellent pastime, the more pleasure Mr Knoppert seemed to find in it.

'I never cared for nature before in my life,' Mr Knoppert often remarked – he was a partner in a brokerage firm, a man who had devoted all his life to the science of finance – 'but snails have opened my eyes to the beauty of the animal world.'

If his friends commented that snails were not really animals, and their slimy habitats hardly the best example of the beauty of nature, Mr Knoppert would tell them with a superior smile that they simply didn't know all that he knew about snails.

And it was true. Mr Knoppert had witnessed an exhibition that was not described, certainly not adequately described, in an encyclopaedia or zoology book that he had been able to find. Mr Knoppert had wandered into the kitchen one evening for a bite of something before dinner, and had happened to notice that a couple of snails in the china bowl on the draining board were behaving very oddly. Standing more or less on their tails, they were weaving before each other for all the world like a pair of snakes hypnotized by a flute player. A moment later, their faces came together in a kiss of voluptuous intensity. Mr Knoppert bent closer and studied them from all angles. Something else was happening: a protuberance like an ear was appearing on the right side of the head of both snails. His instinct told him that he was watching a sexual activity of some sort.

The cook came in and said something to him, but Mr Knoppert silenced her with an impatient wave of his hand. He couldn't take his eyes from the enchanted little creatures in the bowl.

When the ear-like excrescences were precisely together rim to rim, a whitish rod like another small tentacle shot out from one ear and arched over toward the ear of the other snail. Mr Knoppert's first surmise was dashed when a tentacle sallied from the other snail, too. Most peculiar, he thought. The two tentacles withdrew, then came forth again, and as if they had found some invisible mark, remained fixed in either snail. Mr Knoppert peered intently closer. So did the cook.

'Did you ever see anything like this?' Mr Knoppert asked.

'No. They must be fighting,' the cook said indifferently and went away. That was a sample of the ignorance on the subject of snails that he was later to discover everywhere.

Mr Knoppert continued to observe the pair of snails off and on for more than an hour, until first the ears, then the rods, withdrew, and the snails themselves relaxed their attitudes and paid no further attention to each other. But by that time, a different pair of snails had begun a flirtation, and were slowly rearing themselves to get into a position for kissing. Mr Knoppert told the cook that the snails were not to be served that evening. He took the bowl of them up to his study. And snails were never again served in the Knoppert household.

That night, he searched his encylopaedias and a few general science books he happened to possess, but there was absolutely nothing on snails' breeding habits, though the oyster's dull reproductive cycle was described in detail. Perhaps it hadn't been a mating he had seen after all, Mr Knoppert decided after a day or two. His wife Edna told him either to eat the snails or get rid of them – it was at this time that she stepped upon a snail that had crawled out on to the floor – and Mr Knoppert might have, if he hadn't come across a sentence in Darwin's *Origin of Species* on a page given to gastropoda. The sentence was in French, a language Mr Knoppert did not know, but the word *sensualité* made him tense like a bloodhound that has suddenly found the scent. He was in the public library at that time, and laboriously he translated the sentence with the aid of a French–English dictionary. It was a statement of less than a hundred words, saying that snails manifested a sensuality in their mating that was not to be found elsewhere in the animal kingdom. That was all. It was from the notebooks of Henri Fabre. Obviously Darwin had decided not to translate it for the average reader, but to leave it in its original language for the scholarly few who really cared. Mr Knoppert

considered himself one of the scholarly few now, and his round, pink face beamed with self-esteem.

He had learned that his snails were the freshwater type that laid their eggs in sand or earth, so he put moist earth and a little saucer of water into a big wash-bowl and transferred his snails into it. Then he waited for something to happen. Not even another mating happened. He picked up the snails one by one and looked at them, without seeing anything suggestive of pregnancy. But one snail he couldn't pick up. The shell might have been glued to the earth. Mr Knoppert suspected the snail had buried its head in the ground to die. Two more days went by, and on the morning of the third, Mr Knoppert found a spot of crumbly earth where the snail had been. Curious, he investigated the crumbles with a match stem, and to his delight discovered a pit full of shiny new eggs. Snail eggs! He hadn't been wrong. Mr Knoppert called his wife and the cook to look at them. The eggs looked very much like big caviar, only they were white instead of black or red.

'Well, naturally they have to breed some way,' was his wife's comment. Mr Knoppert couldn't understand her lack of interest. He had to go and look at the eggs every hour that he was at home. He looked at them every morning to see if any change had taken place, and the eggs were his last thought every night before he went to bed. Moreover, another snail was now digging a pit. And another pair of snails was mating! The first batch of eggs turned a greyish colour, and miniscule spirals of shells became discernible on one side of each egg. Mr Knoppert's anticipation rose to a higher pitch. At last a morning arrived – the eighteenth after laying, according to Mr Knoppert's careful count – when he looked down into the egg pit and saw the first tiny moving head, the first stubby little antennae uncertainly exploring the nest. Mr Knoppert was as happy as the father of a new child. Every one of the seventy or more eggs in the pit came miraculously to life. He had seen the entire reproductive cycle evolve to a successful conclusion. And the fact that no one, at least no one that he knew of, was acquainted with a fraction of what he knew, lent his knowledge a thrill of discovery, the piquancy of the esoteric. Mr Knoppert made notes on successive matings and egg hatchings. He narrated snail biology to fascinated, more often shocked, friends and guests, until his wife squirmed with embarrassment.

'But where is it going to stop, Peter? If they keep on reproducing at this rate, they'll take over the house!' his wife told him after fifteen or twenty pits had hatched.

'There's no stopping nature,' he replied good-humouredly. 'They've only taken over the study. There's plenty of room there.'

So more and more glass tanks and bowls were moved in. Mr Knoppert went to the market and chose several of the more lively-looking snails, and also a pair he found mating, unobserved by the rest of the world. More and more egg pits appeared in the dirt floors of the tanks, and out of each pit crept finally from seventy to ninety baby snails, transparent as dewdrops, gliding up rather than down the strips of fresh lettuce that Mr Knoppert was quick to give all the pits as edible ladders for the climb. Mating went on so often that he no longer bothered to watch them. A mating could last twenty-four hours. But the thrill of seeing the white caviar become shells and start to move – that never diminished however often he witnessed it.

His colleagues in the brokerage office noticed a new zest for life in Peter Knoppert. He became more daring in his moves, more brilliant in his calculations, became in fact a little vicious in his schemes, but he brought money in for his company. By unanimous vote, his basic salary was raised from forty to sixty thousand dollars per year. When anyone congratulated him on his achievements, Mr Knoppert gave all the credit to his snails and the beneficial relaxation he derived from watching them.

He spent all his evenings with his snails in the room that was no longer a study but a kind of aquarium. He loved to strew the tanks with fresh lettuce and pieces of boiled potato and beet, then turn on the sprinkler system that he had installed in the tanks to simulate natural rainfall. Then all the snails would liven up and begin eating, mating, or merely gliding through the shallow water with obvious pleasure. Mr Knoppert often let a snail crawl on to his forefinger – he fancied his snails enjoyed this human contact – and he would feed it a piece of lettuce by hand, would observe the snail from all sides, finding as much aesthetic satisfaction as another man might from contemplating a Japanese print.

By now, Mr Knoppert did not allow anyone to set foot in his study. Too many snails had the habit of crawling around on the floor, of going to sleep glued to chair bottoms, and to the backs of books on the shelves. Snails spent much of their time sleeping, especially the older snails. But there were enough less indolent snails who preferred love-making. Mr Knoppert estimated that about a dozen pairs of snails must be kissing all the time. And certainly there was a multitude of baby and adolescent snails. They were impossible to count. But Mr Knoppert did count the snails sleeping and creeping on the ceiling alone, and arrived at something between eleven and twelve hundred. The tanks, the bowls, the underside of his desk and the bookshelves must surely have held fifty times that number. Mr Knoppert meant to scrape the snails off the ceiling one day soon. Some of them had been up there for weeks, and he was afraid they were not taking in enough nourishment. But of late he had been a little too busy, and too much in need of the tranquillity that he got simply from sitting in the study in his favourite chair.

During the month of June he was so busy he often worked late into the evening at his office. Reports were piling in at the end of the fiscal year. He made calculations, spotted a half-dozen possibilities of gain, and reserved the most daring, the least obvious moves for his private operations. By this time next year, he thought, he should be three or four times as well off as now. He saw his bank account multiplying as easily and rapidly as his snails. He told his wife this, and she was overjoyed. She even forgave him the ruination of the study, and the stale, fishy smell that was spreading throughout the whole upstairs.

'Still, I do wish you'd take a look just to see if anything's happening, Peter,' she said to him rather anxiously one morning. 'A tank might have overturned or something, and I wouldn't want the rug to be spoilt. You haven't been in the study for nearly a week, have you?'

Mr Knoppert hadn't been in for nearly two weeks. He didn't tell his wife that the rug was pretty much gone already. I'll go up tonight,' he said.

But it was three more days before he found time. He went in one evening just before bedtime and was surprised to find the floor quite covered with snails, with three or four layers of snails. He had difficulty closing the door without mashing any. The dense clusters of snails in the corners made the room look positively round, as if he stood inside some huge, conglomerate stone. Mr Knoppert cracked his knuckles and gazed around him in astonishment. They had not only covered every surface, but

thousands of snails hung down into the room from the chandelier in a grotesque clump.

Mr Knoppert felt for the back of a chair to steady himself. He felt only a lot of shells under his hand. He had to smile a little: there were snails in the chair seat, piled up on one another, like a lumpy cushion. He really must do something about the ceiling, and immediately. He took an umbrella from the corner, brushed some of the snails off it, and cleared a place on his desk to stand. The umbrella point tore the wallpaper, and then the weight of the snails pulled down a long strip that hung almost to the floor. Mr Knoppert felt suddenly frustrated and angry. The sprinklers would make them move. He pulled the lever.

The sprinklers came on in all the tanks, and the seething activity of the entire room increased at once. Mr Knoppert slid his feet along the floor, through tumbling snails' shells that made a sound like pebbles on a beach, and directed a couple of the sprinklers at the ceiling. This was a mistake, he saw at once. The softened paper began to tear, and he dodged one slowly falling mass only to be hit by a swinging festoon of snails, really hit quite a stunning blow on the side of the head. He went down on one knee, dazed. He should open a window, he thought, the air was stifling. And there were snails crawling over his shoes and up his trouser legs. He shook his feet irritably. He was just going to the door, intending to call for one of the servants to help him, when the chandelier fell on him. Mr Knoppert sat down heavily on the floor. He saw now that he couldn't possibly get a window open, because the snails were fastened thick and deep over the windowsills. For a moment, he felt he couldn't get up, felt as if he were suffocating. It was not only the musty smell of the room, but everywhere he looked long wallpaper strips covered with snails blocked his vision as if he were in a prison.

'Edna!' he called, and was amazed at the muffled, ineffectual sound of his voice. The room might have been soundproof.

He crawled to the door, heedless of the sea of snails he crushed under hands and knees. He could not get the door open. There were so many snails on it, crossing and recrossing the crack of the door on all sides, they actually resisted his strength.

'Edna!' A snail crawled into his mouth. He spat it out in disgust. Mr Knoppert tried to brush the snails off his arms. But for every hundred he dislodged, four hundred seemed to slide upon him and fasten to him again, as if they deliberately sought him out as the only comparatively snail-free surface in the room. There were snails crawling over his eyes. Then just as he staggered to his feet, something else hit him – Mr Knoppert couldn't even see what. He was fainting! At any rate, he was on the floor. His arms felt like leaden weights as he tried to reach his nostrils, his eyes, to free them from the sealing, murderous snail bodies.

'Help!' He swallowed a snail. Choking, he widened his mouth for air and felt a snail crawl over his lips on to his tongue. He was in hell! He could feel them gliding over his legs like a glutinous river, pinning his legs to the floor. 'Ugh!' Mr Knoppert's breath came in feeble gasps. His vision grew black, a horrible, undulating black. He could not breathe at all, because he could not reach his nostrils, could not move his hands. Then through the slit of one eye, he saw directly in front of him, only inches away, what had been, he knew, the rubber plant that stood in its pot near the door. A pair of snails were quietly making love in it. And right beside them, tiny snails as pure as dewdrops were emerging from a pit like an infinite army into their widening world.

Inside the story

Patricia Highsmith is known for her crime novels as much as for her short stories. She is skilled at building a tense, claustrophobic atmosphere, at encouraging bizarre and worrying developments from what appear at first to be ordinary situations. She seems almost detached in her observation of human oddities but that same cool detachment is partly what forces us to read on. There is something inescapable about her stories and it comes as no surprise to find that her first novel, *Strangers on a Train*, was filmed by that master who shared a similar taste for the psychologically disturbing, Alfred Hitchcock. Like Hitchcock she is interested in the way in which obsessions may take over and finally devour her characters.

In pairs or small groups

1 Share your feelings at the end of the story. Do you have any sympathy for Mr Knoppert? Discuss why you feel as you do about his sticky ending.

2 How would you describe Mr Knoppert's feelings about his snails when he first observes their habits? How do they develop? What does he get out of his hobby of snail-watching?

3 Is his interest simply that of anyone who has discovered a new hobby? Is it perverse in anyway? How do *you* react to his obsession?

On your own

Write your own story of obsession. It's largely a matter of focusing on something very ordinary, taking it to extremes and following it through to its logical conclusion. The old lady who is fond of stray cats; the man who shares his packed lunch every day with the pigeons; the obsessed collector of stamps, train numbers, records, pop pictures. There are many possibilities for you to explore.

THE LANDLADY

Roald Dahl

Billy Weaver had travelled down from London on the slow afternoon train, with a change at Swindon on the way, and by the time he got to Bath it was about nine o'clock in the evening and the moon was coming up out of a clear starry sky over the houses opposite the station entrance. But the air was deadly cold and the wind was like a flat blade of ice on his cheeks.

'Excuse me,' he said, 'but is there a fairly cheap hotel not too far away from here?'

'Try The Bell and Dragon,' the porter answered, pointing down the road. 'They might take you in. It's about a quarter of a mile along on the other side.'

Billy thanked him and picked up his suitcase and set out to walk the quarter-mile to The Bell and Dragon. He had never been to Bath before. He didn't know anyone who lived there. But Mr Greenslade at the Head Office in London had told him it was a splendid city. 'Find your own lodgings,' he had said, 'and then go along and report to the Branch Manager as soon as you've got yourself settled.'

Billy was seventeen years old. He was wearing a new navy-blue overcoat, a new brown trilby hat, and a new brown suit, and he was feeling fine. He walked briskly down the street. He was trying to do everything briskly these days. Briskness, he had decided, was *the* one common characteristic of all successful businessmen. The big shots up at Head Office were absolutely fantastically brisk all the time. They were amazing.

There were no shops on this wide street that he was walking along, only a line of tall houses on each side, all of them identical. They had porches and pillars and four or five steps going up to their front doors, and it was obvious that once upon a time they had been very swanky residences. But now, even in the darkness, he could see that the paint was peeling from the woodwork on their doors and windows, and that the handsome white façades were cracked and blotchy from neglect.

Suddenly, in a downstairs window that was brilliantly illuminated by a street-lamp not six yards away, Billy caught sight of a printed notice propped up against the glass in one of the upper panes. It said BED AND BREAKFAST. There was a vase of pussy-willows, tall and beautiful, standing just underneath the notice.

He stopped walking. He moved a bit closer. Green curtains (some sort of velvety material) were hanging down on either side of the window. The pussy-willows looked wonderful beside them. He went right up and peered through the glass into the room, and the first thing he saw was a bright fire burning in the hearth. On the carpet in front of the fire, a pretty little dachshund was curled up asleep with its nose tucked into its belly. The room itself, so far as he could see in the half-darkness, was filled with pleasant furniture. There was a baby-grand piano and a big sofa and several plump armchairs; and in one corner he spotted a large parrot in a cage. Animals were usually a good sign in a place like this, Billy told himself; and all in all, it looked to him as though it would be a pretty decent house to stay in. Certainly it would be more comfortable than The Bell and Dragon.

On the other hand, a pub would be more congenial than a boarding-house. There would be beer and darts in the evenings, and lots of people to talk to, and it would probably be a good bit cheaper, too. He had stayed a couple of nights in a pub once before and he had liked it. He had never stayed in any boarding-houses, and, to be perfectly honest, he was a tiny bit frightened of them. The name itself conjured up images of watery cabbage, rapacious landladies, and a powerful smell of kippers in the living-room.

After dithering about like this in the cold for two or three minutes, Billy decided that he would walk on and take a look at The Bell and Dragon before making up his mind. He turned to go.

And now a queer thing happened to him. He was in the act of stepping back and turning away from the window when all at once his eye was caught and held in the most peculiar manner by the small notice that was there. BED AND BREAKFAST, it said. BED AND BREAKFAST, BED AND BREAKFAST, BED AND BREAKFAST. Each word was like a large black eye staring at him through the glass, holding him, compelling him, forcing him to stay where he was and not to walk away from that house, and the next thing he knew, he was actually moving across from the window to the front door of the house, climbing the steps that led up to it, and reaching for the bell.

He pressed the bell. Far away in a back room he heard it ringing, and then *at once* – it must have been at once because he hadn't even had time to take his finger from the bell-button – the door swung open and a woman was standing there.

Normally you ring the bell and you have at least a half-minute's wait before the door opens. But this dame was like a jack-in-the-box. He pressed the bell – and out she popped! It made him jump.

She was about forty-five or fifty years old, and the moment she saw him, she gave him a warm welcoming smile.

'*Please* come in,' she said pleasantly. She stepped aside, holding the door wide open, and Billy found himself automatically starting forward into the house. The compulsion or, more accurately, the desire to follow after her into that house was extraordinarily strong.

'I saw the notice in the window,' he said, holding himself back.

'Yes, I know.'

'I was wondering about a room.'

'It's *all* ready for you, my dear,' she said. She had a round pink face and very gentle blue eyes.

'I was on my way to The Bell and Dragon,' Billy told her. 'But the notice in your window just happened to catch my eye.'

'My dear boy,' she said, 'why don't you come in out of the cold?'

'How much do you charge?'

'Five and sixpence a night, including breakfast.'

It was fantastically cheap. It was less than half of what he had been willing to pay.

'If that is too much,' she added, 'then perhaps I can reduce it just a tiny bit. Do you desire an egg for breakfast? Eggs are expensive at the moment. It would be sixpence less without the egg.'

'Five and sixpence is fine,' he answered. 'I should like very much to stay here.'

'I knew you would. Do come in.'

She seemed terribly nice. She looked exactly like the mother of one's best school-friend welcoming one into the house to stay for the Christmas holidays. Billy took off his hat, and stepped over the threshold.

'Just hang it there,' she said, 'and let me help you with your coat.'

There were no other hats or coats in the hall. There were no umbrellas, no walking-sticks – nothing.

'We have it *all* to ourselves,' she said, smiling at him over her shoulder as she led the way upstairs. 'You see, it isn't very often I have the pleasure of taking a visitor into my little nest.'

The old girl is slightly dotty, Billy told himself. But at five and sixpence a night, who gives a damn about that? 'I should've thought you'd be simply swamped with applicants,' he said politely.

'Oh, I am, my dear, I am, of course I am. But the trouble is that I'm inclined to be just a teeny weeny bit choosy and particular – if you see what I mean.'

'Ah, yes.'

'But I'm always ready. Everything is always ready day and night in this house just on the off-chance that an acceptable young gentleman will come along. And it is such a pleasure, my dear, such a very great pleasure when now and again I open the door and I see someone standing there who is just *exactly* right.' She was half-way up the stairs, and she paused with one hand on the stair-rail, turning her head and smiling down at him with pale lips. 'Like you,' she added, and her blue eyes travelled slowly all the way down the length of Billy's body, to his feet, and then up again.

On the first-floor landing she said to him, 'This floor is mine.'

They climbed up a second flight. 'And this one is *all* yours,' she said. 'Here's your room. I do hope you'll like it.' She took him into a small but charming front bedroom, switching on the light as she went in.

'The morning sun comes right in the window, Mr Perkins. It *is* Mr Perkins, isn't it?'

'No,' he said. 'It's Weaver.'

'Mr Weaver. How nice. I've put a water-bottle between the sheets to air them out, Mr Weaver. It's such a comfort to have a hot water-bottle in a strange bed with clean sheets, don't you agree? And you may light the gas fire at any time if you feel chilly.'

'Thank you,' Billy said. 'Thank you ever so much.' He noticed that the bedspread had been taken off the bed, and that the bedclothes had been neatly turned back on one side, all ready for someone to get in.

'I'm so glad you appeared,' she said, looking earnestly into his face. 'I was beginning to get worried.'

'That's all right,' Billy answered brightly. 'You mustn't worry about me.' He put his suitcase on the chair and started to open it.

'And what about supper, my dear? Did you manage to get anything to eat before you came here?'

'I'm not a bit hungry, thank you,' he said. 'I think I'll just go to bed as soon as possible because tomorrow I've got to get up rather early and report to the office.'

'Very well, then. I'll leave you now so that you can unpack. But before you go to bed, would you be kind enough to pop into the sitting-room on the ground floor and sign the book? Everyone has to do that because it's the law of the land, and we don't want to go breaking any laws at *this* stage of the proceedings, do we?' She gave him a little wave of the hand and went quickly out of the room and closed the door.

Now, the fact that his landlady appeared to be slightly off her rocker didn't worry Billy in the least. After all, she was not only harmless – there was no question about that – but she was also quite obviously a kind and generous soul. He guessed that she had probably lost a son in the war, or something like that, and had never got over it.

So a few minutes later, after unpacking his suitcase

and washing his hands, he trotted downstairs to the ground floor and entered the living-room. His landlady wasn't there, but the fire was glowing in the hearth, and the little dachshund was still sleeping in front of it. The room was wonderfully warm and cosy. I'm a lucky fellow, he thought, rubbing his hands. This is a bit of all right.

He found the guest-book lying open on the piano, so he took out his pen and wrote down his name and address. There were only two other entries above his on the page, and, as one always does with guest-books, he started to read them. One was a Christopher Mulholland from Cardiff. The other was Gregory W. Temple from Bristol.

That's funny, he thought suddenly. Christopher Mulholland. It rings a bell.

Now where on earth had he heard that rather unusual name before?

Was he a boy at school? No. Was it one of his sister's numerous young men, perhaps, or a friend of his father's? No, no, it wasn't any of those. He glanced down again at the book.

Christopher Mulholland   231 Cathedral Road, Cardiff
Gregory W. Temple   27 Sycamore Drive, Bristol

As a matter of fact, now he came to think of it, he wasn't at all sure that the second name didn't have almost as much of a familiar ring about it as the first.

'Gregory Temple?' he said aloud, searching his memory. 'Christopher Mulholland? . . .'

'Such charming boys,' a voice behind him answered, and he turned and saw his landlady sailing into the room with a large silver tea-tray in her hands. She was holding it well out in front of her, and rather high up, as though the tray were a pair of reins on a frisky horse.

'They sound somehow familiar,' he said.

'They do? How interesting.'

'I'm almost positive I've heard those names before somewhere. Isn't that queer? Maybe it was in the newspapers. They weren't famous in any way, were they? I mean famous cricketers or footballers or something like that?'

'Famous,' she said, setting the tea-tray down on the low table in front of the sofa. 'Oh no, I don't think they were famous. But they were extraordinarily handsome, both of them, I can promise you that. They were tall and young and handsome, my dear, just exactly like you.'

Once more, Billy glanced down at the book. 'Look here,' he said, noticing the dates. 'This last entry is over two years old.'

'It is?'

'Yes, indeed. And Christopher Mulholland's is nearly a year before that – more than *three years* ago.'

'Dear me,' she said, shaking her head and heaving a dainty little sigh. 'I would never have thought it. How time does fly away from us all, doesn't it, Mr Wilkins?'

'It's Weaver,' Billy said. 'W-e-a-v-e-r.'

'Oh, of course it is!' she cried, sitting down on the sofa. 'How silly of me. I do apologize. In one ear and out the other, that's me, Mr Weaver.'

'You know something?' Billy said. 'Something that's really quite extraordinary about all this?'

'No, dear, I don't.'

'Well, you see – both of these names, Mulholland and Temple, I not only seem to remember each one of them separately, so to speak, but somehow or other, in some peculiar way, they both appear to be sort of connected together as well. As though they were both famous for the same sort of thing, if you see what I mean – like . . . well . . . like Dempsey and Tunney, for example, or Churchill and Roosevelt.'

'How amusing,' she said, 'but come over here now,

dear, and sit down beside me on the sofa and I'll give you a nice cup of tea and a ginger biscuit before you go to bed.'

'You really shouldn't bother,' Billy said. 'I didn't mean you to do anything like that.' He stood by the piano, watching her as she fussed about with the cups and saucers. He noticed that she had small, white, quickly moving hands, and red finger-nails.

'I'm almost positive it was in the newspapers I saw them,' Billy said. 'I'll think of it in a second. I'm sure I will.'

There is nothing more tantalizing than a thing like this which lingers just outside the borders of one's memory. He hated to give up.

'Now wait a minute,' he said. 'Wait just a minute. Mulholland . . . Christopher Mulholland . . . wasn't *that* the name of the Eton schoolboy who was on a walking-tour through the West Country, and then all of a sudden . . .'

'Milk?' she said. 'And sugar?'

'Yes, please. And then all of a sudden . . .'

'Eton schoolboy?' she said. 'Oh no, my dear, that can't possibly be right because *my* Mr Mulholland was certainly not an Eton schoolboy when he came to me. He was a Cambridge undergraduate. Come over here now and sit next to me and warm yourself in front of this lovely fire. Come on. Your tea's all ready for you.' She patted the empty place beside her on the sofa, and she sat there smiling at Billy and waiting for him to come over.

He crossed the room slowly, and sat down on the edge of the sofa. She placed his teacup on the table in front of him.

'*There* we are,' she said. 'How nice and cosy this is, isn't it?'

Billy started sipping his tea. She did the same. For half a minute or so, neither of them spoke. But Billy knew that she was looking at him. He body was half-turned towards him, and he could feel her eyes resting on his face, watching him over the rim of her teacup. Now and again, he caught a whiff of a peculiar smell that seemed to emanate directly from her person. It was not in the least unpleasant, and it reminded him – well, he wasn't quite sure what it reminded him of. Pickled walnuts? New Leather? Or was it the corridors of a hospital?

'Mr Mulholland was a great one for his tea,' she said at length. 'Never in my life have I seen anyone drink as much tea as dear, sweet Mr Mulholland.'

'I suppose he left fairly recently,' Billy said. He was still puzling his head about the two names. He was positive now that he had seen them in the newspapers – in the headlines.

'Left?' she said, arching her brows. 'But my dear boy, he never left. He's still here. Mr Temple is also here. They're on the third floor, both of them together.'

Billy set down his cup slowly on the table, and stared at his landlady. She smiled back at him, and then she put out one of her white hands and patted him comfortingly on the knee. 'How old are you, my dear?' she asked.

'Seventeen.'

'Seventeen!' she cried. 'Oh, it's the perfect age! Mr Mulholland was also seventeen. But I think he was a trifle shorter than you are, in fact I'm sure he was, and his teeth weren't *quite* so white. You have the most beautiful teeth, Mr Weaver, did you know that?'

'They're not as good as they look,' Billy said. 'They've got simply masses of fillings in them at the back.'

'Mr Temple, of course, was a little older,' she said, ignoring his remark. 'He was actually twenty-eight. And yet I never would have guessed it if he hadn't told me, never in my whole life. There wasn't a *blemish* on his body.'

'A what?' Billy said.

'His skin was *just* like a baby's.'

There was a pause. Billy picked up his teacup and took another sip of his tea, then he set it down again gently in its saucer. He waited for her to say something else, but she seemed to have lapsed into another of her silences. He sat there staring straight ahead of him into the far corner of the room, biting his lower lip.

'That parrot,' he said at last. 'You know something? It had me completely fooled when I first saw it through the window from the street. I could have sworn it was alive.'

'Alas, no longer.'

'It's most terribly clever the way it's been done,' he said. 'It doesn't look in the least bit dead. Who did it?'

'I did.'

'*You* did?'

'Of course,' she said. 'And you have met my little Basil as well?' She nodded towards the dachshund curled up so comfortably in front of the fire. Billy looked at it. And suddenly, he realized that this animal had all the time been just as silent and motionless as the parrot. He put out a hand and touched it gently on the top of its back. The back was hard and cold, and when he pushed the hair to one side with his fingers, he could see the skin underneath, greyish-black and dry and perfectly preserved.

'Good gracious me,' he said. 'How absolutely fascinating.' He turned away from the dog and stared with deep admiration at the little woman beside him on the sofa. 'It must be most awfully difficult to do a thing like that.'

'Not in the least,' she said. 'I stuff *all* my little pets myself when they pass away. Will you have another cup of tea?'

'No, thank you,' Billy said. The tea tasted faintly of bitter almonds, and he didn't much care for it.

'You did sign the book, didn't you?'

'Oh, yes.'

'That's good. Because later on, if I happen to forget what you were called, then I can always come down here and look it up. I still do that almost every day with Mr Mulholland and Mr ... Mr ...'

'Temple,' Billy said. 'Gregory Temple. Excuse my asking, but haven't there been *any* other guests here except them in the last two or three years?'

Holding her teacup high in one hand, inclining her head slightly to the left, she looked up at him out of the corners of her eyes and gave him another gentle little smile.

'No, my dear,' she said. 'Only you.'

Inside the story

In pairs

1 The story begins in a very ordinary way and gradually builds up a sense of menace. Look at the opening of the story – up to the point where Billy decides to walk on to the Bell and Dragon rather than ring the bell at the guest house. Together, list some of the things that suggest the very normal and ordinary nature of the town and of the guest house. What things in particular attract him to the house?

2 It is after this point in the story that we become aware that all may not be as it seems. The author signals the change by telling us 'And now a queer thing happened to him.' Our attention is drawn to the fact that the compulsion Billy feels to ring the bell is peculiar. After Billy does so, the author manages to suggest an air of growing menace without making any other direct suggestion of oddity to us. Together, list the things that happen or that Billy notices that suggest something very strange is going on. There are quite a number. We have noted eighteen – but there may be more! (Keep your eyes open for tense changes as well as the more obvious things.)

3 Discuss what you think might happen next.

On your own

1 Write your version of what you think happens next in the story.

2 Christopher Mulholland, Gregory Temple and now Billy Weaver. We know that the disappearance of the first two has already been headline news. Write the newspaper reports that you think might appear over the next few days regarding Billy. (Think about who has seen him in Bath, who knows he is there, who will notice his absence.)

3 Trying to get a line on the disappearances, a young police officer arrives at the guest house for a routine interview with the landlady about any guests she may have had or anything she may have noticed. How does the landlady handle the situation?

In pairs

The dialogue between Billy and the landlady could easily make an effective radio play. Devise a script that can be tape recorded. You may find it helpful to split the action of the story between, say, four groups to lighten the load. Thus one group could be responsible for the opening scene where Billy arrives in the town and walks down the road. The second group could begin at the point when Billy is dithering on the steps of the guest house wondering whether to ring the bell, and so on. Remember you are writing for radio thus, in this second scene, you may like to include sound effects of Billy mounting the steps, and maybe have him reading the notice over to himself out loud. It may help to have him thinking aloud to himself as he peers in through the window and sees the cosy room. There is a scene break at the point where he goes downstairs to sign the visitors' book and you will have to think about how you will indicate this – and how the listener will know what Billy is reading in the book. Think also about sound effects. Think particularly about the tone of voice used by Billy and the landlady.

FURTHER IDEAS FOR COURSEWORK PROJECTS

The aim of this section is to suggest a variety of possible approaches to short story writers and their work that would be suitable for projects which may be undertaken for examination purposes or for your own interest.

1 Studying a writer's work

Inside Stories introduces you to the work of a number of different writers but, in the compass of a single book, it isn't possible to offer a range of pieces by each one of them. All anthologies are to some extent 'tasters' that offer readers a chance to try different authors and, with luck, whet their appetite for more of the same. If you have particularly enjoyed a story by one of the writers in this book, you could focus on that writer's work and make an in-depth study of it. Here are some suggestions as to how you might approach this project.

Widening your knowledge through reading

1   Select a few of the stories by your chosen writer from the collections they have published. You will find some of these listed in the section about the authors on pp. 197–202 and, of course, the Acknowledgments list gives details of all the book from which the stories in this book were taken. Not all the writers featured in this collection have published collections that are readily available in this country and several of these writers write for adults more than for younger readers, but you should have little difficulty in finding several collections of stories by Ray Bradbury, Margaret Mahy, James Thurber, Jan Mark, Robert Bloch, Patricia Highsmith, Roald Dahl, Italo Calvino, and Natalie Babbitt in any good library or bookshop.

2   Working either on your own or with a partner or small group, read several of the stories. Don't try to tackle too many – two or three in addition to the one(s) you have found in this book will be quite enough. You will probably find it helpful to work with others on this aspect of the project and to share your ideas. In some cases you may be able to prepare a dramatised, taped reading of a particular story using different readers from your group as though for a radio broadcast and to share it with the rest of your class. Ideas about preparing a story for taping can

be found at the end of 'The Wolf and His Gifts' earlier in this book.

Making notes around the story – on your own

Choose one of the stories and jot down notes about your thoughts and feelings, both as you read it and when you reach the end. The easiest way to do this is not to let the note-making interfere with your reading too much but simply to keep a sheet of paper alongside the story and to scribble a single word or a question mark, or whatever seems appropriate to remind you when you have finished, that something flashed through your mind at that point. You will probably be able to reconstruct most of your ideas from these reminders when you finish the story. With the very short stories, you may be able to work directly onto a diagram like the one below.

Spend about ten minutes filling out these reminder notes into something more substantial before the ideas are lost. Reread the story and note any differences in the impression it makes on a second (or third) reading. Compare your notes with those made by a partner or by others.

Sharing impressions – in pairs or small groups

Share your ideas about the story or stories with others. Talk about what the story is about and how it is similar/different to the one that sparked your interest in this particular writer. Is the language used similar or different? Are the feelings you are left with similar or different? Would you have known that the other stories were by the same writer – and, if so, what clues are there?

You may find it helpful to list any common themes or attitudes, or character types, or phrases that recur or seem characteristic of the writer.

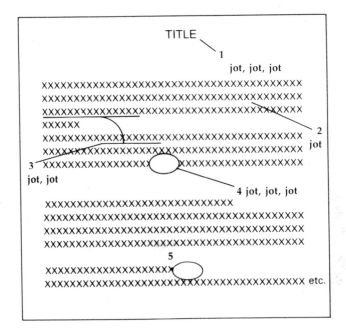

Putting ideas together – whole class

Each group presents their prepared reading (or their tape) of all or part of the story they have chosen to the rest of the class and says what they found interesting.

The rest of the class jot down their own notes about the presentation and ask questions of the presenting group.

The class should now be able to summarise a number of main points about the characteristics of the writer's stories. Even if the rest of the class are not themselves intending to develop a project on this particular writer, the ideas presented to them by the group doing the in-depth study should increase everyone's understanding of the one story that appears in this book.

This is a good point for the group who have undertaken the in-depth study to share their wider knowledge of the writer. When and how were the stories written? What is the writer's background and does it affect the stories? And so on.

2 Focusing your ideas – for groups or individuals

If you have undertaken all or some of the activities above, you should be able to compile a coursework piece on the stories of this particular writer and his or her life and background. You could say what it is that you like about the stories and you could include stories of your own, written as a result of reading that writer's work. Such stories may be simply inspired by the writer's stories (use them as starting points) or they may perhaps be attempts to write in the same style, or even to parody it. In any case, write an accompanying piece to explain what you are attempting to do.

If you are even modestly skilled as an artist, you could design your own illustrations or book covers appropriate to the writer's work and include these.

The whole collection could form the basis of a wall display about the writer's life and work intended to attract others to read some of the stories for themselves.

You could make a short taped anthology of readings from a selection of the stories, presenting it as a radio programme and linking the selections with your own commentary and background information about the writer. Again, the intention should be to persuade others to read the author's work.

3 Themes and types

A number of the stories in this book share similar or closely related themes though they may treat them in quite different ways. There are several stories about the failings of twentieth century society in the section entitled *Present Imperfect* for example; there are several stories about aspects of growing up scattered throughout the book; and there are ghostly stories and stories of terror. What would be contained in your own anthology of stories around a particular theme or story type? If you could put together *My Four Best Ghost Stories* (or *School Stories* or *Science Fiction Stories* . . . or whatever) what would be in there? Notice that there are two possibilities in this assignment: one is to choose your selection according to *theme* and another is to choose it according to story *type*. It would be possible to have a thematic selection of, say, school stories, one of which had a science fiction background, another of which was a ghost story, and so on; or you could simply choose four school stories, or ghost stories or science fiction stories according to type.

Write about your choice, saying why you made it and how the stories you have chosen are similar or different in their treatment of the theme or are representatives of a particular story type.

4 Creative responses

Many of the stories we read remind us of similar or related incidents from which we ourselves could create a story. Some of the stories we read suggest further stories that we could write in response to the original. Sometimes an illustration, drawing or painting may be suggested by a story or an incident in it. During your course, try to build up a selection of personal creative responses to the stories you have read. As suggested, these may take different forms – your own stories, drawings, paintings, collages of pictures from papers or magazines. . . . In each case, you could write an accompanying commentary explaining what triggered your response and what you were trying to do.

5   Shifting the viewpoint

Think about how a story you have read in this book would appear if it were to be told by another character in the story. Discuss what changes this might mean in the way that character and the others in the story are perceived by you, the reader. Rewrite the story from this new point of view. If several pairs work on the same story, each pair can retell it from the viewpoint of a different character and the different new stories can be shared and displayed. Stories like 'Blemish', 'Woof', 'An Honest Thief', 'Charles' and even 'Do Angels Wear Brassieres?' can all be rewritten in this way.

6   Interviewing the cast

Many of these stories provide suitable material for radio or television news interviews using a tape recorder or video recorder. In groups of two or three, prepare a suitable set of questions that will get to the heart of the story and interview one or more of the key characters. It could be something as simple – and illuminating – as an interview with The Good Samaritan and the man he rescued. (Why did the Samaritan behave as he did? What did he think about the people who passed by, leaving the victim at the roadside? What are the innkeeper's views on the affair?) It could be an interview with the snail-watcher's wife as she appears in Patricia Highsmith's bizarre story. Whoever is being interviewed must have time to think about their character and motivation and about what sort of questions they are likely to be asked. Some of the questions might be agreed and known about beforehand but some should require quite spontaneous answers. You will need to think quickly and 'in character'.

7   Picture versions

Change one of the stories into a storyboard, strip cartoon or comic book format, illustrating the key scenes and picking out the bones of the story in speech bubbles within each frame or using brief sentences below.

8   Puppet plays

Change a story into a puppet play or shadow puppet play as described on p.91. Any of the simpler stories can be retold in this way. The four fables by Aesop are ideal, as are almost all the stories in *Section A*. Share your work with the class and maybe with other classes in the school or in a local junior school if appropriate.

9   Storytelling

People love telling stories and to listen to stories well told. You could take one of the simpler stories in this book and think about how you would tell it (not read it) to a group of listeners. How would you settle them into the story and hold their attention? What sort of voice would be appropriate? How slowly or quickly should the story be told? What bits would you emphasise and what bits would you skip? Where would you pause for effect? Can you hold your audience's gaze without faltering? Starting with one of the stories from *Section A*, practise your storytelling technique and, after trying it out on your class, tell your stories in another setting to a younger group or to junior school children.

THE AUTHORS

Aesop is thought to have lived approximately 2,500 years ago in Asia Minor but details of his life are very scanty and accounts of it only appeared two thousand years later. It is believed that he was a servant at the court of King Croesus whose quick wits rapidly earned him promotion and it is even thought he may have worked as a diplomat. His skill as a storyteller allowed him to comment on the faults of the powerful people around him, and by making his characters animal rather than human he was able to criticise without giving offence. Many of the stories were not new even in his day and were based on tales from Egypt, Babylon, India and elsewhere. Aesop never wrote the fables down: for centures they were passed on by people who had been told them.

Natalie Babbitt is an American writer whose stories – particularly her novel, *Tuck Everlasting* – are well known on both sides of the Atlantic. Her two short collections, *The Devil's Story Book* and *The Devil's Other Story Book*, from which the stories in this volume are taken, have won considerable acclaim. She accompanies many of her stories with her own suitably wicked illustrations.

Robert Bloch, born 1917, is an American writer and a master of the brief, macabre tale, often made the more chilling because it begins in everyday life and experience and builds progressively to a horrific revelation. It comes as no surprise to learn that he wrote the story *Psycho* (1959) on which Alfred Hitchcock's film was based. He has received many awards for his work. *The Selected Short Stories of Robert Bloch* appeared in 1987.

Ray Bradbury, born 1920, is one of the great figures of American science fiction and fantasy writing. He has written novels, plays and screenplays for films (John Huston's *Moby Dick* among them) as well as a stream of brilliant short stories, many of which have become classics in their own time. *The Illustrated Man* and *The Golden Apples of the Sun* are two of his best known short story collections.

Timothy Callender was born in Barbados and educated at the University of the West Indies and London University. A writer and painter and teacher both in secondary schools and on the UWI campus, his stories have been published as a collection, *It so Happen*.

Italo Calvino was born in Cuba in 1923 and grew up in San Remo, Italy where, since the 1940s, he established himself as a distinguished writer of novels and short stories. He won the Italian literary award, the Premio Feltrinelli, in 1973. He is an essayist and journalist as well as a novelist and is a member of the editorial staff of a Turin publishing firm.

Robert Carter was born in New South Wales, Australia in 1945. He has enjoyed a number of different occupations including those of patrol officer in Papua, New Guinea, private detective, commercial manager, teacher and school counsellor. Until recently, he worked as a psychologist in a hospital for the terminally ill. He has twice won awards in the National (Australian) Short Story of the Year Competition – in 1983 for 'Within' and in 1985 for 'Prints in the Valley'.

'John Christopher' is the pen name of the British writer, Christopher Sam Youd, born in 1922. A science fiction addict from his teens, he produced his own science fiction fan magazine. He first came to prominence with *The Death of Grass* (1956) and has been one of the major English writers of science fiction for over thirty years. He is well known for his teenage novels, particularly *The Guardians*, *The Prince in Waiting Trilogy* and the *Tripods Trilogy*. Much of his work has been filmed for television. His concern with impending global disaster, and with the shortcomings of our society do not date with the years and his warnings may be, if anything, more timely than ever.

Roald Dahl was born in Wales in 1916, the son of Norwegian parents, and educated at Repton School. He went on an expedition to Newfoundland and later joined the Shell Oil Co. During the Second World War he served in the RAF as a fighter pilot and began writing short stories. His later stories have been translated into many languages and are bestsellers all over the world as are his children's books such as *James and the Giant Peach, Charlie and the Chocolate Factory, Fantastic Mr Fox, Danny Champion of the World* and *The Witches*. He lives in Buckinghamshire and was married to the actress Patricia Neal. He has three daughters and a son.

Jane Gardam was born in Coatham, N. Yorkshire in 1928. She studied literature at London University and became a journalist and writer of novels for both children and adults. She has won numerous awards for her work and received the Katherine Mansfield award for *The Pangs of Love and Other Stories* which was published in 1983.

Ernest Hemingway was born in 1899 in Oak Park, Illinois. He worked for a short time as a reporter on a Kansas City newspaper before serving in the Italian army in World War One. This experience gave rise to his first novel, *A Farewell to Arms*. He settled in Paris in the 1920s and published his short story collection, *Men Without Women*. During the Spanish Civil War he worked in Spain as a newspaper correspondent. His fiction reflects both his interest in bullfighting and his obsession with death. He also fought in the Second World War. He died in 1961.

Patricia Highsmith was born in Fort Worth, Texas in 1921 and moved to New York when she was six. By the age of 23 she had decided to become a writer and her first novel, *Strangers on a Train*, was filmed by Alfred Hitchcock. The Mystery Writers of America awarded her the Edgar Allen Poe Scroll. She enjoys playing the piano, painting and sculpture; she now lives in France.

Langston Hughes was born in Missouri, USA in 1902 and was one of the most eminent black poets of the mid-twentieth century. A graduate of Columbia University, New York and Lincoln University, Pennsylvania, he received many awards. *The Ways of White Folks* was a major short story collection published in 1934. Apart from many collections of poetry he has published 66 short stories. He died in 1967.

Shirley Jackson (1919–1965) was born in San Francisco, California and graduated from Syracuse University, New York. She lived in Vermont and published novels, short stories, plays and some writing for children. She had a particular understanding of young minds and her two books about life with her own children, *Life Among the Savages* and *Raising Demons*, may have some bearing on 'Charles', the story in this volume.

Yashar Kemal was born in 1923 and is Turkey's best known writer. He works as a journalist. In 1952 he published his first volume of short stories, followed by his first novel in 1955. Many of his novels and stories since then have been translated into English by his wife, Thilda.

Margaret Mahy is a New Zealander who lives near Christchurch. She has published over fifty children's books, many of which have been translated into several other languages and has twice won the Carnegie Medal. In 1987 she won *The Observer* Teenage Fiction Award for *Memory*. Only recently has she written short stories designed to appeal to young adolescents and 'The House of Coloured Windows' is taken from her first collection of these, *The Door in the Air*.

Jan Mark was born in 1943 in Welwyn, Hertfordshire and brought up in Ashford, Kent. She attended Canterbury College of Art and then taught for six years in a secondary school in Gravesend. She is now a freelance writer known mainly for her children's fiction. She has won the Carnegie Medal, *The Observer* Teenage Fiction Award, the Penguin/*Guardian* Award, and the Angel Literary Prize. From 1982–84 she held an Arts Council Fellowship in Writing at Oxford Polytechnic. Her works include *Thunder and Lightnings*, *Hairs in the Palm of your Hand*, and many more.

Robert Munsch is a Canadian, born in 1945. He is a full-time writer and teacher known mainly for his children's fiction. From 1975–84 he was Assistant Professor of Early Childhood Education at the University of Guelph, Ontario.

Dorothy Nimmo was born in Manchester and now lives in N. Yorkshire. She has published short stories in *Spare Rib* and *Writing Women* and poems in several magazines and journals.

'Frank O'Connor' is the pseudonym of Michael O'Donovan, who was born in Cork in 1903. He worked as a librarian in Dublin and elsewhere in Ireland and, as Frank O'Connor, became well known for his short stories though he also wrote poems and an autobiography. He died in 1966.

'Saki' was the pen name of Hector Harold Munro who lived from 1870 to 1916. he wrote novels but is best known for his many short stories. In his childhood he was brought up by an aunt – an experience which was to have a profound effect upon his view of the adult world and to influence many of his stories. He went on to a career in journalism and then became a successful writer. He was killed by a German sniper in 1916 while serving with the British Army. Immediately upon his death, his sister, Ethel, destroyed many of his private papers and thus very little is known about his private life.

Olive Senior was born in 1941 in Jamaica. One of ten children of a poor family, she spent her early days partly at home with her brothers and sisters and partly living with better-off relatives, 'pretty much being shifted between the two extremes of a continuum based on race, colour and class in Jamaica.' She began work as a journalist and gained a degree in print journalism in Canada. Later, she became editor of an academic journal and she is now Editor of *Jamaica Journal* and Managing Director of Jamaica Publications Ltd. She has published poetry and, with *Summer Lightning*, the collection from which 'Do Angels Wear Brassieres?' is taken, she won the Commonwealth Writers' prize for 1987.

Iain Crichton Smith was born in 1928 and lives in Scotland. A writer of poems and short stories and contributor to many literary journals, he was a teacher in Scotland before becoming a full-time writer. A member of the Scottish Arts Council, he also writes in and translates from Gaelic.

'Catherine Storr' is the pen name of Lady Bolagh, a British writer born in 1913. She has written novels, short stories and children's fiction. She trained as a doctor and from 1948–50 was assistant psychiatrist at the West London Hospital. From 1966–70 she was Assistant Editor of Penguin Books. She lives in Hampstead.

James Thurber was born in Ohio in 1894. He worked as a government clerk in Washington and then at the US embassy in Paris; this was followed by a spell as a journalist for a Chicago paper's Paris edition. In 1926 he returned to America and worked on the staff of the *New Yorker* magazine until 1933. He remained a lifelong contributor to its pages. He is internationally famous for his humorous stories with their dry, distinctive style and for his witty drawings and cartoons. He died in 1961.

Rose Tremain lives in Norwich. She has written plays for radio and television as well as short story collections and novels. In 1983 she was one of the writers chosen to represent the Best of Young British Novelists.

Catherine Wells is something of a mystery. Her story 'The Ghost' appears in *The Virago Book of Ghost Stories* edited by Richard Dalby, but it is the only story in that splendid collection which has neither acknowledgment nor notes on the author. Perhaps if she or her agents were to get in touch . . .

Jay Williams is American and the author of *The Practical Princess and other Liberating Fairy Tales* published by Chatto & Windus in 1979. As Jack Zipes notes in his introduction to *Don't Bet on The Prince* (Gower Publishing Company, 1986, a collection in which 'Petronella' also appears), 'as a male writing to question present gender arrangements, Williams is concerned about generating respect for women, learning from them and exposing male foibles.'